TARRAGON SHADOWS

Book Four of the Tarragon Series

Elizabeth James

Thrall of Darkness

THE TARRAGON SERIES

CONTENTS

PROLOGUE

The Elder sat weeping as he held the two collars and watched the blood trickle through the walls to collect in a pool at the base of the ancient volcano. The blood sizzled as it struck lava, sending out a mist that would protect the dragons for centuries to come. Most blood only lasted a decade, but this blood was different: centuries old, strengthened by dragon's blood, it would eliminate the need for more sacrifices for a very long time. But still the Elder wept, for the owner of the blood had been like a son to him and the shock of Ashton's death was like a fist to his gut.

He still remembered Ashton when he was a young man and the Elder had taken him as a pet, and how relieved both of them had been when the mountain chose not to take Ashton's life and had taken a small blood sacrifice instead. He remembered the nights they had spent together, with Ashton panting under him begging for release. He remembered teaching Ashton the joys of drinking dragon blood and reclaiming his youth. Those days, once a fond memory, were dead now. Ashton's blood seeped into the chamber until all the Elder could see was crimson.

No one knew the Elder was alive, not since he had found his way into Mount Tarragon over a century ago with Nieve, his beloved green dragon. Nieve's talent of immortality was a gift, but a curse as well in many ways as the days stretched to years and decades and the Elder realized that death would never come, even without dragon blood. Death might not come, but old age had and the Elder knew he would have to kill a dozen dragons before he and Nieve were back to their full strength. He held up a withered hand and sighed. In his mind he was still the vibrant young man he had been for nearly three centuries at the height of his power, when killing dragons was a time-honored tradition and not something to be hidden, but only one century without dragon blood had turned him into a husk. Now that Ashton was gone, it was time to rejuvenate himself and choose a new disciple.

The Elder dried his tears and stood, reaching for his cane. Soon he wouldn't need a cane. The blood had stopped running down the walls and the Elder trembled with rage. Whoever had killed Ashton was going to pay dearly. He would stop at nothing to see Ashton's death avenged. He hobbled to Nieve's side. The green dragon was nearly gray with age and had grown skeletal after a century of isolation within the mountain. He needed a fresh kill as badly as the Elder did, if not more.

They would leave the safety of the mountain, just long enough to find a meal. Even though they were weak, Nieve was still larger than any of the dragons nearby and that would make the difference in a fight. The Elder mounted Nieve, bones aching as he adopted the familiar pose. Nieve crawled through tunnels glowing crimson with lava and blood until a blinding rectangle appeared before them. They both covered their eyes, Nieve with his wing and the Elder with his arm. After several minutes, the light grew manageable and they continued, stopping every few feet for their eyes to adjust. When they finally emerged onto the mountainside, the Elder gasped.

A Queen dragon was having a mating flight and the familiar sight brought tears to his eyes. It was beautiful to watch her shimmering red scales glitter as she darted ahead of the emerald and cerulean splashes of the males. Then he noticed several dragons leaving the campus, heading his way. He leapt off Nieve and urged his dragon into the sky just as they flew by.

Nieve plucked one from the pack like a ripe apple from a bursting tree. He dragged the dragon and its partner to the ground as the dragon screeched and the others scattered. None of the other dragons came to the victim's aid, instead fleeing as quickly as possible. Nieve knocked the great beast unconscious as he slammed it into the ground, making sure not to harm the human riding it. The human slid off the dragon's back and ran towards the Elder, shouting for help. He approached the Elder, then recoiled as if the sight of the Elder was disgusting to him. The Elder wondered how age had deteriorated his once good looks; if the man's reaction was any indication, his handsome face was now quite fearsome.

"Who are you?" the man asked warily, glancing between the Elder and the massive dragon perched atop his unconscious dragon.

"I am the Elder," he replied.

The man laughed uneasily. "That's a myth."

The Elder wondered what he had heard about him, and where he had heard it. His lips stretched into a smile. He gestured for Nieve to kill the dragon. The man screamed and grabbed the Elder's tattered robe.

"No, you can't do this! I may have supported Ashton but I never supported this!"

The Elder paused. "You supported Ashton? Tell me, who killed him?"

The man's eyes glittered. "If I tell you, you can't kill my dragon. I'll bring you other dragons to kill," he added with a hint of desperation.

The Elder nodded. Knowledge was more important than a kill right now. After all, he had waited over a century for dragon blood; a day or two wouldn't matter much. It was much better to get information from this man, especially if he had supported Ashton.

"Jamie killed him," the man said. "He's the Queen who just had the mating flight."

The Elder pursed his cracked lips. Yes, Queens were often a

problem. It would be difficult to kill one, but not impossible. And if he managed to drink her blood – he shivered in anticipation. He had never dreamed of drinking a Queen's blood but the thought was intoxicating. He would gain more power and youth from her blood than several male dragons. He licked his lips. Then his attention returned to the man in front of him, the man who had promised dragons.

"Can you get me dragons that are loyal to Jamie to kill?"

"I can try," the man said. "But I can get you dragons."

"Good. What is your name?"

"Alan."

The Elder gestured to Nieve, who reluctantly got off the unconscious dragon. Nieve bared his teeth to show his displeasure at having to wait for a meal, but the Elder ignored him. There would be food later, if Alan kept his word. And if he didn't, then Nieve would be allowed to hunt Alan freely until he got his meal.

"Well, Alan, I require a dragon. Today. Before the sun sets."

Alan gulped. "Of course, Elder. Once my dragon wakes up I'll bring you a dragon."

The Elder reached out and grabbed Alan's neck.

"You will bring a dragon back here before the sun sets or I will not rest until your dragon is dead, do you understand?"

Alan went white and trembled in his hand. He tried to speak but couldn't, whether from fear or the Elder's grip, the Elder didn't know, but he was pleased with the man's reaction. Perhaps looking like a walking corpse had some advantages after all. The Elder released him and Alan stumbled backwards, nearly falling to the ground.

"If you are loyal to Ashton, then Ashton taught you how to serve," the Elder continued. "You serve me now."

"Yes, Elder," Alan whispered. "I will do as you ask."

The Elder nodded and turned to Nieve. "Bring the dragon here and we will be waiting."

Then he mounted Nieve and they flew a short distance away before hiding in the dense forest as the mist curled around them. When Alan brought the other dragon, the dragon wouldn't suspect their presence at all and he would be able to attack freely. The Elder dismounted and held out his hand as mist twisted between his fingers. It was thick today, and seemed to be on his side. He had lived inside the mountain for over a century and still didn't understand how the mist functioned, but he knew that the mountain often took sides in conflicts and could not always be counted on. Today, though, with Ashton's blood running thick through the mountain, it was firmly on his side and he hoped it would remain like that at least until his strength and youth returned.

While he waited for Alan to bring him a dragon, he pondered the steps he needed to take to reintegrate himself in the Tarragon world. He had been driven out a century ago by fools who thought that his ways were outdated and corrupt, fools who thought that sacrificing dragons was a thing of the past. They didn't understand the pleasures of dragon blood or the necessity of having a powerful leader to guide Tarragon society over the centuries. Only Ashton had understood, and he had filled the Elder's shoes neatly when the Elder was forced to flee into the mountain. And now Ashton was gone, no doubt killed for the same reasons the Elder had been forced into hiding. Killed by a young, foolish Queen who didn't understand how Tarragon society was supposed to work.

Well, there had to be another human who could understand. Alan was too weak; the Elder already knew. He was a servant, nothing more. The Elder needed someone strong, someone powerful, someone with a dragon that others would look up to. It was too bad the Queen was responsible, because having a Queen on his side was exactly what he needed. He had always dreamed of having a Queen dragon as an ally, to share in the true pleasures of being a dragon. Perhaps the Queen could be persuaded to join him, but he would never forgive this Jamie for killing Ashton. No, Jamie would die, and he would have to wait until another Queen was born.

Unless, of course, there were two Queen dragons, but that was highly unlikely. It was rare enough to have a single Queen dragon, having two would be a miracle. He dismissed the idea and his thoughts turned to his hunger. He hadn't allowed himself to feel hunger for decades, but now that dragon blood was so close at hand he felt the ache in his bones and belly sharply. If Alan didn't hurry up, he would find himself being served as dessert.

He heard a flapping of wings and Nieve's ears perked up. Two dragons appeared and landed where the Elder had told Alan to meet. Nieve silently slid out of the mist and approached. In a few short minutes, the Elder heard a scream, then power filled him and he knew Nieve was drinking the dragon's blood.

It filled his body entirely, washing through his veins and restoring his strength like ambrosia bringing immortality to a god. And he was a god, for all intents and purposes. He shut his eyes and focused on the sensation he had dreamed about for a century. Fiery hot pinpricks sparked across his skin and his hair stood on end. His cock grew hard as a fierce arousal consumed him, and his muscles tensed almost to the point of pain. Then they relaxed and as they relaxed he felt his skin tightening to conform to them, the wrinkles vanished ever so slightly, his youth showing through just a little. More dragons would be needed to restore him to his full youth; this was just an appetizer.

He walked to the clearing with the dead dragon and saw that Alan had killed the other dragon's partner: a practical choice since the man would have likely attacked Alan once his dragon was killed. But Alan was smart enough not to kill the human until Nieve had fully drunk his blood. Alan would be a good servant, it seemed. Ashton must have trained him well. The Elder wondered idly if Alan had been one of Ashton's pets or if he were simply a lackey. Alan was attractive, with hints of red in his hair that sparkled in the dying sun's rays and clear, deceptive eyes, but he didn't seem like Ashton's usual type.

As the Elder entered the clearing, Alan turned to him and his eyes widened as if he were surprised to see the effect that one dragon's blood had on the Elder. So Ashton had not shared the pleasures of dragon's blood with him. He wasn't likely a pet, then, but he would still make a good servant.

"You have done well," the Elder said. "But I will require more dragons. Can you produce them?"

Alan trembled as if he knew that if he answered no, he and his dragon would be eaten on the spot.

"Of course, Great Elder," he said, bowing. "Many dragons are fleeing the campus right now to escape Jamie's notice and it isn't hard to lure them here. But if you want more dragons, you may need to relocate. There is a new school being built in Spokane that will not be watched as carefully as this, and many of the dragons who are hiding from Jamie will be flying that direction. If you want dragons that won't be missed by anyone, you would do well to head there as well."

The Elder tapped his fingers against his lips. Alan was telling the truth, but he disliked the idea of leaving the mountain that had been his home for the past four centuries. It was be an enormous change and a dangerous flight across Washington. He vaguely remembered Spokane, which had been a small town when he had entered the mountain. If another school were being built there, however, that must have changed. What else had changed in the century when he was dormant in the mountain? Perhaps Alan would be even more useful by helping him adjust to the new century.

"Very well," the Elder said. "We will remain here several more days, and then relocate to Spokane. I only hope you are telling the truth, because if you are lying to me..."

He let his voice trail off and Alan went pale. The Elder didn't need to continue his threat; Alan already knew it. Losing one's dragon was the most painful thing that could happen to some-one in Tarragon society and the Elder knew Alan would do any-thing to keep his dragon alive. That would make him a very obedient servant and right now, that was just what he needed.

The Elder thought of Ashton's blood dripping down the walls and meeting with the lava deep in the mountain below. The mountain would be able to sustain a second school, he knew, and when that school started, he would be there to guide it.

CHAPTER ONE

In His Arms

D erek leaned back into Chris's arms with a sigh. He and Chris had just celebrated their second month together in the most spectacular way. Derek smiled at the older man and was rewarded with a kiss on the forehead. Derek could hear Jettie and Yaris cuddling in the large Queen's chamber down the hall and knew that for all four of them, it would be a relaxing evening that would help ease his mating flight, which Chris estimated would happen in only a couple of months now. It was midway through spring semester and she should have her flight around the start of summer. He just hoped the other council members would accept Chris as their leader without any qualms and it wouldn't resort to violence.

There were problems not having a strong enough council on campus here in Spokane, but generally the men, women, and students who had transferred to the new school policed themselves. At Derek's mating flight, however, when it was the council members who would lose control, there would almost certainly be problems. He just hoped the lust that they experienced and weren't able to release wouldn't be inflicted on students. Otherwise Jamie and Scott might have to come to campus again and the sight of those two, so happy together, was always a blow to Derek, who still had plans to make Scott his.

He knew he was in charge of this campus – Jamie had told him as much when the campus was founded – but sometimes he suspected Jamie had only sent him here to keep him away from Scott, Jamie's beautiful and sexy boyfriend and mate. Derek had his own lover, of course, and Chris was certainly desirable, but even he paled in comparison to Scott. It might have been because Scott was Derek's first, or because Derek had lusted after Scott for so long, but Scott was the ultimate prize in this game that he and Jamie were secretly playing.

Derek relaxed against Chris in the bed and felt a little guilty for thinking about Scott while lying in bed with another man. But he had confessed his feelings to Chris once and Chris hadn't belittled them; in fact, Chris had said that as the partner to a Queen dragon, Derek shouldn't lock himself into the conventions of a single mate. Queens often took multiple mates, Chris explained, and he shouldn't feel ashamed or embarrassed about lusting after multiple people. It was his dragon's nature showing through.

Chris ran his fingers across Derek's shoulder and followed his touch with kisses. Derek wondered what his mating flight would be like, and how it would be different from their lovemaking. He knew that the longer the flight, the better, but he also knew that committed pairs tended to have shorter flights. He was determined to lay as many eggs as Marisol, however. He would hate for Marisol to be better at him in this as well as everything else.

Derek fingered the long scar on his belly that was exposed as he lay naked with Chris. His father's friend Alan had tried to kill him because he couldn't bond with Jettie the way that Jamie and Marisol were bonded, because, as Alan said, he was a queen and not a Queen. He was still sensitive to everything that proved Alan right.

Chris's hand hovered over his.

"Thinking about that again? You shouldn't worry so much. You and Jettie are exactly what this campus needs."

Derek relaxed against the older man.

"Just wondering about her mating flight, and how many eggs

she'll lay."

"The main campus will always have more because they have the old hatching grounds," Chris pointed out. "They don't even really need Marisol's eggs. Jettie's eggs will matter much more than Marisol's do."

Derek smiled. It was true; Jettie's eggs would bring life to the campus while Marisol's were only making life a little easier for a few students on the main campus. Chris always knew what to say. He gazed up at the muscular man behind him, caught again by his blond hair and blue eyes, so beautiful in the moonlight. He was so different than Scott. Scott was dark, with hazelnut skin and black hair and eyes. Scott was the type of man Derek usually went for, but Chris was different. Chris always seemed to know what to say to him, how to reassure him and inspire him. Chris was always there for him.

His smile faded. There was a subject both of them had been avoiding the past few weeks, claiming that they needed to get the school settled before they took any action on it. After all, the chaos of getting an entirely new school set up might account for the strange incidences. But the school was running smoothly now and they had to deal with it. There was no more putting it off.

Dragons were disappearing. At first it was one upperclassman immediately upon arriving at the school and everyone assumed his dragon had flown out of the mist and been killed. Then nothing for a week, then another dragon vanished without a trace and everyone assumed she had also strayed too far. No one knew what the mist did to dragons who didn't remain within its protective borders; it was reasonable to assume that dragons couldn't survive without the mist on this strange new campus. But adults came and went from the campus freely; there had to be something else at work.

When the third dragon vanished, it became clear that this was a problem, not just a quirk of the mist. There was no indication of what happened to the dragons, just that they vanished, but it was clear that they died shortly thereafter because their humans, who they inevitably left behind, soon went into a panic and had to be subdued. Two of them lost their minds from grief. Everyone was on guard but still a fourth dragon vanished and Derek knew something drastic needed to be done to take care of this situation. After all, this campus was his concern and he needed to deal with it. But he had already taken every step he knew how to take, and dragons were still vanishing. There had to be something else he could do.

Chris sighed and rolled onto his back as if he knew that the time for cuddling was over and Derek was ready to talk business. He sat up and began to dress. Derek did the same, somewhat reluctantly. He knew he could pull Chris back into bed and lose himself in another pleasurable night, but something had to be done about the dragons. He was in charge of this campus now; it was his responsibility.

"I'm sorry," he said.

"Don't be," Chris replied gently, reaching out to stroke his shoulder. "I know this has been weighing on you."

"It's just, we don't know what happens or why certain dragons are targeted. If anything were to happen to Jettie-"

His voice caught and tears filled his eyes. He would die if anything happened to Jettie. One of the girls had died after losing her dragon, and the ones who survived only did so physically, not mentally.

"Nothing will happen to Jettie," Chris said firmly. "She's protected at all times by at least two other dragons. The other dragons were always alone when they vanished."

Derek nodded and took a deep breath. Of course nothing would happen to her. He was letting his fears get the better of him.

"However," Chris continued, "We may have to tell Jamie what's going on. Perhaps he can speak to the dragons and find out what's happening."

Derek pouted. He hated allowing Jamie any power over the Spokane Academy. It was yet another reminder that Jamie had more power than him, and that Jamie had Scott.

"Maybe I could ask Scott to come investigate," he said, brightening at the thought. "Since Marisol just laid her eggs and isn't able to leave Portland."

Chris smiled. "Why don't you? I think that's a wonderful idea."

"You won't mind?"

"Of course not. You deserve to have whatever you want," he murmured, kissing Derek's cheek.

Derek flushed. Chris was so understanding. Even though they were lovers, Chris never grew jealous of Scott and Derek's fixation on the man. He encouraged it, even, as he was doing now. He was exactly the type of man Derek needed and Derek was thrilled beyond words that Chris had been bold enough to approach him that long-ago day after his father had been killed. He couldn't imagine his life without Chris and Chris's always sage advice.

"I'll do that then," Derek announced, feeling a weight lift off his shoulders.

The disappearing dragons wouldn't be his problem alone anymore, now he could share them with Scott. And with Jamie, even. He flashed a smile at Chris.

"Well, now that that's decided," he said, extending a hand to Chris, "I don't much feel like getting up after all."

Chris laughed and began pulling off his clothes as Derek did the same, his breath quickening in anticipation as he saw the firm muscles he loved running his hands over. He adored Chris's body and the instant they were naked together Derek put his hands on Chris's shoulders and shoved the man back into the bed. Chris grinned and held out his arms as Derek straddled him. Though Derek was usually the bottom in their relationship, he was frequently on top in their foreplay and he liked it like that. He loved the feeling of power he got from straddling a man and feeling his arousal harden and strengthen below him as he played with his body. He only wished this was Scott beneath him.

Derek leaned down and kissed Chris again and again on the lips, then let his kisses trail against the hard stubble of Chris's jawline to his sensitive neck. Chris moaned and shifted underneath him, eager for more as Derek allowed himself to suck gently on Chris's neck, tasting the sensitive flesh as he sought the most erotic spots to make his lover hard. One of Chris's hands tangled in his hair and pulled him close as his lips and tongue worked their way down to his collarbone and struck a particularly sensitive spot. Chris was panting now, hard against Derek as Derek leisurely took his time playing with his chest, letting his hands trace the contours and come closer and closer to his nipples without ever touching them.

Then he lowered his head and sucked hard on one of his nipples and Chris arched his back and cried out in pleasure. Derek twirled his tongue around the nub of flesh and nibbled gently, then went to the other nipple as Chris started humping against him. Chris was more than ready and Derek sat up and examined his lover, breathless and flushed with arousal. It was time. Derek scooted next to him and lay on his back and in an instant, Chris was above him, pressing his legs to his chest and pressing his cock to Derek's entrance. He barely hesitated before plunging into Derek's willing body and Derek let out a pleased grunt at the pressure.

He shut his eyes and imagined this was Scott. A smile curled his lips as he remembered to breathe. He wrapped his arms around the man over him and opened himself fully to the experience, inviting the pain as well as the pleasure, soaking up every inkling of their lovemaking: the sweat on his lover's brow dripping onto his, his lover's mouth covering his in desperate kissing, the constant thrust against his most sensitive parts. Pure pleasure, and soon it would be Scott above him. Chris moaned and thrust sporadically as he came, and Derek wasn't far behind him.

They lay in the bed together, gasping for breath and slowly recovering from the strenuous activity. Chris ran a hand across Derek's cheek and kissed his forehead.

"My lover," he whispered.

Derek cuddled against him in return. He was Chris's lover now, but soon he would be Scott's. Nothing would prevent him from making that happen.

CHAPTER TWO

Disappearances

Scott stared at Jamie's silhouette in the window and wondered if he would be going to Spokane anytime soon. He knew Jamie resented how often Scott had been there since the campus was set up three months ago over winter break. It was set up quickly and only held experienced students right now, but next fall a batch of freshmen would be entering who knew nothing about Tarragon society and the academy had to have all the kinks worked out by then.

He knew that Jamie, though he hated Scott going to the campus, also recognized the necessity. Marisol had laid her second batch of eggs and was guarding them, and besides, Jamie was needed on the main campus to ensure that things went smoothly with the main council. Jamie had to continuously prevent them from slipping back into the old ways, which were so alluring for so many of them.

Margot was the most dangerous, he and Jamie had decided. She was supremely rational but somehow at the end of her explanations things stayed exactly how they were: benefitting the council and the girl's academy in particular. Scott had learned to be especially on guard against her and knew that Jamie shared his sentiments. There were just too many unknowns about her. She had warned about Jamie's kidnapping, after all, but in such a vague way and too late for Scott to prevent it. Had her warning been part of the plan or had it been a sincere effort on her part to stop the kidnapping? And why had she insisted that Jamie be the one to kill Ashton? Scott knew that Jamie was still haunted by nightmares of killing Ashton and his anger for Margot was partially fueled by that, but was his anger causing him to have a negative view of her when she had really just been trying to help? He didn't know, but he was on guard at all times around her.

Jamie sighed and turned to face him. Scott knew he would be going to Spokane soon. It was written across Jamie's face in the worried creases by his lips and the glint of anger and helplessness in his eyes. Jamie had been watching the situation there for weeks, ever since dragons had begun disappearing. Derek hadn't officially informed him of the problem yet, but the dragons followed their own code and had informed Jamie immediately.

The dragons were usually young dragons, just learning to fly, always alone, and belonging to freshmen. Scott knew Jamie was determined to find the cause. But even with his gift of speaking to all of the dragons, Jamie had confessed to Scott that he had no clue what was happening. The dragons just went silent, and then their human partners started going insane and screaming that their dragons were dead. But no bodies were ever found; no trace of violence ever spotted.

It had to do with Ashton's minions, Scott was sure. Nearly forty dragons had fled the campus after Ashton's death and during Marisol's mating flight when Narné couldn't stop them. Rumor said they were hiding near Spokane and waiting for a chance to take over the fledgling academy. Scott didn't doubt those rumors; it was a good plan but one he wouldn't allow to happen. Not while he was the Queen's mate.

He felt a usual flicker of fear at the thought of what would happen when Derek went through his mating flight and there was another Queen's mate to deal with. The other man wouldn't have as much authority as Scott, but he would still be a threat. And if one of Ashton's hidden men won the flight, the Spokane academy could easily become home to a second Ashton. He was determined not to let that happen to Derek. He knew Jamie disapproved of his relationship with Derek but he would do everything in his power to prevent Derek from becoming like his father. Derek deserved a better life. He deserved his own fate, not to be bound into becoming a cruel, sadistic monster like his father. Derek was a good person.

Jamie shook his head and turned back to the window, obviously distressed. Scott approached from behind and wrapped his arms around his love. Jamie melted into him and sighed.

"What's wrong, Jamie?"

"You may have to leave again," Jamie said. "But I don't want you to."

Scott smiled and kissed his cheek. "You know I'll always be back. Sometimes I think you worry I'll stay away forever. But I'll always be back in your arms. You need me to check in on Derek and the dragon situation?"

"I need to know what is happening to those dragons. But be careful. I couldn't survive if anything happened to you or Narné."

"I'll stay with other dragons at all times," Scott assured him. His own heart skipped a beat at the thought of anything happening to Narné. "But I will figure it out."

Jamie turned into Scott's arms and embraced him. Scott kissed him firmly on the lips, feeling Jamie withdraw slightly as he always did before these visits, as if he truly were afraid that Scott wouldn't return. He wished there were something he could say or do to reassure Jamie, but he didn't know what other than continue to tell Jamie he loved him and continue to return after every trip. He knew Jamie still bore serious emotional scars and knew that he was responsible for some of them, but he would do everything in his power to help Jamie heal.

In the back of his mind he knew that someday he might have to choose between helping Derek and helping Jamie, but he pushed the thought aside and deepened his kiss, trying to pull

Jamie out of his depressing thoughts so that he could see Jamie's bright smile before he left. Jamie must have known what he was doing because he did smile, but his eyes were still sad. Scott kissed him tenderly and stroked his hair.

"I'll be back, my love, as soon as I figure out what's happening to the dragons."

He left quickly after that, not wanting to extend his goodbyes. He already had a bag packed in case of emergencies and he grabbed it, then went to the dragon chamber where Marisol and Narné were sharing their own goodbye. The two dragons split apart and Narné allowed Scott onto his back, then they emerged into the sunlight and Scott sneezed at the sudden brightness.

They flew for the better part of a day, stopping occasionally to stretch, always accompanied by a small tendril of fog that made them appear a tiny cloud in the sky. Finally, when darkness had fallen for several hours, the lights of Spokane loomed on the horizon. They flew over the city and outlying towns and reached the mountain where the campus was located. There were several ski slopes near the campus but the mist completely shrouded the campus and prevented errant skiers from wandering in. To everyone in the area, Mount Spokane looked exactly like it always had. But to anyone with a dragon, the campus was clearly visible.

He and Narné landed in the designated landing area beyond the football field where students wouldn't be able to see them – a necessary precaution once they started having new freshmen on campus. Mike was waiting for him and as always a rush of conflicting emotions ran through Scott at the sight of his first lover. He had hated Mike for so long after Mike had raped him, but after everything Mike had been through and sacrificed in order to save Jamie and the campus, Scott's petty concerns seemed to melt away and he found himself wanting to start over with the man. But Mike was still caught up in mourning and no one had been able to pull him out of his depression. Yet.

"We've been expecting you," Mike said with a forced smile.

"Derek and Jettie would like to speak with you immediately."

"Of course," Scott said, a little surprised.

They sent for help from Jamie this morning, Narné informed him.

Scott nodded and followed Mike as Narné hopped off to his usual quarters when he visited. Mike's shoulders were hunched slightly and Scott longed to reach out and ease some of his tension, but he knew he couldn't. Someone else would have to help Mike; Scott had his hands full with Jamie and Derek.

"Do you know anything about what's going on?" Scott asked.

Mike was a keen observer and undoubtedly knew more than many of the people on campus. Any insight he had would be invaluable in figuring this out. Mike hesitated, then glanced at Scott.

"Ashton told me something, once," he said in a rough voice. "I haven't told anyone yet because it's something that Ashton said."

Scott stopped walking and devoted all of his attention to Mike. "What did he say?"

Mike lowered his eyes and faced Scott. "There was an ancient dragon that not even the Queens could reach. None of the dragons knew he even existed, but he did. And when he awakens again, the world will be awash with blood."

Scott shivered. "What do you mean, the Queens couldn't reach him? You mean they can't communicate with him? And what is supposed to wake him up?"

"I don't know," Mike said wearily. "That's all he ever said. But he sounded hopeful when he talked about it, as if speaking of an old friend."

Scott placed a hand on his forehead. The dragons who vanished went silent. If there was a dragon that none of them could reach, not even the Queen, not even Jamie, then it would make sense. But it would also mean that an ancient being had been awakened and Ashton had predicted great violence with that awakening. Scott shook his head as if trying to deny Mike's story. He didn't want to accept it, but it seemed to fit. An ancient dragon luring in young dragons and killing them. But why kill them? What was the purpose? There were still so many unknowns, but at least now he had a place to start.

"Thank you, Mike," Scott said, patting the man on his shoulder.

Mike looked surprised by the gesture and touched his shoulder where Scott's hand had been. Had he fallen so deep into despair that he was unused to human contact? Scott hoped not. Mike used to be a vibrant, sexual man who enjoyed all of life's pleasures and to see him like this was shocking. If Ashton weren't dead, Scott would kill him on the spot for what he had done to Mike. But Mike would recover, slowly, and with help.

"Is that you, Scott?" a voice cried, and suddenly two arms wrapped themselves around his neck and thoughts of Mike were thrown aside as Derek threw himself into a hug.

Scott couldn't help but grin at the enthusiastic hello and didn't even mind when Derek kissed his cheek – especially since Derek didn't try to kiss his lips as he sometimes did. No matter how many times he explained that they couldn't be more than friends, Derek continued to chip away at the wall of friendship as if determined to find a lover underneath. He just didn't understand how tightly bound Scott and Jamie were.

"At your service, queen," Scott said, backing up to bow as was proper protocol.

Derek took his hand and, with barely a glance at Mike, started leading Scott towards his apartment. Scott would have to remind Derek how important and delicate Mike was right now. Scott, for his part, managed a warm goodbye to Mike before being dragged off. They passed a blonde man that Scott knew to be Chris, Derek's boyfriend, and Scott couldn't help but wonder how Chris put up with Derek flirting with Scott so much. But Chris didn't seem to care, he even encouraged it at times. Very unusual.

Scott was determined to get to know Chris a little better on this trip, since it was becoming clear that Chris would mate with Derek in Derek's first mating flight. Jamie said Chris still had loyalties to Ashton, though not enough to make him a threat, and Scott wanted to be sure that he was good enough for Derek before the mating flight happened. For right now, though, he was just glad to see Derek so happy and he allowed himself to be led past Chris into the apartment.

Once inside, Derek closed the door and the happy façade dropped.

"Scott, this situation is out of control. Another dragon disappeared. We have to do something, and now."

CHAPTER THREE

The Other Campus

J amie was tired of everyone acting as if he were broken somehow. He had been physically scarred most of his life and was
used to hiding his scars; hiding his emotional scars wasn't
much different and he wished people would give him the freedom to hide those scars without constantly inquiring after him.
He couldn't pretend to himself that he was fine after killing
Ashton and losing Kale, but he wanted to be able to pretend to
everyone else.

Yet everyone who talked to him seemed hesitant, as if worried
that they might say the wrong thing and trigger some unwelcome reaction in him. The only one who didn't was Margot,
and he couldn't express how much he appreciated it. He didn't
necessarily trust her, and he knew Scott didn't trust her at all,
but he welcomed her presence. And she might know about the
disappearing dragons, he thought as he headed out of dragon
canyon towards the girl's college. After all, she had been second
to Ashton on the council. He hadn't approached her before because Derek hadn't officially asked for his help, but now that
Derek had, Jamie was eager to find out what Margot knew.

The mist was thick as he walked the path between the col-
leges, but it thinned in the direction he needed to go, acting as
an escort to him. It seemed to take forever before the mist finally
thinned again and he saw the other campus, just as classic and
elegant as the boy's. Margot lived in the apartments but he

headed towards the school buildings, since he knew she taught a class at this time of day. It was rare for a council member to teach anything other than one-on-one sessions with upperclassmen, but Margot preferred getting to know the freshmen and taught one of the basic writing classes. Jamie respected her for that.

Her class was just letting out when he arrived and the flux of female students emerging from the room temporarily stunned Jamie, partially because he wasn't used to being surrounded by women and partially because many of them looked at him with open jealousy. He knew that most of them thought that Queen dragons should be partnered with women, not men, and resented both him and Derek, and he also knew that many of the students were jealous of his relationship with Scott, but he hadn't expected the students to be borderline hostile towards him. It was quite a change from the boy's school where everyone practically worshipped him.

As soon as the students passed him by, he entered the classroom to see Margot packing up her books into a small tote bag. She glanced up at him without expression.

"I thought that might be you," she said. "Little else gets the girl's attention like that."

Jamie blushed. "I had some questions to ask you."

"Of course. Why don't you come to my office?"

Jamie nodded and followed her out of the classroom towards the rows of doors that held teacher offices. He was a little curious about her office, and as he entered he had to pause to take the entire room in.

The books were the first things he noticed. Every wall save one was covered in floor-to-ceiling bookshelves crammed with more books than could possibly fit. They were shoved in haphazardly at all angles to get them to fit, and he couldn't see any organization pattern at all. The ones that were standing upright seemed to be in alphabetical order, but the ones piled on top of them were in no order at all and far outnumbered the neatly stacked books.

The single blank wall was taken up by an L-shaped desk covered in papers and one of the latest models of computer. Margot sat in the over-stuffed arm chair and gestured for Jamie to take the wooden chair across the desk from her. He obeyed, his eyes darting to the books, wondering what she considered important enough to keep in her office. There were the usual books that she must use for class, and some Shakespeare and Dante, but most of the books had simple bindings and titles that almost seemed to be in a different language. Either that or they all referred to things Jamie had never heard of before.

"Now then," she began, taking off her glasses and rubbing them on a soft cloth she retrieved from her desk. She looked surprisingly young without her glasses. "What did you want to ask me?"

Jamie hesitated. He didn't trust her entirely, but she was wise and knew a lot, and could certainly help him. Plus, she was now the head of the council and he would have to involve the council in the dragon disappearances eventually. Better do it now, when he might actually gain something from it.

He began telling her about the disappearances, how it started with one dragon in Spokane and everyone thought it was a fluke, but then how it continued and now, with the most recent disappearance occurring today, how they were certain someone was targeting young dragons. She placed her glasses back on her nose as he spoke and watched him impassively as he explained, but he could almost see her thinking and putting pieces together. She knew something. When he finished, he took a deep breath and waited for her to speak.

She took several moments, then looked at the books to her right.

"There is a legend," she began, and told him about a great evil that was said to hide inside Mount Tarragon, destined to waken and bring doom to them all. Scott had already spoken to Marisol about Mike's warning and it sounded very familiar. Coming from two sources, Jamie grimly realized that it was probably true. They had awakened something and it was seeking blood.

"You don't look surprised, young one," Margot said as she finished telling the legend.

"I had my suspicions," Jamie said, purposefully not mentioning Mike or where he had heard a similar story. He didn't want Mike to get caught up in this.

"Then you believe this myth?"

"You do, don't you?"

A sly smile stole across her face. "I believe the facts. It could very well be that one of Ashton's minions has taken up Ashton's practice of eating dragons. Have you eliminated that possibility?"

"I have," Jamie said. "I can sense all dragons and I would know if one of them were doing it. Or at the very least, the dragons would know and they would tell me."

"So the thing killing these dragons is beyond your abilities to sense?"

Jamie paused, unwilling to admit to a weakness in front of her. She didn't seem to care, however, and just nodded as if he had answered yes.

"I assume Scott has been sent to deal with it. If it is a dragon whose ability places him outside of your reach, you will need to be extremely careful. We cannot lose our Queen or our Queen's mate."

"I'm surprised you care so much about Scott," Jamie said without thinking.

Margot laughed. "His presence keeps that men's campus in line. If you didn't have a strong attachment to someone and your mate was determined solely by the mating flight, the mate would change every year and it would be chaos. We need stability, and Scott is a good choice. Surely you know I have no intention of splitting you up."

"I know," Jamie said, cheeks flushing again. "What about Derek's mate?"

"Derek seems to have formed a strong connection with one of the council members in Spokane," Margot said. "There will be little fighting over that position either."

Jamie nodded. He hadn't considered the consequences of Derek's mate changing with every mating flight, but chaotic would be an understatement. Each one of Derek's mates would try to win the most control in their year before they were inevitably replaced. Then Jamie would truly feel sorry for Derek. It was good that Derek was making connections, then, even if the man he was seeing still had some loyalties to Ashton. As long as it wasn't Scott who won Derek's mating flight, however, Jamie didn't really care.

There was a quiet knock on the door and a soft smile lit Margot's face. She must know who it is, Jamie thought as he turned in his chair to see the person opening the door. It was a young woman, most likely a senior or recent graduate, with golden tresses and warm brown eyes. Her skin was tan and had a speckling of freckles across the nose and she had an athletic build as if she spent a lot of time working outside in the sun. Jamie felt a little self-conscious with his pale skin and lack of strong muscles. The woman was quite beautiful, and grew more so when her eyes met Margot and a smile curled her lips. Looking between the women and suddenly understanding the smile, Jamie blushed. They must have been lovers, or at least in love, to have those gentle smiles.

"Do you need something, Clara?" Margot asked in a voice like honey, not at all like her usual commanding tone.

"The women's council has requested your presence," Clara said. "Apparently one of the freshmen is having difficulties with her dragon again."

Margot sighed and turned to Jamie.

"If you'll excuse me, Jamie. I am needed elsewhere. Should you have any more questions, please let me know, but I've told you all I know."

"Thank you, Margot," he replied politely, standing and scooting around Clara.

Clara smiled at him as she shut the door and he wondered if a freshman really were having problems or if Clara had just said that to get rid of him. It didn't really matter either way; he had his information and was ready to return to the boy's campus. As he turned to leave the building, he heard a squawking sound and turned towards it in surprise.

A large grey and white cat was trotting through the hall of the academic building with a live bird in its mouth. Jamie gasped.

"Put that bird down right now," he commanded, and to his surprise, the cat seemed to listen, setting the bird down right at his feet.

The bird, a large swallow, seemed dazed for a few moments and then started fluttering its wings. It lifted from the ground and made a beeline straight for the open door down the hallway. The cat made no movement to catch it and was instead watching Jamie with a gleam in its eyes, as if waiting for Jamie to congratulate its hunting skills or something.

Jamie had never really been around cats but he knew a little about them, and this one seemed tame even if it didn't have a collar. After all, it was inside the building so someone must have let it in. It had to belong to someone. He extended his hand cautiously and the cat leaned forward and sniffed it, then butted its head against his palm. Jamie smiled and scratched behind the cat's ears. A warm purring sound erupted from the creature and Jamie relaxed a little. This had to be someone's cat. A wild cat wouldn't act like this.

He scratched the cat for a few more seconds, then got up to leave. The cat followed him. He left the building and the cat still followed him. He turned around and considered going back inside to ask around and see who the cat belonged to when Margot and Clara emerged from her office and paused. Margot seemed surprised to see the cat so close to Jamie and she studied him with a hint of a smile.

"She likes you," Margot said, leaning down to rub the cat's back. "She's been hanging around our campus for days now but hasn't adopted anyone yet. Perhaps she's been waiting for you."

"I can't have a cat," Jamie said. "I have a dragon."

"Dragons and cats get along better than you might expect," Margot said. "Why don't you take her back to your campus and at least keep her while Marisol is at the hatching grounds? It will be good for you to have some companionship."

Jamie stared at the cat, who stared back with a hint of a challenge in her eyes as if daring him to leave her. He knew she was going to follow no matter what he did, so why not adopt her, just for a little bit? He hadn't really given any thought to how lonely it would be without Marisol and without Scott, and perhaps a cat would be good company.

"What's her name?"

Margot laughed. "She's a cat, not a dragon. You have to name her."

"I thought she was someone's pet."

"No, she's one of the feral cats from this campus. The men's campus doesn't have cats, but here we have a small community. We spay and neuter as many of them as we can to keep their numbers down, but there are always more. She seems to like you a lot," Margot observed.

Jamie was a little nervous about accepting a feral cat into his rooms, but from the cat's stance he didn't think she was going to give him a choice.

"All right. Come on, kitty," he said, turning towards the path and pleased to see that the fog parted for the cat as well. As they walked, he tried to think of a good name for her. They walked in almost complete silence, broken only by the occasional meow from her when he walked too fast. As they entered the boy's campus, he was aware of people staring at the cat oddly. He had to walk all the way across campus to the dragon canyon but when he arrived at his rooms, the cat leapt up onto his couch and curled up as if she knew she were home. She let out another meow.

"That's right, kitty, this is where you live now," Jamie said, inwardly calculating what all he would need to keep a cat. Food and water, first of all. A litter box. Maybe some toys. Since he didn't have money and all of his belongings were purchased through the council, he would have to go to them for permission. He just hoped his cat wouldn't mind the slight delay.

He gazed at her sleeping on the couch, paws twitching slightly, and grinned. It would be nice having another creature in his rooms while Marisol and Scott where away. He could feel Marisol's indulgent acceptance of the newest member of their family and hoped Scott wasn't allergic or anything. With a sigh, he headed back out to the council to get supplies for his new cat.

CHAPTER FOUR

Predator

C hris smiled at Scott as the other man arrived on campus, then continued on his way to the student whose dragon had just gone missing. They were all gathering to try to prevent her from killing herself, but his thoughts lingered on Derek and Scott as he walked. As Ashton had predicted, Derek was a double-edged sword and had to be wielded carefully. Before Ashton's death, the man had hand-selected the people who would be allowed to participate in his son's mating flight and become the new Queen's mate, and he had given them many instructions on how to treat his son and channel his abilities.

Derek was a powerful man, though he often didn't realize it. People naturally looked up to him and he was a natural choice for a Queen. Even though he didn't have the same power as Jamie, he would still be formidable. But only if he could be controlled properly, as Ashton had warned again and again. Derek had grown up soft, valuing other people's opinions and lives, and he needed to be hardened. But subtly, in a way that wouldn't be obvious to anyone.

Chris still remembered Ashton's advice on bringing out Derek's predatory nature as a way of channeling him properly, and that was precisely what Chris was doing when he allowed Derek to see Scott. Scott was a wildcard, since Derek had such a blend of possessive and gentle emotions for him, but almost always the predatory nature won out as Derek began viewing

Scott as the prize in a contest between him and Jamie. Exactly what Chris – and Ashton – wanted. There needed to be a balance to Jamie's power or else the old ways of the campus would vanish and everything Ashton had spent lifetimes building would be destroyed.

On a more personal level, Chris didn't want the old ways to end because he had sacrificed so much under them. He still remembered the ritual of joining the council, when Ashton had raped him in front of most of the council. Such practices were banned now under Jamie and Chris knew that as soon as a council member joined and didn't have to undergo such torturous proceedings, he wouldn't respect that new member nearly as much. It was something that bound them together, something that kept them in line. They were all Ashton's; it was why they served on the council so well. He couldn't imagine a council where people weren't bound by such dark initiations.

Luckily, the only person who was likely to be accepted onto the council in the near future was Mike, and he had undergone the same initiation in order to take over the first-year exam. So Chris would have years before he would have to hold back resentment every time he looked at the new council members and viewed them as less. And in the meantime, perhaps he and Derek could restore some of the old ways in Spokane without Jamie's knowledge, though Jamie seemed to know everything thanks to his communication with the dragons.

Chris arrived at the hospital suite where the girl was being kept. He had been hearing screams for quite a while on his walk, and hoped the other students weren't panicking. So far they had managed to keep this somewhat contained, but it wouldn't be long before complete panic broke out and parents began insisting that their children go to the main campus instead of this campus. He wouldn't let that happen. If there was only one campus, Derek would have no power at all, and Derek needed to have power to stand up for himself if any of Ashton's dreams for his future were to come true. Ashton might be dead, but Chris's loyalty to the man was unwavering. He was loyal to Ashton, now he was loyal to Derek and the man that Derek had the potential to become.

"Please let me die," the girl was screaming.

She was a little thing, and her dragon had likely been small as well. Sophomore. Brunette, with wide-set brown eyes and a rather large nose that looked exotic on her little face. He vaguely remembered her. It was his job to know all the students on his campus and he squinted and pulled her name from his memory – Brittany. First in her family to enter one of the academies, though her family had been a part of Tarragon society for generations. They were not going to be pleased, though at least none of them knew about dragons and would assume that she, like all members of their family, had simply died young if she did indeed die.

The nurses and psychiatrists reasoned with her as he hung back and watched. He didn't know what to say. If he were to lose Yaris, he would want to die as well and resent anyone trying to keep him alive. He sent a quick message to Yaris to reassure himself that the dragon was with other dragons and Yaris snorted in reassurance. He did have some confidence in his dragon, however: Yaris's gift was to transport himself instantly to another location as long as that location was within sight, so if something attacked him, he would be able to jump out of danger. The enemy wouldn't be expecting it. But better safe than sorry, especially where his beloved Yaris was concerned.

Jettie too was always protected – the entire Tarragon society would be devastated by the loss of a Queen. Compared to her, he was no one, and he was literally no one until the mating flight confirmed that he was the Queen's mate. He was just the Queen's lover, a position with no power whatsoever, until the mating flight which was due to happen in a couple of months. Of course, mating flights had been known to happen early, so Chris was sure to stay near Derek at all times just in case, but there wasn't any danger of anyone besides Scott beating him and he doubted

Scott would even enter the mating flight. Jamie would never forgive him if he did, and for all of Scott's attraction to Derek, Scott seemed oddly fixed on Jamie. Having Derek go after Scott, therefore, weakened Jamie and was a delightful turn of affairs for Chris.

The girl started screaming with increased intensity and Chris's attention returned to her. She was writhing in the bed, her hands and feet securely bound to the bed in cloth restraints. The veins in her neck stood out prominently as she threw her head back and screamed. Her whole body arched like a curved board had been placed beneath it and he was amazed that she could hold that rigidity for so long as she quaked, then collapsed back into the bed as the screaming stopped. Briefly.

"My Lyssa's gone," she sobbed. "Let me go, let me follow, don't keep me here without her."

Her body arched again, the veins protruding from her flesh until Chris was sure they would burst. She collapsed again but her attitude had changed and now she snarled and tried to break free.

"You bastards, let me go. Fuck you for keeping me here, I'm going to follow her no matter what you think!"

She started smashing her head backwards against the pillows and the doctors and nurses surged forward to stop her, even though Chris couldn't see how she could possibly harm herself on a pillow. But with them distracted, he suddenly found that she was looking straight at him.

"Please," she whispered directly to him while the rest of the room was in chaos.

His heart wavered. He knew they needed her alive, not just because it was good to be alive but because they needed to return her to her parents to prevent the family from growing too angry. Plus, they needed to question her about what had happened immediately before the attack. But her pain spoke to him clearly, her desperation, and he found himself clutching her hand as if to comfort her.

If he ever lost Yaris, he hoped someone would be kind enough to put him out of his misery. He wouldn't want to live after that, even if he had knowledge to help prevent future deaths, even if his living body would help ease his parents' worries. His soul would be dead, and forcing him to exist beyond that would be cruelty beyond measure. He understood this young girl's pain and her wish. And he would fulfill it.

He had worked in a hospital for a short time after leaving the academy and before returning as a council member, and he knew how dangerous air bubbles in the blood stream could be. There were plenty of needles lying around; a simple injection into her vein would end her pain simply and quickly. She was still spasming and slamming her head and the room was still in chaos, so it didn't take long to grab an unused needle and suck some air into it. Her hand was still in his, and he posed the needle against her vein. Odd how the rest of her body was thrashing so violently yet she was so still here, as if she knew he was helping her. He put his finger on the needle.

When human partners died, the dragons were killed instantly to prevent them pain. He had killed dragons before. It was a painful task, but it prevented even more pain as the dragons were unable to live without their partners. This was no different, he assured himself. This was not killing a human; this was killing a human partner whose dragon had just been killed. He took a deep breath. He could do it. Whatever the consequences, he could do it.

A hand landed on his shoulder and he jerked back in surprise. He looked up to meet Derek's understanding gaze. The girl's screams increased again as if she realized that she had just lost her last ally in the room. Derek took the needle from Chris's hand and he allowed it. Sweat was rolling down his brow. Then he noticed Scott a few steps back, but Scott's attention was all on the girl. He hadn't realized what Chris had been about to do. Only Derek had noticed, and he knew that Derek not only understood,

Derek would never tell. But it was too late for the girl now; she was doomed to live.

"Brittany," Derek said in a stern yet understanding voice. "We need to talk and then the doctors will help you sleep."

She quieted down. "How long will I sleep?"

"Until you are ready to face the world again."

"Forever, then," she sighed, and the tension left her body. "What do you need to know?"

"Tell me what happened. Everything."

She shivered. "I was with Lucero and Natalie. Lyssa was flying by herself near the stables. I know you said not to let our dragons be by themselves, but she was within sight of the stables the whole time."

"Then what happened?"

"Lyssa said a mist surrounded her and she was frightened, then – without warning – I couldn't communicate with her at all, and then a few seconds later she was screaming and then she was gone!"

Brittany's lip trembled and tears ran down her face, but she kept it together. "I started running for help as soon as the mist happened but it was too late and she's gone!"

She wasn't going to be able to keep it together for much longer, Chris could tell. He was amazed she could talk about it at all after the ferocity of her actions before and her desperation for death. He pondered what she had said. What role did the mist play? Normally the mist protected the dragons, but in this case it seemed to be actively disorienting them and leading to their deaths. Was it because they were in Spokane, too far from the source of the mist? Or was there someone nearby whose dragon could control the mist, as had sometimes happened in the past? A true mystery, one that even Jamie didn't seem able to solve if he had sent Scott here to investigate.

"Can I sleep now?" Brittany asked with an edge of desperation in her voice.

Derek placed his palm on her sweaty forehead. "Yes, thank you for your help. The doctors will monitor you and make sure you remain healthy until you're ready to return to the world."

She laughed bitterly. "They'll be waiting a long time."

Derek, Scott, and Chris left the room as the doctors got to work. Chris knew from one of the other survivors that it would in reality only be about a month before Brittany was ready to face existence without a dragon at her side. It was a devastating loss, but not one that required death. He remembered the needle in his hand, the death he had been about to deal, and felt ashamed. They had nearly lost out on valuable information because his emotions got in the way and made him sympathize with the girl's plight too much. Ashton was right: it was better to be hard and use logic, not emotion. He was just glad that Derek had been present to prevent him from making a mistake.

He glanced over at Derek, but the man's attention was solely focused on Scott. Good, Chris thought. Let his predatory nature come out and let him seduce Scott away from Jamie. It was just one more step closer to the future that Ashton had predicted. Chris smiled at them as they headed off to the stables to look for any signs of the enemy. He headed back to his and Derek's chambers to move some of his more obvious belongings out of the way so Scott wouldn't be faced with obvious reminders of Chris's presence. After all, he wanted Derek to succeed in his seduction. Humming quietly to himself, he began packing up his clothes to move to his personal rooms next door and wondered if Derek and Scott would find anything.

CHAPTER FIVE

Misty Encounter

D erek didn't blame Chris for what he had been about to do to the girl, but that didn't mean he forgave the man. Chris had been about to end the girl's life, and not only would that have cost them precious information, not only would it have been a morally questionable act, it would have meant that Chris couldn't see a future for the girl when Derek knew she was only in temporary pain and was fully capable of living a long, fulfilling life. Just because things looked bleak now didn't mean that they would always look that way for her.

Derek's best friend in high school had tried to kill himself when they were freshmen. He hadn't been able to see anything in the future worth living for, and he had tried to take his own life. Derek, luckily, had seen the warning signs and gotten him help. Once Jake was on medication for his depression – which no one had even suspected him of having – he began to see the beauty of life again and in just a few years he was enjoying life again.

Derek had no question that when Jake acted and tried to over-dose on pills before Derek had caught him, life had seemed like it would never go anywhere. But now Jake had a future, just as the girl would have a future once she got past this momentary disaster. It would just take time, and maybe medication, and a lot of love from her family and friends, but she would recover.

Yet even though he believed that with all his heart, he knew that she would never fully recover, never fully be the same. She had lost a part of her soul that she would never regain. She might start enjoying life again, but she would always be missing her dragon. Time would dull the pain, but it would never entirely go away. He shuddered and thought of what would happen if he lost Jettie. He would certainly want to die, but he could imagine himself surviving, living a half-life without her, able to function but not fully living life. It would be terrible, but it would be better than death, he thought. After all, Jettie wouldn't want him to die. She would want him to live and be happy.

He felt a mental nudge from her and knew she didn't like where his thoughts were headed.

I am safe, she assured him. *The others protect me at all times.*

He nodded.

"Are you all right?" Scott asked.

Derek had been so caught up in his thoughts he had nearly forgotten Scott at his side. He took a deep breath and inhaled the spicy scent of his former – and future, he hoped – lover.

"Just a little shaken," he admitted.

He could admit his weaknesses to Scott. Scott understood him and wouldn't judge him, and besides, Scott enjoyed protecting people so showing Derek's vulnerability was a good way to get Scott on his side. He suspected that was one reason Scott was still with Jamie – Jamie just needed him more than Derek did.

Scott put his arm around Derek as they walked.

"You handled that very well. She'll survive and maybe one day be happy that she's still alive."

Derek nodded. He was glad that Scott shared his sentiment. It chilled him a little that Chris was prepared to kill the girl, even though he completely understood Chris's motives.

They were almost at the stables when they heard horses shrieking and a dense mist surrounded them. Derek clutched Scott tightly and the man cradled him in his arms. Derek would have enjoyed it more if he hadn't been terrified of the mist and if the horses' screams weren't piercing the invisible white cone around them. A heavy wind raced around them but didn't lift the mist and Scott grabbed him tighter as if trying to root them to the ground. There was a sudden sucking sensation as if they were being pulled in one direction and they wavered, on the brink of falling, as the sound of an inhalation surrounded them. Then there was a snuffling sound and the sound of something enormous taking off. The mist traveled upwards and the ground was visible, then their knees, then all of them, and a great ball of mist traveled upward and away into the sky.

It was awe-inspiring, as if a dragon were surrounded by the mist itself and had its own personal cloak. Derek pushed free of Scott and took a few steps towards the mist that was rapidly leaving the area. Was it a dragon? The inhalation, almost as if a large dragon had sniffed them to inspect their scents. Scott had a dazed look on his face and Derek knew his own expression must be similar.

"Narné has no idea what that was," Scott said. "But he sees blood in the future."

Derek shivered. Narné's gift of telling the possible future was not very comforting this time. At Derek's shiver, Scott's attention snapped back to him.

"Derek, are you okay? You're pale. Are you hurt?"

"I'm fine," he said. "Just a little shaken."

In truth he was terrified. There was a dragon in his territory that Jamie couldn't reach or speak to, that traveled in its own personal mist and couldn't be seen or stopped, and that was feeding on his dragons with impunity. What if it came after Jettie? After all, it had sniffed him and Derek. What if it would now target their dragons even if their dragons remained in groups? And with the power and size this dragon seemed to have, why bother attacking lone dragons? It could probably take on a group.

"Let me get you back to your room, Derek," Scott said, wrapping his arm around Derek's shoulders and leading him away from the stables. As his arm landed on Derek's shoulder, he made a tutting sound.

"You're shaking, honey. But you're safe. I won't let anything happen to you or to Jettie."

"How can we stop something like that?"

"We'll find a way."

Derek sighed and took comfort in Scott's arm. He often dreamed of Scott touching him like this, but for once he was too genuinely shaken to enjoy it. He had not counted on that when he invited Scott to come to Spokane. He had expected it to all be about seduction; a monster dragon was an unwelcome visitor.

When they reached Derek's rooms, he immediately noted that Chris had removed all of his items and he was silently thankful for the man. Scott didn't notice anything, of course, and that was the point. It looked like Derek's room, not a shared room with Chris. Scott escorted him to his bedroom and Derek's heart hitched. The fear began to fade.

"You should get some rest after a shock like that," Scott said.

"Will you help me undress? My hands are shaky," Derek said, holding up hands that were legitimately shaking.

Scott looked at him for a long moment as if calculating whether or not this was a good idea, then approached him and began unbuttoning Derek's shirt. Derek inwardly cheered, though he had to admit that he really needed the help, since he didn't think he could manage the buttons in his current state. He really was shaken up. Scott's hands were cool and professional, but Derek could see a flicker of lust in his eyes even though Scott tried to hide it.

He knew that Scott was still attracted to him even though Scott claimed to belong to Jamie, and it gave him hope. If Scott only liked him as a friend, he would give up and accept friendship. But moments like these were what sparked Derek on and gave him the courage to keep pushing for more. Scott's hands were gentle against his skin but he lingered a little too long as he unbuttoned, another sign. When his shirt was finally undone, Scott pulled it off and eyed his shirtless body.

"You're still shaking," he said, placing a hand in the center of Derek's chest.

Derek moaned and leaned into the unexpected touch. Yes, Scott was still interested. There was no other reason for this touch except as an excuse to feel Derek up. Scott blushed, but kept his hand there and grabbed Derek's bare shoulder with his other hand. He pushed Derek back into the bed and began removing Derek's shoes. Once they were off, he arranged Derek's feet on the bed and pulled the covers over him. Derek was a little disappointed Scott wouldn't be stripping his pants off, but maybe that would be too obvious a come on for the shy Scott.

After Derek was tucked into bed, Scott sat in a chair a few feet away.

"I'll stay until you're safely asleep," he said. "I'll just be talking to Narné and Marisol."

"Thank you," Derek said.

Scott smiled at him and Derek knew he would remember that open, carefree smile for a long time. Scott wasn't thinking about Jamie or disappearing dragons or anything else – he was only thinking about Derek. It was a smile not to be forgotten.

Derek shut his eyes and soon enough, sleep took him. It felt as though mist were covering his senses and for a moment he panicked because of the lingering fear from earlier in the day when the mist had been protecting such a terrible beast. Then he realized it was the same mist, only he could see inside it now. He reached out to Jettie and found that she was with him, seeing the same thing he was seeing. He could reach through the mist, somehow, and in an instant he saw the beast within the mist.

It was terrible and beautiful all in one. Massive. Far larger than any dragon he had ever seen, including Marisol. It was a gray-green color and looked skinny, as if it hadn't been getting enough to eat. He could count its ribs and he wondered how large it would be if fully fed. The dragon was flying through a dark tunnel and soon it reached a large cavern with a platform in the middle, where a man stood.

The man reached out to caress the dragon, then turned to face where Derek was. It seemed as though he stared straight into Derek's soul.

"You've brought a visitor, my dragon," the man said in a low, rich voice. "I assume you are the Queen we scented earlier. Welcome, Queen."

Derek tried to speak but no words came out. He was asleep, after all, though this was like no dream he had ever had before. He could sense Jettie struggling to speak as well but facing the same dilemma. They were both mute. Thousands of questions were piling up but all Derek could do was study the man and hope to recognize him and perhaps tell someone about him when he woke up.

The man was older, perhaps Ashton's age. He appeared Asian, with light tan skin and almond eyes. He wore a cloak with a hood so it was difficult to see much of his face. Like his dragon, he seemed starved and skinny under his robes. Derek tried to look around and figure out where they were but the cavern was poorly lit and all he could see was the platform they were on, made of earth. Useless.

"We will meet again, my Queen," the man said with a smile. "At your mating flight. I intend to become your mate."

Anger burned through Derek at that comment. How dare this man assume that he was even invited in Derek's mating flight? Let alone assume that he would win it? Chris was going to be Derek's mate; it was all but decided. Everyone knew, and everyone had silently agreed to give a good flight but let the Queen decide her own mate, which would be Chris.

But fear filled him as well as he studied the dragon. Because it was so huge, and so much larger and stronger than the other dragons, he knew this man would have an immense advantage in the mating flight. Would Chris be able to outfly this monster even if Chris had Derek's blessing? Fear overcame him and he felt the mist covering his senses. He must be waking up. Everything faded and when he opened his eyes, it was nighttime and Scott was asleep in the bed beside him.

Derek sighed and looked at Scott. At least he had a little more information on the disappearances now.

CHAPTER SIX

Jettie's Gift

Scott awoke with Derek cuddled against him. He didn't move at first, afraid that he would awaken the boy. He silently cursed himself for falling asleep next to him. Of course Derek would curl into his arms like this. Even if Derek had done it unconsciously, it was a perfectly natural position for the two of them after everything they had shared. He would just have to hope that it was unconscious and Derek didn't realize they had slept together – again – and Scott would have to be careful extricating himself from this delicate position.

But as soon as he pulled away, Derek's grip on his forearm tightened and the boy moaned in disappointment. Scott stayed where he was and Derek stirred in his arms, then rolled out of their spooning position to face him. His face was still white with residual fear, Scott noted, and the usual predatory gleam was gone. He looked frightened. Scott pulled him closer and hugged him.

"I had a vision, Scott," Derek whispered. "I want it to be a dream, but it was too real. Jettie saw it too. We saw inside the mist."

Scott inhaled sharply. Jettie had shown no sign of her ability yet; was this it?

"What did you see?"

"A dragon," Derek said in the same hoarse whisper. "An enormous green dragon so old it was grey. And a man who recognized me. The dragon was his."

"Who were they?"

Scott tried to keep the urgency out of his voice but he could feel Narné pressing for the information. If Marisol knew the name of the dragon or the rider, she could read them the same way she could read the other dragons. The other dragons were part of Tarragon society and their names were commonly known by all dragons, but because this strange dragon wasn't known by any others, Jamie and Marisol were blind to it.

"I don't know," Derek said, and Scott shut his eyes in defeat. "But he said," Derek continued in a low, frightened voice, "He said he would see me at my mating flight, that he intended to become my mate."

Scott's eyes snapped open again and he pulled back to examine the terrified Derek. No wonder Derek was still pale. He knew Derek was frightened of the mating flight even though Derek's flight was all but decided given the boy's preference for Chris. It was a frightening experience. Jamie's first mating flight had been chaotic, to say the least, and Scott had barely won even though he was Jamie's choice. Jamie's second mating flight hadn't been any better and Scott knew that Jamie was secretly afraid all of his mating flights would be traumatic events. And if Jamie was terrified of his mating flights even with Scott at his side, Derek must be doubly so.

"Can you tell me anything about him, Derek?"

Derek described what he had seen and Scott pondered. A long tunnel leading to a cavern. It would make sense for a dragon and his partner to be hiding in a cave nearby, but where? And who was this man Derek had described?

"Is that Jettie's power, Scott? Letting me see into the mist?"

Scott allowed his mind to return to the present for a moment instead of dwelling on the future and he stroked Derek's shoulder.

"I believe so. If you can see into the mist wherever it is, then it is a very powerful gift because the mist follows dragons all over the world. Perhaps you can even control the mist if you try hard enough."

"But how did he see me, and why couldn't I speak? Was I really there?"

"You were here the whole time," Scott reassured him. "You were only there in spirit. I don't know how he saw you," Scott admitted, "But you weren't in any danger. And if he intends on being in your mating flight, then I don't think Jettie is in any danger either."

Derek let out a slow, shuddering breath. "I don't want him in my mating flight. I think he's the one who's killing the dragons. He looked so skinny, like he was starving, and I can't help but think that he's been killing the dragons to feed on. It's just this sense I have."

"You may be right. If he is an ancient being, then he may follow the same laws that Ashton followed and eat live dragons," Scott said with a shudder. "We cannot allow him to win your mating flight. We have to find him before that happens."

Derek nodded vehemently, then his body relaxed and seemed to contour to Scott's body in an extremely intimate and arousing way. Scott inhaled and tried to prevent his body from responding. He was in bed with Derek to comfort the boy, not to seduce him. Derek snuggled closer and ducked his head under Scott's so that his breath tickled Scott's neck. Derek's hands wrapped around his neck and began rubbing his shoulders. Scott shut his eyes and his breathing sped up. He needed to end this, right now, but it felt so good.

Jamie rarely cuddled with him like this anymore, though he didn't know why. Jamie had been through so much, though, it was hard to question anything he did or didn't do. Scott was just glad that Jamie still loved him. But he missed moments like this with Jamie, when sex was out of the question but they still wanted to be close to each other and share each other's bodies.

His hands tightened on Derek's shoulders almost without his permission as he clung to the boy and inhaled the clean scent of his dark hair.

Then, reluctantly, he pulled away. Derek looked disappointed but not surprised as Scott got up from the bed and straightened his clothing. Derek also got up and put a shirt on, then toed on his shoes. They had slept through the night and already the sun had risen outside. Scott had not meant to spend the entire night here and he hoped no one had noticed, or at least no one who would report it back to Jamie. The dragons would tell Jamie if Jamie asked, but dragons weren't the type who volunteered information. Occasionally it was annoying having Jamie be on such good terms with all of the dragons, since the dragons would tell Jamie anything and everything he asked because they considered him one of their own, but most of the time it was a boon.

Like now, he thought as Narné informed Marisol of Derek's vision and Jettie's gift. Her gift was unusual, but would serve them well, especially if Derek could manipulate the mist as well as see into it. They would have to test his ability to control the mist today to learn the extent of Jettie's powers. After breakfast, of course.

Jettie ate an entire cow as her crowd of guards looked on and Derek and Scott nibbled on sandwiches at the edge of the pasture. Normally they would eat away from the carnage, but Derek was a little jumpy after his vision and he wanted to be close to Jettie, and Scott didn't want to argue with him. So he tried to ignore the cow as he ate his sandwich and drank a soda. Derek looked a lot better after he ate, or maybe it was just being near Jettie that improved his mood and appearance. Scott could appreciate how frightening it was living somewhere where dragons were being plucked off one by one; Narné was with them in the pasture and Scott was glad that he was with them and with a large crowd of dragons.

They were going to see if Derek could control the mist after breakfast, but they didn't want to accidentally summon the killer dragon so they had almost a full wing of dragons present to attack if the killer dragon did appear. The dragons were watching Jettie eat right now, but they were constantly vigilant. As soon as she finished her meal, she flew over to the fence where they sat and nuzzled two of them until they moved aside and let her sit between them. Narné was a couple dragons down on the fence. They looked like enormous crows on a telephone wire and Scott smiled. Then it was down to business.

Derek's first task was to see if he could see into the mist while awake. But as much as he tried, he couldn't see anything. When Jettie began to get irritated at being told to relax and see into the mist, they switched to the other part of the training: controlling the mist. One of the councilmembers, an older woman with short hair who vaguely reminded Scott of Margot, was leading Derek's lesson.

"Now I want you imagine a ball of mist in your upturned palm," she said.

Derek rolled his eyes but kept his hands palm up and seemed to be concentrating. Then he shouted. A wisp of mist had appeared over his right palm.

"Very good," the woman said without any emotion. "Now imagine it growing into a ball."

Derek narrowed his eyes as Scott watched in amazement. He had always assumed that the mist obeyed no one but the mountain, but here was proof that it could be manipulated. The mysterious man with the killer dragon must also be able to control the mist, he thought, or else the mist wouldn't protect his dragon the way it did.

The wisp of mist turned into a ball that began expanding rapidly, growing to encompass Derek's entire arm and shoulder.

"Not so fast," the woman said. "Imagine it shrinking."

But the ball was growing now and within seconds Derek's entire body was encased in mist. The ball did stop then, and they

41

heard Derek's frightened shout.

"Help," he cried. "I can't stop it; I can't see anything!"

"Imagine the ball of mist shrinking," the woman said, still in that emotionless voice as if she'd taught this lesson a hundred times before. "Imagine you are popping the bubble of mist with a pin and the mist is escaping outward and shrinking."

There was an audible popping sound and suddenly the ball of mist began shrinking as if someone had let the air out of it. It appeared that the second part of the woman's advice had worked. Soon the mist was a small ball in Derek's palm again and he was staring at them in awe and fear.

"I want you to envision the mist in your hand circling Scott," the woman said.

Scott blinked. He hadn't been expecting this. Derek looked at him and blushed as though he were going to refuse, then he tossed his hand so the wisp of mist flew towards Scott and landed at his feet. At the woman's instructions, Derek made it large again and soon mist covered Scott's senses. He was lost in a field of grey-white mist, unable to see his own hand in front of his face. He was blind, and barely able to hear anything. The mist was a guide on campus but now it was a weapon and he realized that Derek had truly been given a double-edged sword. Derek could protect people with this gift by hiding them in the mist, but he could also blind his enemies and make them helpless.

Scott didn't cry out for help, however. He stood bravely until the mist shrank, though he did take a deep breath as soon as it was gone. He hoped he would never experience that kind of fuzzy blindness ever again and he wondered how the killer dragon could fly in it. The dragon must have an excellent memory of where to go – and he must not be going very far. They would have to scour the area around the stables for any signs of a cave or cavern. The humans would have to do it, since any dragon in the area was at risk of being eaten, and it would take much longer, but it had to be done.

When the lesson was over, Derek was beaming. He looked delighted, as did Jettie. Scott knew that Derek had been genuinely worried about Jettie not having a gift because of Ashton's comments that Jettie wasn't a true Queen, and he hoped this would calm any of Derek's remaining fears. Just because Jettie and Derek weren't bonded as deeply as Jamie and Marisol didn't lessen the fact that they were Queens, or at least that's what Scott thought. Jamie and Marisol would always be the first Queens, but Derek and Jettie would always be respected and valuable.

He bid Derek a temporary farewell and headed towards the stables to meet up with a group of other dragon partners ready to search the area for any signs of Lyssa, the last missing dragon, and to search for signs of a tunnel that a large dragon could fly into. Derek was in a much better mood and Scott hoped it would continue. He hated seeing Derek frightened. He still didn't know what to do about Derek's mating flight if they didn't find the strange man in time, but at least they knew that the stranger would show himself and it would be a chance to catch him and bring him to justice. And if they happened to find out his name or his dragon's name beforehand, then Jamie would be able to track them and prevent them from being in the mating flight completely.

Filled with resolve, Scott set out to find the stranger and prevent the blood that Narné and Mike had warned was coming.

CHAPTER SEVEN

Forgotten Continent

The cat stared at him, then at his bowl of cereal. She meowed. With a sigh, he pushed the bowl towards her. Jamie was finished and there was just milk left, but he usually enjoyed drinking the milk. It seemed that he would no longer have that privilege now that he had a cat.

As she drank her milk, he thought about Scott and Derek together in Spokane and squelched the jealousy that threatened to overtake him. Derek had discovered his and Jettie's power, and he would need help channeling it. Scott might have to stay even longer while they followed up on the lead Derek had given them. He did feel sorry for Derek, though, since he knew how frightening the thought of the first mating flight could be, especially when it seemed like the flight would be won by someone undesirable.

Scott had originally been banned from Jamie's first flight and only a trick had allowed him to participate, so Jamie had needed to mentally prepare himself to sleep with someone else. It hadn't come to pass, luckily, but just the threat had weighed Jamie down heavily. He couldn't imagine the fear that Derek felt, knowing that a ruthless killer had set his sights on Derek's mating flight and seemed poised to win. They had to find the man before the mating flight. If he won the mating flight, he would have far too much power and they would be unable to deal with him.

Jamie shivered. Deal with him. Kill him, the words meant, and Jamie wondered if he, as the Queen, would again be expected to strike the killing blow. He hoped not. He still remembered how difficult it had been to pierce Ashton's skin, then how easily the blade had seared through once the blade had severed the outer layer. He had nearly decapitated the man in his attempts to kill Ashton. The blood that had splattered across his face and body and hands would never leave him. In some ways he didn't want it to leave him; when he felt that phantom blood, it was a reminder of what he had done, what he had become. What made him any different than this man in Spokane?

The cat finished her milk and meowed at him, batting a paw at his face as if trying to force him out of his thoughts, and at the same time Marisol sent an indignant snort his way.

You are nothing like this man, she said. *He kills for pleasure. You did it out of necessity, to protect, and only because you had no choice.*

The cat meowed again, almost as if she could hear Marisol and agreed with her words. Jamie mentally shrugged and stroked the cat's head. They were right, of course. He was nothing like the man with the killer dragon. But he had killed, and that set him apart from everyone else on campus. If only Kale were here. Kale would understand. But Kale was dead, killed by Ashton, and Kale's lover Mike was still recovering from that death. Tears of sorrow and frustration welled up in Jamie's eyes. He knew life wasn't fair – he had learned that lesson long ago when his parents died – but why did it have to be so incredibly unfair? Why did so many bad things have to happen to so many good people?

A knock sounded at the door and Jamie sniffled. He mentally pulled himself together and petted the cat several more times before another knock sounded. He vaguely remembered that he had a meeting scheduled for this morning. Taking a deep breath, he went to the door and opened it. A handsome black man stood on the other side dressed in an orange and green robe. The vibrant colors were a stark contrast to the clothing worn by most of the councilmembers, who preferred shades of grey and especially black, with only occasional flashes of red. He blinked and invited the man in.

"Thank you for your time, Queen Jamie," the man said in a gorgeous African accent. The words just seemed to flow off his tongue like honey and Jamie suddenly realized that even though Tarragon Academy represented students from around the world, very few of them had accents.

"My name is Akwa Falana, and I come to you from Nigeria to represent the peoples of Africa."

Jamie nodded, and sent a thought to Marisol to get information about this man and his dragon. To his surprise, Marisol replied that the man didn't have a dragon and Jamie's eyes widened.

"How are you here without-"

Jamie paused as the rest of the story flooded in from other dragons. Akwa had been a student here many, many decades ago and Ashton had chosen him as a sacrifice. His dragon had been killed but he had managed to escape the mountain. No one saw him for years and everyone assumed that he had been sacrificed with his dragon as planned. Jamie was disturbed as usual by the dragon's willingness to accept the human sacrifices as part of the pact that protected them. It was only the fact that Ashton had been drinking dragon blood that made them turn against Ashton, not the fact that Ashton had been killing humans and dragons for centuries. But this man in front of him had possessed a dragon, and lost it in the most horrific way possible, and Jamie had rudely brought up that fact.

"I'm so sorry," he said quickly.

Akwa looked at him with a stoic expression. "It's true, then, that you can speak to the dragons? They've told you about me?"

"Yes. I'm so sorry. I didn't know."

"I am not offended. You are a child, after all."

Jamie stiffened.

"You must not be offended by my words, Queen," Akwa said, raising his hands. "You have undoubtedly experienced too much of this world for your age, but your wisdom has yet to be tempered by time."

Jamie nodded. Even he could agree that he was too young for the weight that he carried and he only hoped that time did make it easier. Jamie escorted Akwa to the formal sitting room and offered him some tea, which the man accepted. While Jamie prepared the tea, he thought about the man's beautiful accent and wondered again why there weren't more accents on campus. Many of the students came from other countries, but they all spoke flawless American English. He knew that part of living in Tarragon society was learning English no matter where in the world you lived, but surely more people would have accents. He brought the tea back in the room and Akwa rose to take it from him.

"You have no servants?" he asked.

"No," Jamie said. "I don't need any."

"You are a refreshing change," he said. "Perhaps the change we need."

He took a sip of tea, smiled, and set his tea down. Then he leaned back and placed his hands on his knees. It was time for business, whatever his business was.

"You see, Jamie, for the past sixty years, ever since I escaped this place, I have forbidden my African brethren from coming here even though it means they are doomed to live shortened lives. It is better to die in your twenties than experience the loss I experienced."

"You mean, no one from Africa goes to this school?"

Jamie's mind whirled but he realized with shock that almost everyone at the school was white. There were Asians, and Native Americans, but everyone else was European or American. Surely, though, some of the Americans would be black, but as Jamie thought about all the students, he realized that they weren't. It wasn't that unusual for a lack of racial diversity in the Pacific Northwest, so it hadn't occurred to him before, but it was definitely something he intended to change.

The other part of Akwa's message suddenly hit him. If people of Tarragon descent didn't bond with a dragon, they inevitably died young, usually in their twenties. Old enough to pass on their genes to the next generation, but not old enough to take care of that generation.

"You see our dilemma, I'm sure," Akwa said. "We are still a tribal society and we welcome outsiders into our tribes to take care of our young communally, but everyone knows who is part of the clan and who is an outsider. We have managed to avoid urban life for the most part, though it creeps in at times, and we hold true to the traditions that have kept Tarragon society strong for thousands of years. But our children think dragons are a thing of the past and they are doomed to die. We need to give them hope. We need to give them life. Will you help us?"

"Wait, you teach them about dragons? They would be coming to campus already knowing about dragons?"

"We are not a society like yours that scorns such myths. We believe in many of the old stories."

Jamie thought of the other clans he had learned about in his classes, and how the teachers had been so dismissive of the truth of those myths even while he wondered if perhaps they were true. Maybe having believers in the class would be a good experience. And he had been toying with the idea of slowly introducing the idea of dragons to the first year students so that the exam wasn't such a shock.

"It would be a huge adjustment for them," Jamie said slowly. "We would need to restructure a lot of things here. How many eligible students do you have?"

"We do not follow a traditional school system, but I have been to college and know the standards you use. We have just less than two hundred students who would do well at Tarragon

Academy."

On the one hand, it was a large number, since each campus could only hold one hundred freshmen each year. There was no way he could take all of them, especially since he had to take students from the rest of the world. But on the other hand, it was a remarkably small number. Germany, a single country, had over six hundred, and Africa was an entire continent. Clearly many of the Tarragon descendants had died without leaving children in the past sixty years since they had stopped coming to the academy. It was almost sickening that they had been deprived of their survival.

Jamie tried not to blame the man in front of him for those deaths, but it was hard. Akwa had valid reason for keeping his people away from Ashton, but leaving them to die? Ashton wouldn't have sacrificed all of them; most of them would have survived and an entire continent's worth of people could have been saved. But he saw the sadness in Akwa's eyes and knew the man blamed himself and Jamie didn't need to heap any more blame on him. Akwa had made a terrible decision and had to live with it, just as Jamie was learning to live with the terrible decisions he was being forced to make.

"I don't know how many we can take," Jamie said honestly. "The council has a committee in charge of recruiting students and I was planning on telling them to just double whatever they usually do."

Akwa waved his hand dismissively. "They recruit based on the wallet. Those with the highest bribes get in. Their children are usually already living in the United States and many have been chosen by Ashton as future councilmembers. If you wish to help people, put the countries in charge of recruitment. There will still be bribes, but at least the academy will be clean."

Jamie swallowed hard. He hadn't ever thought that the council was getting kickbacks from the parents of students. He had assumed that they studied each student's resume and chose the best for the academy. But now that Akwa said it, it was obvious.

After all, the recruitment committee was the most sought after committee to be on, even though Jamie had assumed it was the most work. Akwa's suggestion was a good one. Each country had a lead dragon and partner. If he put that man or woman in charge, then the academy couldn't be accused of bribery. And he didn't want to start his first year as Queen with bribery charges floating around.

"Thank you for the suggestion," he said. "I will take everything you've said into consideration. I can assure you, however, that Africa will be included when it comes time to recruit for next year."

"Thank you, Queen Jamie. That is all I can hope for."

Akwa stood and shook hands firmly, then Jamie led him out. The cat watched from the kitchen table, where she hadn't moved. As soon as the stranger left, she hopped down and twirled around Jamie's feet. He needed someone in the council to talk to in order to figure out what to do about students, but there were very few people he could trust. Mike was in Spokane, and he was Jamie's first choice, but Eric was here and he could generally be relied on. He was new, and might not know a lot about recruitment of students, but he would at least know how to handle the council during the transition into a bribe-free environment.

The council was going to be pissed, Jamie thought with a wry smile. But it had to be done. If it meant a fair, equal campus, he would see it done.

CHAPTER EIGHT

Nightmare

Derek snuck back into his room for a quick nap. He was exhausted after channeling the mist. Even though the mist was insubstantial, it had felt like he was sculpting something enormous and heavy with his mind the entire time, and he was drained. Besides, he hadn't been getting sleep lately and he had gotten in the habit of taking quick naps throughout the day. He passed Chris on the way to his room and glanced down awkwardly, a little embarrassed at the thought that he and Scott had slept in the same bed last night, the very bed that he and Chris usually slept in.

But Chris didn't look upset at all. He clapped a hand on Derek's shoulder and waited until Derek met his gaze.

"How are you doing, Derek?" he asked seriously. "Are you better?"

"Yeah," Derek said. "I was a little freaked out after that dream with the stranger, but I feel like I have my powers under control now. Jettie's power is pretty cool, isn't it?"

Chris smiled. "Yeah, it is. You'll be able to monitor what dragons are doing all over the world."

Derek perked up a little. He hadn't thought through all of the advantages of Jettie's power yet. Dragons used the mist as protection whenever they left the academy, so it would make sense that he would be able to see them wherever they went. That could be a definite advantage. Jamie might be able to talk to all the dragons, but he would be able to see them and that wasn't bad. He smiled and Chris shared his smile.

"Taking a nap?" Chris asked, gesturing towards their room where Derek was headed. Derek nodded. He was a little shy about Scott knowing he was taking a nap, but Chris knew all about his daytime naps.

"Sweet dreams," Chris said, kissing his cheek. "I'm going to see if Scott needs any help."

"Good luck," Derek said, kissing him back.

Derek watched Chris leave, then slid inside his room and shut the door softly. He leapt onto the bed in a fit of happiness. He couldn't believe his luck. He had the best boyfriend ever, and the best crush. He was in love with two people and both of them seemed to be okay with him being with the other. Of course, Scott wouldn't admit that he was one of Derek's loves, but after this morning it was hard to argue. They had slept together yet again and there had been definite attraction. Derek clutched a pillow to his chest and replayed the moment when Scott's body had seemed to melt against his and for the briefest moment, they had felt like two lovers entwined after sex. It had been so brief, but it had been there, that moment of intimacy that defined their relationship.

Derek cuddled the pillow and let his eyes drift shut. It felt as though a warm mist surrounded him and he sighed happily and tried to imagine Scott's arms around him. But the feeling wouldn't come, and for some reason he felt a gust of air as if something enormous was breathing on him. He opened his eyes and gasped in fear.

The grey-green dragon was staring at him with dark gold eyes as it shifted in a large hollowed out place in the earth. It settled its enormous head back on the ground and breathed out, the warm air gusting over him again.

"Well, Queen, it looks like you've returned," a voice said from behind him, and Derek whirled, terror spiking as he already knew what he would see.

A man dressed in robes and a hood stood as if he had been expecting to see Derek, his arms crossed and one finger tapping his wrist as if he had been waiting impatiently. Derek tried to remain calm. He wasn't here, not really. The man couldn't hurt him. The man didn't want to hurt him, he reminded himself. The man wanted to be in his mating flight and that couldn't happen if he or Jettie were injured.

The man walked closer and held his hand out, and Derek fully expected it to pass right through him, the way it happened with ghosts in movies. After, Derek wasn't really here. Scott had assured him that his real body was still in bed. This was only his spirit. But the man's hand hit his shoulder with gentle force and stopped. Derek felt as if his confidence were leaking through his feet and he were shrinking. If this man could touch him, there was no telling what he could do.

"I'm not going to hurt you," the man whispered as though he could sense Derek's sudden panic.

Derek wanted to run, but his feet were locked in place. He didn't know how to move in this strange dream-like trance. All he could do was stand still as the man stroked his shoulder. The touch wasn't harmful, but it was commanding, as if the man were claiming him as his own. Derek tried to move away but his body – or whatever he had in this strange dream – refused to budge.

The man leaned close and Derek could feel his breath on his ear and smell the slightly sweet scent of blood as he spoke.

"You're so beautiful, Queen. It will be a pleasure to win your mating flight."

Derek shuddered, but his body didn't move. This man was the killer; the blood on his breath gave him away. And he was going to win the mating flight unless something was done to him beforehand. Someone needed to kill him, soon. The man released Derek's shoulder and placed both hands on his hood, pulling it

53

back to reveal an incredibly handsome Asian man. Under other circumstances Derek would be quite attracted to him, but not like this. Then the man pulled his robe apart and it fell to the floor, exposing his nude body.

He was incredibly built, and Derek couldn't help but stare as the man flexed his impressive muscles and seemed to watch Derek's gaze travel over his gorgeous body. He had to be at least fifty, but his body was solid with muscle and appeared younger. He wasn't thick with muscle; he was slim in exactly the way Derek liked, lightly but powerfully muscled. And his cock was incredible. Derek couldn't help but stare and knew that the man enjoyed his gaze as the man started to harden as he watched.

Derek knew that he was gifted in that area, but this man made him look below average. He couldn't even imagine having sex with this man, the thought made him squirm with imagined pain and pleasure. It would be excruciating, yet he could imagine it being incredibly good, too, especially if the man knew what he was doing, which he almost certainly did.

The man approached him and Derek's eyes snapped up to his face. The man embraced him and pressed their bodies together, rubbing slightly, cheeks against each other. Derek couldn't help but respond to such a beautiful display of manhood being ground against him and he felt shame that he was responding, but he couldn't help it. The man was gorgeous.

"That's it, Queen," the man murmured, his hands traveling around Derek's body to cup his ass and increase the pressure on his hardening cock. "Feel me."

Derek gasped as the man seemed to know exactly what to do to arouse him and fire began to flood his veins. He didn't want to be turned on by this but the man was so skilled. He let out a moan – although no sound escaped his lips – and part of him gave up and submitted to the touch. He couldn't fight and it felt so good, why not enjoy it? The man's fingers ground into his ass perfectly and the friction between their cocks was exactly what he needed to get hot. His breathing was starting to quicken and he knew his heart was racing. He shouldn't be feeling this, not with this man, but he had no choice in the matter. The man was irresistible.

The man leaned back, then shifted his head and kissed Derek. At first Derek resisted as much as he was able, but he wasn't in control of his body and his body was in heat and eager for the additional pleasure. His lips opened of their own accord and the man's tongue slid inside, and Derek felt his whole body jerk at the unexpected jolt of pleasure that ran through him. But there was also disgust as the taste of blood filled him, and no matter how amazing the kiss was, he couldn't get over the blood. It was everywhere until he felt he was drowning in the substance. Even as the man's tongue traced deep stripes on his own tongue, it felt as though he were only tracing the taste of blood deeper and deeper into his throat.

Derek involuntarily gagged and to his surprise, his body reacted. The man pulled away from the kiss and began kissing his cheeks and forehead which were flush and sweaty, his hands still massaging Derek's ass. Derek focused on a single word which he prayed would put an end to this. He envisioned the word as part of the mist, carried outward the same way he had sent the mist to entrap Scott earlier in the day. He sent the word spiraling outward until it rang through the room.

"No."

The man stopped abruptly as if shocked, and leaned back enough to stare at Derek. A flicker of a smile appeared on his lips as his hands slid from his ass to his back.

"You are powerful, Queen. I will do as you ask, but the day will come when you beg for me." He leaned until his lips brushed Derek's ear. "It will happen."

Derek flinched and shut his eyes. There was a whirling sensation and he opened his eyes immediately. He was back in his room, in just as aroused a state as he had been in the vision. He groaned and leaned into the pillow. He needed someone badly, someone who could reassure him it wouldn't happen, someone who could cleanse him of the taste of blood. He needed Scott. But would Scott be here for him?

Jettie, get Scott. I need him, he said.

He could sense Jettie's hesitation but also her need and he realized that if she were more mature, the vision he had just experienced would have sent her into her mating flight. Was that what the man wanted? Derek shivered. He was frightened at the thought of the man entering his dreams at will and pushing Jettie into a mating flight, frightened at his own lust, and only Scott could reassure him. But would he? Would he put aside his relationship with Jamie and see that Derek needed him desperately?

Derek shut his eyes and shivered. If anyone else slept with him right now, he knew without question that he would still have the memory of the man in the cave hanging over him and would live in fear, but if Scott slept with him, those fears would be erased because Scott would care for him and keep him safe. Scott would protect him. Wouldn't he? A tear ran down Derek's cheek. If Scott rejected him now, he wasn't sure what he would do. He would just have to wait and see if Scott came for him.

CHAPTER NINE

Derek's Need

Scott examined the ground where a large footprint was impressed into the slightly moist soil. It was at least twice the size of Narné's print and he was beginning to feel uneasy about the enemy they were facing. Before, when the killer was just a vague dragon and rider who were "large," as described by Derek, it was one thing. But now, seeing exactly how large the dragon was, he was chilled and realized that the dragon could probably easily win the mating flight unless something drastic were done to stop it. He didn't want to kill any dragons or riders, but it was looking like that was the only solution.

He was kneeling in the dirt when Chris came up to him and whistled, looking at the print as well. He wasn't sure how he felt about Chris. He was glad that Derek had someone like Chris in his life, but Chris was one of Ashton's men and according to Marisol still had some loyalty. But unfortunately, Chris had sunk his fangs into Derek so quickly after Ashton's death that Scott hadn't been able to steer Derek towards a more suitable lover. He didn't especially like Chris, but Derek could have done a lot worse.

"Do you have a plan yet?" Chris asked. "Derek's frightened. He may not say it, but I can see it."

Scott considered lying, or acting superior and dismissing Chris, but he knew that Chris might be an ally in the future despite his loyalties in the past, and besides, Chris was likely going to be Derek's mate and they would be working together. He didn't want to start out on the wrong foot. Honesty was the best answer.

"No," Scott said. "Jamie can't get a read without more information and I wouldn't dream of sending Derek back to get more information. If Marisol were here she might be able to smell something from this track, but she can't leave the eggs and Narné said the scent is too delicate for the other dragons to catch. We just have to keep watch and hope that we can catch the dragon now that we know what to look for."

"That's not very reassuring," Chris said. "But I suppose it's something. Derek will want to help."

"And when he can control his powers better, he can. But I don't want to risk hurting him or sending him back there before he can control the mist properly."

Chris nodded and stood up. Scott stood as well. They looked at each other and Scott was about to say something, he didn't know what, but he was going to extend some sort of olive branch when Narné's voice filled his mind and the outside world vanished for a moment.

Derek needs you, Narné said, and the sexual undertone left no doubt how Derek needed him. Scott at first shrugged it off, but Narné refused to let go of his attention.

If you ignore Derek now, if you leave him alone, he will side with the killer when the killer reveals himself. I have seen it, Narné said urgently. *You must go and be with Derek now.*

Scott blinked in shock. Why would Derek possibly side with the killer?

The killer will seduce him and without you to counterbalance him, Derek will be lost, Narné explained impatiently.

But what about Jamie? Scott asked. *I can't lose Jamie.*

Narné was silent for a moment. *I have not seen how this will effect Jamie. The future is not clear to me. But Derek's future is clear. If you do not go to him now, he will unite with the killer and we will have a war on our hands, a far deadlier war than our battle with*

Ashton.

Scott's mind whirled. He started walking towards Derek's room even though he hadn't decided what to do yet. He wouldn't do anything to risk his relationship with Jamie, but surely Jamie would understand. He tried to reach Marisol but she was asleep and wouldn't rouse. He silently cursed her for being asleep now, at the moment when he needed her most. He needed to know Jamie's reaction and he had no way of predicting it. Jamie had to understand, though. This would prevent another war, prevent Jamie from having to kill more people. It was a sacrifice, but it would save them from even greater sacrifices. Jamie *would* understand, he decided. But maybe he didn't have to have sex with Derek. Maybe just being there for Derek would be enough.

Suddenly he was aware of Chris at his side, walking with him and watching him carefully.

"Are you going to him?" Chris asked. "My dragon told me that Derek is in need and requested you, but if you refuse I should go to him."

Scott blushed. But perhaps there was a way out of this without sleeping with Derek. It would be scandalous and perhaps Jamie would be even more shocked than Scott having sex with Derek, but it could work.

"I've promised Jamie I won't have sex with Derek," Scott said honestly, "And I don't want to break that promise if I don't have to, but I will be there for Derek."

He hesitated and stared at Chris, wondering if he actually had the courage to say what he was thinking.

"So?" Chris prompted. "Do you need me or not?"

"Derek needs me," Scott said. "But I won't sleep with him. But I am willing to be there for him."

"I don't think he's looking for cuddling, if the dragons are correct."

Scott squirmed. "If I could be there for him but you could be the one actually – loving him, perhaps it would work."

Chris stared at him for a long moment, then laughed. "A threesome? You're suggesting a threesome?"

Scott felt his cheeks turn bright red as blood rushed to his face. He turned away and wished he could erase everything he had just said.

"Wait," Chris said, his laughter ending abruptly, "I'm sorry. That seems like a perfect solution. He wants you, but he also wants what you can't give him and I can. But are you sure about this? Are you sure you don't just want him yourself? Can you really share him?"

"I don't have much of a choice," Scott said stiffly. "Narné warns that something drastic will happen if I don't sleep with him, but I can't break my word to Jamie. Maybe if I'm with him but not, you know, with him, we can avoid the potential future and I can stay true to Jamie."

"You know how forceful Derek can be, don't you?" Chris asked seriously. "He may not be satisfied with you staying out of the action."

"Then you'll have to keep him busy," Scott said, blushing again.

Chris grinned and gestured towards Derek's room. They were only a few steps away. Scott took a deep breath.

Narné, he asked, *if I do this, will Derek still turn against us? Will this be enough?*

I don't know, Narné said. *I see no future for this turn of events. But at least you know that it won't inevitably end in failure.*

Scott nodded. So this might or might not work, but that was true of anything. He looked over at Chris and felt the heat rising in his cheeks again. His sexual experiences were fairly limited but he had a feeling that Chris was quite confident and experienced, and he just hoped he didn't look naïve in front of the man. Besides, this was his first threesome – he shook his head a little in disbelief that he was partaking in a threesome – and he didn't quite know how it was supposed to work. But he knew Derek, and knew that he couldn't let Derek down even as he couldn't break his promise to Jamie.

He and Chris entered the room and found Derek crouched on the bed, naked and hard as a rock, in the fetal position and terrified. Immediately all fears about the threesome fled Scott's mind and he and Chris both raced to Derek and began coaxing him out of the fetal position. He fell into Scott's arms and clutched Scott tightly. Chris stepped back and while a brief flash of jealousy crossed his features, he composed himself quickly.

"Hush, Derek, you're safe now," Scott crooned as he rocked Derek in his arms.

"He was there again," Derek said in a gasping voice. "And he touched me and made me feel things and I need you so bad right now!"

Scott let his hand drift down to Derek's erect penis and stroke it gently. Derek let out a pained moan and then his body softened against Scott's and some of the fear began to fade from his face.

"He said I would beg for him," Derek whispered.

"Never," Scott said in an equally quiet voice, well aware that Chris could hear both of them.

Scott lay flat on the bed and pulled Derek down with him so that they were lying flush against each other. He kissed Derek and Derek kissed back hesitantly at first, as though afraid of something, then his kisses became desperate. Scott kept one hand on Derek's cock as the boy began to relax into his touches. Then Chris came over and lay behind Derek, sliding his hands along Derek's back. At first Derek's eyes opened wide in surprise and he broke away from the kiss to see who it was, but when he saw Chris he smiled a little.

"You're both here," he said.

"You have a lot of people who care about you," Chris said in a husky voice Scott had never heard.

Derek's cheeks pinked and Chris kissed his forehead before running a hand along his jawline and directing his head back towards Scott. Derek obeyed and soon was kissing Scott again, with Chris massaging his back. The tension in Derek's body was almost entirely gone, but his arousal still demanded attention that Scott knew he couldn't give without breaking his promise to Jamie.

Derek seemed to gain some confidence by the touches of his two lovers because he grabbed Scott's hands and forced Scott flat on his back, straddling him. Chris lay to one side but quickly took up a position behind Derek, also straddling Scott, who felt doubly dominated. Derek's hands on his wrists were gentle as Derek kissed him deeply and he was aware of little else until Derek began taking Scott's shirt off. Scott hesitated for a moment, then began helping him. He didn't know what he had been thinking, but of course he was going to end up naked in this incident. Chris moved off both of them and stripped as well, seemingly quite aware that both Scott and Derek were watching him. Chris was a couple decades older than them, but handsome and well built, and Scott was a little envious that Derek had such a man for his first real lover. Of course, Scott had had Mike as his lover and Mike was incredible, but Derek was lucky as well.

With the clothes safely away, Derek took up his position straddling Scott again, this time their hard cocks rubbing up against each other. Derek leaned close against Scott's chest until Scott could feel his breath against his nipples and the delightful sensation made him harder. Chris was behind Derek, probably preparing his opening for penetration because of the little gasps of pleasure Derek was making. Derek alternated between simply breathing on Scott and kissing his chest, and then he fixed on Scott's nipples and Scott hissed at the sudden pleasure. One of Derek's hands reached between them and stroked their cocks and Scott wondered what would be considered sex in this strange threesome and what he would be able to tell Jamie. Nothing, he decided as he arched his back against Derek's hand and mouth. He would tell Jamie nothing.

Derek's lips traced back up his chest until they met his lips again, and then Derek drew away from him slightly and he hissed, his whole body going tense as Chris slid into him. Scott's hands rubbed small circles against Derek's hips to ease the penetration and then Derek let out a pleased sigh and returned to kissing Scott. Chris also sighed and started moving rhythmically against Derek's aroused body. The movement ground Derek into Scott, and the pressure was building inside his balls. He had not expected on cumming, but it now seemed inevitable unless they changed position and Derek seemed quite pleased where he was.

The steady rhythm grounded Scott as he kissed Derek and gave them purpose in their kisses, and allowed him to massage Derek's body in a more teasing way, knowing exactly when Derek was at the peak of his pleasure. Chris began alternating strokes and Scott could tell when Derek's prostrate was struck by the boy's reaction, and soon he realized that Chris would nod to him before doing so, allowing him to play with Derek's body and triple Derek's pleasure. Derek's cock quivered but never came even as Scott felt himself sliding closer and closer to release. Then, suddenly, Derek began pushing against both of them and struggling for a new position. Both Scott and Chris, ever ready to adjust for Derek's needs, paused. Derek kissed down Scott's body and began repositioning himself lower on the bed as Chris withdrew and scooted down as well.

At first Scott didn't realize what was happening. Then Derek's lips closed around the head of his penis and he gasped. He started to push Derek away from his cock, to insist that Derek not suck him off, not have oral sex with him because that would violate his promise with Jamie, but it felt so incredibly good and the look on Derek's face was one of hope and joy and Scott couldn't say anything. He caught sight of a knowing smirk on Chris's face, and then Scott closed his eyes in pure bliss as Derek's touch surrounded him. Would Jamie ever forgive him?

CHAPTER TEN

Threesome

C hris breathed in and out with his thrusts as he penetrated Derek's willing body and watched Scott writhe in pleasure underneath them. Scott might have said that he was just doing this to help Derek and not because he wanted the boy, but it was obvious that Scott had strong feelings for Derek and was getting significant sexual pleasure out of this experience. When Derek began moving down on Scott's body, Chris immediately knew that Derek was going to suck Scott off. He also knew from the bewildered look on Scott's face that Scott didn't realize what was happening until Derek's lips finally made contact with the man's cock and a blast of realization and fear overshadowed his eyes. Scott opened his mouth as if to protest, then shut his mouth and his eyes and seemed to give himself over to pleasure.

Chris, for his part, allowed Derek to readjust and get a good grip on Scott before he grabbed Derek's hips and gently, smoothly entered the boy again. Derek sighed as he entered him fully and Chris felt him squeeze against the pressure, a delightful touch that made Derek his favorite lover. He gave Derek long, full strokes, knowing how much Derek enjoyed that, and tried to time it with Derek's strokes of Scott's cock. He wanted Derek to feel the full pleasure of being completely filled on both ends. Chris himself had been the center in a threesome like this before, with Ashton and another man, and he knew how incredibly hot it could be. He wanted to give that experience to Derek and he was grateful to Scott for cooperating, however initially unwilling Scott was.

He watched Scott biting his lip as if trying to hold back his pleasure and wondered how the man was going to explain this to Jamie, his formal lover and boyfriend. Would Jamie insist that the two of them be in a threesome to catch up on sexual experience? Chris thought of Jamie and the image of him from the mating flight flooded his mind: Jamie, naked and writhing, begging for Chris to touch him. Yes, he would be willing to help them out with a threesome if they asked; anyone on campus with a dragon would be willing after seeing Jamie like that. But it was unlikely. Jamie seemed stricter about sex, despite the image of him that had projected to everyone with a dragon around the world. Everyone wanted him and although Queens in the past, Queens like Derek, would have embraced their sexual freedom and enjoyed that popularity, Jamie was stuck on Scott. But Scott apparently didn't feel the same way, or else he wouldn't be panting under Derek's tongue.

At first Scott's hands were wrapped tight into fists against the sheets, but as Chris watched – and sped up his thrusts – Scott moaned and grabbed Derek's head, tangling his fingers into Derek's curls and directing the boy into even more pleasurable rhythms. Chris watched carefully and maintained his strokes to match what Scott was doing, even though by now he was starting to lose control and it was getting harder and harder to keep his strokes steady and even and not just hump Derek until he came. But he wanted Derek to have the full experience. Still, he wasn't going to last much longer.

He reached down to Derek's cock and it sprang up into his hand, eager and dripping. He used the precum to slick it up and started stroking even as he stroked into the boy's body and Derek sucked on Scott's cock. He especially played with the ridge between the shaft and the head, enjoying the slightly rough edge between the two as his hand slid up and down along Derek's member. He squeezed tight to give Derek enough pressure and

Derek let out a moan as he sucked Scott. Perfect. Chris started pumping his hand faster as his strokes into Derek's body increased in speed as well. He could feel Derek responding and, through him, Scott.

Scott came first, crying out and twisting, pressing Derek's head close against him as Derek swallowed and then lapped up his cum. But Derek didn't have much time, because he was already panting heavily and moaning from the combined pressure of the hand on his cock and the cock in his ass. He came second, shivering heavily and letting out a huge sigh of pleasure as he spurted across the bed. And then, finally, Chris allowed himself to cum deep inside Derek's sweet body, kissing his back and letting out a moan as he did. The three of them collapsed against each other for several long moments.

Chris looked at his two lovers. Scott was red and looking away and Chris knew he had no idea what to do or say, so he took charge. He sat up and gathered Derek into his arms, kissing him soundly and gesturing for Scott to sit up as well. He passed Derek to Scott, who also kissed him soundly. The taste of Scott's cum was on Derek's lips but it was arousing, a reminder of what they had just shared. Then Chris leaned across Derek and kissed Scott quickly and lightly on the lips. Scott accepted the kiss awkwardly, but he did accept it and Chris was glad. He wanted there to be no hard feelings between them and no misplaced jealousy, and it seemed there wouldn't. Awkwardness, maybe, but nothing else.

"Scott and Derek, why don't you take the first shower?" Chris asked, gesturing towards the bathroom.

There was a gleam in Derek's eye but Chris knew that they wouldn't be having sex in the shower. Still, it would give them alone time to talk about what had happened and they probably needed it. Scott agreed and the two of them entered the bathroom. In a minute, the water started running and all he could hear was muffled voices. Chris, for his part, bundled up the sheets and tossed them in the laundry, then remade the bed with

66

clean sheets. He went to the window and looked out. Derek's room was several stories off the ground so he didn't have to worry about the fact that he was completely naked, and it was invigorating to look out at the beautiful day and not worry about clothing.

Inwardly, though, he was worried about what had caused Derek's sudden lust. It had to be a dream about the killer, but that meant the killer was capable of sending Derek into a lustful state at will. While that wasn't a problem now – he and Scott could take care of it – it would be a problem when Jettie matured. The level of lust that Derek had just shown would easily trigger a mating flight in Jettie in even a couple of months. She could even be pushed into a premature flight, which could have disastrous consequences for her eggs and her overall growth. Dragons needed to complete growing before they entered mating flights. But if Derek was kept in a state of high arousal, it was likely that Jettie would enter a mating flight the instant she was capable, not when she was fully ready. And a dragon who didn't mature first might have stunted growth, stunted abilities, let alone the consequences to the eggs of that batch and future batches. Something needed to be done to protect Derek from his dreams and from that killer.

He was so busy thinking about the dangers to Jettie that he must not have heard the water go off, because suddenly Derek was at his side, wearing a towel around his waist.

"Scott left," Derek said. "Are you okay?"

Chris smiled at him and kissed his forehead. "Are you okay?"

Derek blushed in a way that Chris found absolutely charming. "Yeah, I'm good," he said. "Thank you."

"Anything for you. Take a shower with me?"

Derek chuckled. "I just took a shower."

"Not like mine, I assure you."

The boy nodded and held out his hand. Chris accepted it and led him into the bathroom and the overly large walk-in shower.

He started the water, which was still hot from Scott and Derek's shower. Then he took Derek by the shoulders and began kissing him. He didn't know why, but he wanted to claim Derek as his. He didn't mind sharing Derek with Scott, that wasn't it, he didn't think, but he needed to know that this boy belonged to him in some way. He supposed that it hurt a little to know that when Derek was in desperate need he had called on Scott for help, not Chris. He wanted Derek to depend on him, not Scott. But it wasn't jealousy, he reassured himself. He wasn't the jealous type. Ashton had beaten that out of him over the years and it wasn't coming back now.

Derek responded to his kiss and upped the ante by pressing him against the wall of the shower and sliding his tongue into Chris's mouth. Chris grinned into the kiss. Derek was always so forceful during foreplay. It made his surrender during sex so much more appealing. Derek grabbed the soap and ran it across Chris's body, soaping up his hands before replacing the soap and letting his hands do the work lathering up Chris's body, starting at his chest and arms before descending to his hardening cock. Derek swiped his fingers between Chris's legs until they spun around his opening and Chris widened his stance to give him permission to do what he wanted. Derek's eyes widened slightly as if surprised to be given the go ahead and he swirled his soapy fingers around Chris's opening cautiously, gently, as if approaching a wild animal. Chris couldn't help but smile at the thought and at Chris's smile, Derek seemed to draw the strength to slide a finger inside. Chris sighed.

Derek's sweet, cautious invasion of his body was incredibly arousing. He had been fingered before, many times, but always by men like Ashton who took what they wanted and paid little attention to his emotions. But Derek was completely different, watching him keenly to see if he was going too far or too fast. Chris leaned his head back and started rubbing Derek's back to encourage him to explore Chris's body more, and soon Derek had a second finger inside of him, stretching him and making him feel better than he had since he had been inside Derek just an hour ago. Not much could compete with that, but this was close.

Derek laughed lightly and kissed Chris again, his fingers sliding out of Chris and returning to their task of soaping him up. Chris kissed him and began his job of cleaning Derek, only he focused most of his attention on Derek's cock and soon had the boy hard and sweating in the hot shower. Derek leaned his head against Chris's forehead, breathing hard.

"Please," he whispered.

Chris acquiesced immediately and stroked hard and fast until Derek's body went rigid and his cock exploded against the shower. Derek cried out and clutched Chris to him, then went limp as Chris clung to him and held him upright, cleaning him again and then escorting both of them out of the bathroom. He had Derek wrap a towel around his waist again and sit on the toilet while Chris dried himself off, well aware of the boy admiring his body. Even Scott had admired his body, he thought with a touch of pride. He was older than both of them, but he still looked good and he was glad that his workouts every day paid off. Once he was dry and dressed, he helped Derek, who was still languid from his orgasm. And once they were both dressed, he brought Derek back into the main room and held him in his arms.

"You can always call for me, you know," Chris said gently, not wanting to pressure Derek but wanting Derek to know he had options besides Scott.

"I know, now," Derek said. "Thank you."

"I think one of us should be with you at all times, even when you're asleep," Chris said.

"Scott said the same thing," Derek said with an expression of annoyance. "I don't need a babysitter."

"No, you need a lover and a guardian."

The annoyance faded from Derek's face.

"I guess you're right. Scott said to ask you if you'd stay with me for a while. Is that okay?"

"Of course," Chris said, but he was a little upset that Scott had once again beat him to the punch in this back and forth game they seemed to be playing. Even though he was the one spending time with Derek, it was at Scott's request. "What is Scott doing?"

"Researching something, I think," Derek said with a slight wobble in his voice. Probably researching how to prevent Derek's dreams from ending up with that killer, Chris thought. A worthy pursuit. Chris would be happy to take care of Derek while Scott took on the seemingly impossible task of researching the killer.

"Well, I would love to spend time with you. Why don't we see how the new buildings are doing around the quad?" he asked, knowing that Derek was curious about the construction of the college, especially the main student area where upperclassmen and freshmen would mingle during the upcoming year. It was the only place on campus where such mingling would exist and it would pose certain problems, since upperclassmen would have to watch what they said about dragons around the freshmen, but both Jamie and Derek had agreed that it was a necessary part of college life to have a mingling place so it was being built as quickly as possible, and the nearby buildings were being renovated as well.

Derek brightened and grabbed Chris's hand. "Yeah," he said. "There's something I want to show you as well."

Chris followed, cheered considerably by the change in Derek's mood but still wondering about the ramifications of what had just happened between him, Derek, and Scott. Things had changed for the three of them, but how would it impact their futures?

CHAPTER ELEVEN

A Growing Distance

J amie stroked the cat and stared at her for several hours after Narné spoke to him. He understood what Scott had done and why Scott had done it and if Scott had managed to ask him for permission, he probably would have given it. But it hurt just the same. Scott and Derek had been together. And Chris had been involved, of all things. Maybe it made sense to Scott, but it didn't make sense to Jamie and right now all he could feel was a numbness in his heart that extended to his fingertips as he stroked the cat.

He had chosen a name for her, but the joy of that choice was lost now. She was Janna, and she seemed to like the name immensely, but he had no one to share the name with now. Scott was busy searching for ways to prevent Derek from being drawn to the killer and no one else cared. That was what Scott didn't understand. For Jamie, there was no one else. Derek had Chris to turn to, or any number of his friends, but Jamie had no one. He was all alone.

There was a knock at the door and he looked at it despondently, not even having the energy to get up and answer it. Whoever it was would go away after a few minutes and leave him in misery, he thought. To his surprise, though, the sound of a key jangled and the door opened. Only Scott and one other person had a key to his apartment, but Amar had no reason to visit him. Yet as the door opened, Amar entered and waved with a bright smile on his face. His smile flattened a little as he took in Jamie's crossed arms and slouched position.

"What's up? I heard you got a cat and I wanted to stop by."

"Yeah, now's not a good time," Jamie said, not moving except to continue stroking Janna's head. She nuzzled him, then jumped off the table and walked over to Amar, her tail held high as if showing off to him. She rubbed against his legs as he petted her.

"Wow, she's friendly. What's her name?"

"Janna," Jamie said, smiling a little that he got to share her name with someone. Maybe he did have other people in his life.

"Hey Janna," Amar said, crouching down until he was at eye level with her. "You're sure a pretty kitty. So what's up, Jamie?"

Jamie lowered his head again as tears filled his eyes. He had been hoping Amar would just leave, but maybe Amar had been given a heads up by his dragon and knew Jamie was in need of a friend. Amar rubbed Janna's head and seemed to know that Jamie needed a minute to compose himself. He had been such a good friend over the past year and a half and Jamie was so incredibly grateful. He had really lucked out getting Amar as a roommate when he started here. Whoever had decided roommates had done an amazing job.

"I don't know what to do about Scott," Jamie confessed. "I think I want to break up with him."

Amar nodded. "He's been spending a lot of time away lately. Anything you want to talk about?"

Jamie thought of the sordid details of their relationship and the recent addition of Scott's threesome. No, he did not want to talk to Amar about it. He wanted to forget it had ever happened. But he did need to process it somehow, even if he didn't verbalize it and tell Amar all the details.

"He cheated on me," Jamie said, voice trembling. It was such an understatement, such a simple description of the betrayal he felt.

Amar's eyes narrowed and his jaw tightened. His hand that wasn't rubbing Janna curled into a fist. Jamie was rather glad Scott wasn't there or else he was sure Amar would have punched Scott out. Maybe Scott needed it, the way he had been behaving. But it was somewhat gratifying having a friend who cared so much about him, who was willing to fight for him.

"I never liked him," Amar said. "The things he's done to you over this past year, but you've always looked past it somehow. If he's hurt you, you know I'll protect you."

"I know, Amar, and I don't need any help even though I do appreciate it. I just need some time away from him, I think. I don't even know if I can break up with him since he's Marisol's mate and all."

"They can't force you to be with someone you don't want, no matter what happened during your mating flight."

"But think of what it'll do to the campus. It was hard enough getting them to accept Scott, and if he's not with me, what will happen to him? Will he lose everything?"

"You have to worry about yourself, not about him and what might happen to him. If he's not treating you right, then he deserves what happens to him. And the campus will survive without him. I know he's doing a lot right now, especially in Spokane, but there are others willing to do his job."

"Exactly," Jamie cried. "Who will take his place as my mate? Who will win the next mating flight if not him? I don't want anyone else, I just want him! But it seems like he doesn't want me, doesn't care for me at all. What am I supposed to do when the person I love doesn't love me in return, but I have to stay with him or risk being with someone I hate?"

Amar was silent, his eyes big as he thought about Jamie's dilemma. Jamie had never quite spoken about his feelings like this before and it helped hearing it said aloud. He was with someone who seemed not to love him, even though he loved Scott with all his heart. But he had to stay with Scott no matter how much it hurt because otherwise he would be trapped with someone else who was probably only using him for his title. He couldn't forget that everyone he met – everyone in Tarragon society – had seen him naked and lustful, and their emotions were partially based on that. He had plenty of options besides Scott, sure, but they were all insincere.

"There's a new kid here, you know," Amar said in a seemingly complete change of subject. Jamie stared at him in confusion.

"From Africa," Amar continued. "He came with the representative. Even though he's not a student, he already knows about dragons and everything."

"What?" Jamie said faintly, his mind whirling.

He couldn't believe the representative's gall in bringing a prospective student here, and then in not mentioning it to Jamie at all, but more than anything he couldn't understand how it related to Scott and his dilemma.

"He doesn't know anything about you or Scott," Amar said, finally bringing everything together. "Why don't you spend some time with him? It might be a nice change hanging out with someone who doesn't know who you are."

Jamie blinked. He hadn't thought of the younger students as options, but they hadn't seen him in the mating flight and they wouldn't know about his title. They would be entering the academy in the fall, and would know about dragons in time for Marisol's next mating flight. If he did find someone in the younger class, it might actually work out. After all, the council was willing to accept Scott and he was young, maybe they would accept someone even younger as the Queen's mate.

"His name is Tareq and he seems pretty cool," Amar said. "I think you need to meet some new people anyway, get out of this groove you're in. You're taking things so seriously lately. You need to relax. Janna agrees," he added as the cat leapt over the Jamie and nuzzled him.

No one knew about the missing dragons, so of course no one

knew why Jamie had been so serious lately, but it was nice hearing Amar's concern. And Amar had a point, after all. Jamie had become so absorbed in his own problems that he was losing track of the good things in his life, like Marisol and Janna. And Amar. He did need to take a step back and maybe meet some new people. Maybe he wouldn't meet a new boyfriend, but perhaps he could at least meet a new friend.

"I think I will meet him," Jamie said. "Is he staying in the dorms?"

"He's at the dragon canyon right now, looking at the blue dragons. Tephis is showing him around. I think he'll have an easy time bonding with a dragon."

"That's good to know," Jamie said, remembering too late Amar's gift of seeing whether or not people would be able to bond with dragons in the future. "Tell Tephis to bring him here."

Jamie straightened and stood, scratching Janna behind her ears and moving into the kitchen to quickly clean things up. There were a few pans and dishes out; with Scott gone there was no reason to clean. Amar helped straighten the pillows and throw blanket in the living room and before long there was a knock at the door.

"Do you want me to stay?" Amar asked.

"Yeah," Jamie said, suddenly shy.

Jamie went to the door. He knew the African students lived in tribal communities and he was curious to see what the student would be wearing. He opened the door and tried to contain his surprise.

The student was about six inches taller than him with beautiful chocolate skin and thick black hair. He wore a t-shirt and jeans, but it was the expensive headphones wrapped around his neck that caused Jamie's surprise, especially since they were connected to the latest model of hot new phone. He looked like he just got off the plane from New York, not Africa. Even the t-shirt, now that Jamie examined it, was of immaculate design and the jeans were stylishly distressed. His shoes were the hippest brand and were nearly glowing they were so clean. Jamie could not have been more surprised by his appearance.

"Hello, I am Tareq," he said in a lilting voice, extending his hand to Jamie, who took it and had to shake himself before shaking the hand.

"Hi Tareq, I'm Jamie," Jamie said, wishing he had a cool accent.

"I understand you are partnered with the beautiful Queen dragon," Tareq said. "It is an honor to meet you."

"Thanks," Jamie said, hoping Tareq wouldn't treat him differently just because he was the Queen.

"Hi Tareq," Amar said. "What did you think of the canyon?"

They chatted for a while, eventually moving to the lush couches in the living room. Amar took the loveseat and Tareq and Jamie sat at opposite ends of the larger couch. Jamie watched Tareq as he spoke, finding himself drawn to the dark and handsome man. He was considerate and friendly, and always polite. But even as they talked Jamie couldn't help but miss Scott and wonder what Scott was doing, and he knew that it would be a long time before he even started seriously thinking about someone else. Scott may have broken his heart, but his heart still belonged to Scott, broken or not. The shattered pieces were Scott's to do with as he may. Jamie just hoped that Scott was gentle with him.

CHAPTER TWELVE

Confessed Love

Derek's heart fluttered as he and Chris examined the new buildings and casually chatted about the construction with the workers. His mind was still in the bedroom and he kept flushing every time he glanced over to see Chris looking at him. Luckily the workers didn't seem to notice anything unusual or if they did, they had the wisdom to keep it to themselves. Let them gossip after Derek left. After all, everyone knew he and Chris were an item; it wouldn't be that unusual for him and Chris to be sharing intimate glances in public. They didn't have any idea what was really making Derek blush.

Chris. Scott. Together. Above him and below him. Cradling him. Surrounding him. Enveloping him in a cocoon of love so tight he never wanted to escape. He could still taste Scott's surrender and feel Chris's controlled thrusts. The combination of the two was literally breathtaking, and Derek had to constantly remind himself to take deep breaths as the memory sucked away his air. Scott below him with his usual initial resistance that faded as Scott got more and more into it, a slow surrender that always made Derek hotter than anything else in the world, and on top of that, his lover caressing and loving him in the masterful way that Chris had, both controlling him and letting him control, giving him freedom but definitely taking charge. Derek knew nothing would ever compare to that experience again and he could only pray that it would be repeated.

As he and Chris left the workers, he sidled up to the taller man and wriggled their fingers together. He felt like a high school kid again with his first boyfriend, free to be seen in public with another man for the first time. Even though homosexuality was never an issue in Tarragon society, he had still grown up in a conservative town in Washington that tended to judge people by the people they loved. He had escaped the worst of it by attending a school with other Tarragon children and being Ashton's son on top of it all, but when he first came out there was still a lot of jeering and bullying. He had always been so alone, and having to preserve his virginity made it impossible to get dates with the few guys that would date him – the ones who wanted to take advantage of him.

But now he was free to hold hands with his boyfriend – his lover – in public, and bask in the glow of the afternoon they had just spent together, and with Scott. He wondered how Scott was handling this. Scott was nowhere near as liberated in his sexual mores as Chris or even Derek. And Scott had Jamie to think about, too. Maybe Scott had left earlier not to investigate but to have time to himself to deal with this situation in private, or with Jamie. That would make sense. He wondered what Jamie's reaction would be and felt a little smug.

It was becoming increasingly clear that Scott belonged to Derek, not Jamie, and it was one thing Derek had over Jamie. He didn't have much, after all, with his weaker bond with Jettie – that he had accepted, but still felt as a lack when comparing himself to Jamie – and his lack of a mate since Jettie hadn't had her mating flight yet. He shivered at that thought, though. The killer wanted to be his mate and no matter how wonderful their threesome had been, Chris and Scott couldn't erase the memory of the killer touching him. Caressing him. Seducing him. He would die before he let that man win the mating flight.

"Everything alright, sweetheart?" Chris asked as he squeezed Derek's fingers.

Derek forced a smile, then let himself look at Chris more fully and remembered that sweet face next to his, breathing in time with him, thrusting into him. His smile became genuine.

"Yeah," he said. "Just thinking."

"Are the new buildings up to your standards?"

Derek laughed. "I like them. It'll be the coolest place on campus. Everyone will want to go there. It's just too bad this is the only time the dragons will get to go there. I think they like perching on the tall buildings and especially that crane."

"Yeah, the crane operator didn't seem too pleased with that," Chris said with a laugh. He was so beautiful when he laughed. "Was there something you wanted to show me?"

Derek blushed. He had found a spot on the mountain a little way away from everything else with a view of the entire area for miles and miles, a little clearing surrounded by pine trees where the mist tangled gently among the tree trunks and everything felt peaceful. It was dangerous being on his own, he knew, but he had stumbled upon the spot on accident before they fully realized the threat and now that he had Chris with him, surely he could return. He just hoped it was as beautiful as it had been a month ago.

Still holding Derek's hand, he began leading Chris off campus. They had to pass through the campus first and Chris was fine with that, but when Derek began pulling Chris into the woods at the edge of campus, he resisted.

"We can't leave campus, Derek. It isn't safe."

"Our dragons are still here, and besides, we're together. What could go wrong?"

Chris stared at him. "We're dealing with a cold-blooded killer, Derek. I don't want to scare you, but he's after you and he wants you alive. If he gets you – actually physically gets his hands on you – nothing will stop him from winning the mating flight. As it is right now, he has to fight his way through campus to get to you before he can win, even if his dragon outflies all of ours."

Derek's mouth went dry. He remembered hearing rumors of

Ashton kidnapping Jamie last year in an attempt to lock his mating flight and prevent anyone else from winning. Would the killer try it? Of course.

"But you'll be with me," Derek said in a shaky voice.

"And why exactly would he hesitate to kill me, since he's killed so many others? My life means nothing, Derek. He'd kill me even if my dragon is safe if it meant he could get his hands on you."

Derek shook his head in futile denial. He knew it was true. Chris would be killed and for what? A pretty place in the mountains with a nice view. He shivered. It seemed like all of the academy was closing in around him and entrapping him. First he couldn't go anywhere without Chris or Scott, and now he couldn't go to the places he wanted to go for fear that they would be killed and he would be kidnapped. His world was growing smaller and smaller.

"Just focus on your classes, okay sweetheart?" Chris said. "Scott and I will be working on the killer. We don't want you to be afraid."

"How can I not be afraid? It seems like every time I go to sleep he's there, and he's getting more aggressive each time. What happened today was – I mean, it was incredible, but I'm not foolish enough to think it'll happen every time. And one of these times Jettie's going to notice what's going on, either from what the killer does or from what you do, and she's going to start her mating flight and it'll all be over. What happens then?"

"Your mating flight is not the end of the world, Derek," Chris scolded him. "Even if the killer's dragon is the largest and fastest, all he can do is stall until Jettie gets exhausted and leaves her mating mood or the killer manages to get to you physically. And we won't let him get to you. You may have to go through a couple of mating flights where no mating actually takes place – and I've heard that these are relatively painful for the dragon in question – but you can survive it if it means keeping that killer away from you. And eventually he'll slip up, another dragon – my dragon –

will get in and mate with you. After all, I am your preference, right?"

He asked it in a kidding voice but there was some question, too, and Derek grabbed his shoulder and kissed him.

"You know you are."

"I'm sorry you can't show me what you wanted to."

"We'll save it for later," Derek said, hoping there was a later. "After this mess with the killer gets sorted out."

"I would like that," Chris said, smiling as he kissed Derek sweetly.

Derek clung to the kiss for a long time, pressing against Chris and cherishing the feeling of being loved. It was a feeling that was missing from the killer, even though the killer set his body on fire. He only wanted to be turned on by love, not lust, and he hated his body's weaknesses. As he kissed Chris, a warm, fuzzy feeling suffused his soul and he let his hands trail idly along Chris's chest. When he had been young and dreaming of love, this is what he had imagined. He had tried to find love with Scott, but Scott, though he was the focus on Derek's desire, did not return the feeling in the same way and only by returning the feeling could this extraordinary feeling be created. He knew that Chris would do anything for him and as he dug deep to analyze this feeling, he realized he would do anything for Chris.

"I love you," he whispered, barely pulling away from the kiss to say it.

Chris blinked in surprise, then a brilliant smile lit his face. Derek didn't even need to hear the words to know Chris's response, though hearing them helped ease the fear that crept in as soon as Derek had said the words and realized that his feeling might not be reciprocated.

"I love you, Derek," Chris said.

Derek grinned and kissed Chris again, and again. Chris wrapped his arms around Derek and leaned forward until Derek was falling backward in his arms, supported by the man he realized he loved dearly. It was such an odd realization that he loved someone this much, and so unexpectedly. He would have expected to fall in love with Scott, not Chris, but Chris had stolen his heart. That warm, fuzzy feeling returned and his heart felt as though it were going to explode from love.

Jettie, in her room, was nuzzling Chris's dragon in approval and sent warm thoughts to him as well. She approved of his feelings. But there was an underlying fear in her thoughts just as there was in his. Now that he realized how much he cared for Chris, he didn't want anything at all to happen to the man. He couldn't take any risks with Chris, and that involved leading him out in the woods alone. He took Chris's hand and led him back to the main campus where they would be surrounded by people.

Chris didn't protest and seemed a little eager, if anything. He had probably realized his feelings for Derek long ago, Derek realized, and was on edge anytime Derek did anything dangerous like lead them to the edge of campus. So many things could have gone wrong just then, and thinking about them brought back the fear and diminished the happy glow he felt from saying "I love you" for the first time. But he was still pretty giddy, and when he saw one of his teachers walking to his classroom Derek waved and smiled and the teacher looked puzzled. Probably because Derek rarely spoke in class and was extremely shy around the teacher.

In class, everyone tended to swarm Derek because he was the Queen and he could handle the students. But he couldn't handle the teachers fawning over him and most of them quickly learned that he wanted to be treated like a student and they treated him as such. This was one teacher who had never fawned over him and always treated him like a student – and a troublemaker as well since his presence disrupted the class – and that was probably why he was so surprised by the wave. But Derek was in too good a mood today. First the incredible sex, and now telling his boyfriend that he loved him. Everything was going perfectly and nothing could put a damper on his day.

CHAPTER THIRTEEN

Forced Flight

S cott searched the grounds for marks of the killer dragon as thoughts raced through his mind. The feel of Derek's lips closing around him haunted his thoughts. The thought of Jamie's sweet surrender when they made love clung to him as well, and he couldn't reconcile the two. His feelings for Derek were so raw and lustful, and his feelings for Jamie were so filled with longing and respect. He loved both of them, he did, but in such different ways that he didn't know which was true love, if there was such a thing as true love. There had to be such a thing as true love, because he couldn't describe what he had for Jamie any other way. But Derek, he cared for Derek so much it had to be love as well.

Narné nudged him mentally. *Focus on the killer,* he said. *He may still be around, watching you.*

Scott nodded and focused his attention. He could focus on his feelings later. This was a time for concentration. He was taking a bit of a risk coming here before the others arrived, but it was still on campus, just the edge of campus. The others would be joining him shortly to help him look for clues as to the killer dragon's identity. Narné wasn't with him either, since it was far too dangerous for a dragon to be alone. Instead, Narné was with the others, preparing the search party. Scott had gone ahead in order to get some room to breathe after what had just happened.

A branch snapped to his left and he whirled. Nothing. He

edged closer, on edge. He had brought a sword, as the council had instructed him to do, and he drew it carefully. He wasn't the best, but he had held off Ashton well enough and was gaining in confidence with his skills. A prickling sensation inched up his neck as he neared the brush where the branch had snapped. It was probably an animal but what if it wasn't? His shoulders tensed as he entered the woods lining the clearing. Trees surrounded him. A dark shadow fell over him.

He turned to see the cause of the shadow and gasped. Blood drained from his face as he saw an enormous dragon hidden in the trees with almost perfect camouflage. The dragon's claws darted towards him and he stumbled backwards, dropping his sword. Two talons closed around him and he waited for them to pierce him, but instead they tightened around him and the dragon lifted from the ground with him in its grasp.

Narné! He cried out to his dragon, who had already been alerted by his partner's distress. He tried to memorize the ground so Narné could follow him but mist surrounded them and he was blinded and disoriented. His senses were of no use to Narné, who growled in frustration. The great dragon flew for what seemed like hours but may have been as short as twenty minutes in the disorienting mist. Narné was with him mentally the entire time, reassuring Scott that the killer must want him alive and wouldn't kill him. But that worried them both – why did the killer want him alive? Marisol comforted him as well and he had never been as grateful for her voice as he was during that terrifying flight caught between the massive dragon's claws.

The dragon let go of him abruptly and he gasped, expecting to fall to his death. Instead, he fell only a few feet and the impact jarred him. He fell hard on one arm and it felt as though he twisted his right wrist in the fall. The mist cleared, and he stared up at a tall man in dark robes, the same man Derek had described to him. Only this was more terrifying, because he was here in reality, not in dreams, and there was no reason this man had for leaving him alive.

Scott was aware of Marisol straining to see through his eyes and feel through his senses to capture everything that she could about the man and he hoped she could sense enough to be able to identify the dragon and partner and begin tracking them the way she could track all other dragons. He was aware of Narné's comforting presence at the forefront of his mind, calming and reassuring him even while he could feel Narné's tightly concealed panic. As for Scott, he was almost beyond panic, pushed into a state of calm acceptance. If he was to die, so be it. At least Narné wouldn't be butchered first.

The man stared at him for several minutes as Scott laid on the floor, not moving. Then Scott shifted into a more comfortable position so that his wrist wasn't under his body and he winced. It was definitely twisted, hopefully not broken.

"I apologize for the injury," the man finally said, gesturing towards Scott's wrist. "No harm was intended. Please, stand."

Scott stood hesitantly. The man's voice was rich and deep, and he was clearly used to being obeyed. Scott was tempted to continue laying down just to spite him, but he wanted to be standing so he could be on equal terms with the man.

"Who are you?" Scott asked as soon as he was on his feet, nursing his sore wrist.

The man smiled, the shadows from his hood playing across his features.

"You may call me the Elder."

Scott's eyes narrowed. That was no help at all. A name was power within the dragon community. With a name, Marisol would have been able to track him. With a title like this, though, she couldn't. Which he likely knew very well, and that was why he had given himself that title.

"What do you want?"

"We'll get to that. May I see your wrist?"

Scott hesitated. He knew nothing about this man other than

the fact that he killed dragons and drank their blood. That was hardly a good recommendation for extending a vulnerable body part. But the massive dragon behind him hissed when he didn't obey, and bared its teeth. Clearly the dragon didn't like when its partner was disobeyed and Scott knew his life was on the line, so Scott obeyed and extended his arm.

The man's touch on his wrist was light and exploratory, and after gently running his fingers over the sore area he nodded.

"It isn't broken, but you should go easy on it for a while."

"Thank you," Scott said, not knowing what else to say. He found himself trusting the man's pronouncement even though he had no reason to trust. The man was simply so confident, it was hard to doubt him.

Scott pulled his arm back and cradled it in his other arm, looking around curiously. They were in a cave of some sort, with light filtering through from several openings on the sides and top. The cave extended a way back, shrinking into a passage too small for the dragon. There was a bed and table closer to the back where the man must live. Scott wondered where they were and how long the man had been living here. It couldn't have been too long, he figured, because surely the man would have left for human company. But then again, the killings had been going on for months. How did the man survive?

"You are the Queen's mate, are you not?" the man asked.

Scott was startled and nodded. He had some doubts about whether Jamie still wanted him after the incident with Derek, but he was officially the Queen's mate and one indiscretion couldn't change that. But was that why he was here? Why would he want the Queen's mate? Scott knew he was trying to win Derek's mating flight; did he think Scott would try for Derek's flight as well and so he was trying to capture his competition?

"You will be staying here a while, I think," the man said, watching him keenly. "Do you know why?"

"No," Scott said honestly. "I'm not going to be in the Spokane mating flight."

The man smiled. "But you are head of the council, and the council decides who can participate in each mating flight. I would like permission to be in the new Queen's mating flight."

"No offense, but it isn't going to happen."

The man's eyes flashed. "I will be in the flight with your permission or without, and I will win. But if I have your permission, I will play by your rules and respect the council during my time as Queen's mate. And I will spare your life. If she enters her flight before I have your permission, however, you will forfeit your life and I will rule as I see fit. I assure you, it will not be the way you wish me to rule."

"You've killed dragons," Scott said, knowing he was taking a risk with the accusation but also knowing that his life was on the line anyway and his situation couldn't get much worse. "The council will never accept someone who has killed dragons."

"The council will accept who you tell them to accept. You have more power than you realize, I think. But you do not need to decide immediately. Perhaps some time to think will help you reach a decision."

A cold smile lit his lips and he grabbed Scott's arm. Scott flinched even though the man wasn't hurting him and easily could be hurting him. Instead, the man led him to the back of the cave into a small chamber with a wooden door. He pushed Scott inside, shut the door, and locked it from the outside.

"You will find everything you need inside. Take your time. The Queen will not enter her mating flight for at least a month, and I am well prepared to keep you here that long."

Scott stared at the door in shock and pushed against it in vain before turning to look at his cell. A flattened rock was the bed, and there was a bucket that must be the toilet. He wrinkled his nose at the thought. There was nothing else in the room. Worse, there was no light from above; all the light came through the wooden door and it was already quite dark inside. It would be pitch black soon, and for most of the day. He would have nothing to do but lie in bed and discuss options with the dragons, which was precisely what the man – the Elder – wanted him to do.

He reached out to Narné, who had been listening closely to the conversation. He could sense Marisol but only vaguely. She must be talking to Jamie, he thought, and felt a ball of sorrow in his throat at the thought of not being able to see Jamie. What if he died and never got to see Jamie again? What if this fight were the last thing between them? He had to make amends with Jamie. It couldn't end like this. Thoughts of Jamie led inevitably to thoughts of Derek, and the Elder's request. There was no way he was leaving Derek to a man like this. This man could not be Derek's mate. There had to be another way. But was Scott willing to die for that, especially since there was a chance the Elder would win even if Scott died? He didn't know. He couldn't know until he thought on it more.

Scott lay down on the stone bed and winced. It was too hard, and his wrist hurt, and he was inexplicably thirsty. He just had to hope that the Elder would remember to give him food and water. Until then, he would try to sort things out with Narné and see if Narné had seen any potential futures they could work with.

CHAPTER FOURTEEN

Reflections

C hris was a little peeved at Scott for getting himself kidnapped by the killer. More than a little, really. He was furious. Chris had been so careful with Derek, making sure Derek didn't go off campus, and then Scott just wandered off on his own in exactly the same way he had prevented Derek from doing and Chris's prediction had come true – the killer had struck. Chris was just glad the killer hadn't harmed Scott, or at least the dragons were saying that Scott was fine. His own dragon was very reassuring about the situation, and the dragons all seemed to think that Scott was safe from harm for now.

Derek didn't know about it yet. Jettie knew, but she was reluctantly keeping it a secret from Derek at the command of Marisol. Chris completely understood why. If Derek knew what had happened to Scott, he might try to manipulate the mist and face off against the killer before they had a plan of action and the consequences would be disastrous. No, Derek needed to be sheltered from this. For now. Until they figured out what to do.

Chris was a little honored that he was being kept in the loop on this ordeal, but he knew it was because he was the only one capable of keeping Derek's interest away from Scott. Derek's confession of love still rang through his ears and heart, and he knew the boy was sincere. He knew he was sincere in his response. He did love Derek, and he would protect Derek from this mysterious killer and no matter what happened, he would be Derek's mate in Derek's first mating flight. Nothing, not even an enormous dragon and a powerful ancient evil, could stop him.

Right now, Derek was working on homework as Chris cleaned their home. His things were still in the nearby apartment that was technically his, because he didn't want Scott to see his things in the apartment and get spooked away. He wanted Scott and Derek together because it weakened Marisol's power and made Jettie – and therefore Derek and Derek's mate – stronger. But was that all he was doing anymore? He had a strong urge to mark the room, leave some sign of possession so that everyone would know that Derek was his. He would share Derek, certainly, but he wanted people to know that Derek belonged to him first and foremost.

It was the confession of love, he suspected. He was feeling extra possessive because Derek had confessed his feelings and Chris had realized that those feelings were returned. He had initially targeted Derek as a way to ensure that Ashton's dreams didn't die with Ashton, but now he was emotionally invested. He wanted what was best for Derek, regardless of what Ashton would have wanted. Of course, Ashton was a genius and his goals for Derek's eventual ascension to the height of Tarragon society were in everyone's best interests, so he was still doing as Ashton had commanded him, but he was in it for a different reason now. He was in it for love. And if Derek found out that Scott had been kidnapped, Derek would unthinkingly put himself in danger and Chris couldn't live with that.

"Hey, can you help me with this?" Derek asked, holding out a book and a piece of paper.

Chris smiled and sat beside the boy, explaining the dense essay about the history of Tarragon society and making it relevant to current society. Chris had almost been tapped as a teacher but he had backed out at the last minute – he had been intimidated by the thought of all those students turning to him for the answers – so he was fairly good at explaining the material to Derek, and he enjoyed doing it. It was easy explaining things one on one. It was just when he stood in front of an entire class that he began to get nervous and start doubting his own knowledge. And while it was fine for teachers to be expanding their knowledge while teaching students, it wasn't fine to be in a constant state of delirious self-doubt and stumble through a lecture you were barely confident in. The students picked up on things like that, he knew, and would rip him to shreds. So instead he took his place on the council and helped pick out the curriculum for the college of liberal arts. Much easier, and he still got to be a part of the teaching process.

It was a delight seeing the knowledge bloom on Derek's face as the previously unfathomable essay turned into something relevant and approachable and Chris felt his heart lighten somewhat. He helped Derek formulate responses to the reading, making sure to always let Derek take the lead and come up with his own ideas instead of dictating what Derek should think about the ideas, and soon Derek was finished and the sun had set. Derek stretched, shut the book, and turned to him.

"I didn't expect Scott to take this long. Do you think he's okay?"

"He's fine," Chris assured him.

"I mean, after this morning," Derek continued in a quieter voice, a cherry red flushing through his cheeks.

Chris ducked in and kissed him.

"He's fine," Chris repeated. "He was going with some others to explore the mountain for a few days. It might be a while before he comes back."

"Is that safe?"

"He won't be alone," Chris said, wishing he didn't have to lie as he said the words Marisol had instructed him to say. "And," he added, "it has nothing to do with this morning."

Marisol hadn't added that part but he could see Derek's hesitation and worry that somehow the threesome had ruined his relationship with Scott. It had been pretty clear, however, that the relationship between Scott and Derek was far from ruined. If anything, the relationship between Scott and Jamie was the one that was ruined, and Chris wondered how the kidnapping was going to affect that. Would Jamie even fight to get Scott back? Or would he value his fellow Queen, Derek, over his disobedient lover? Chris licked his lips. Despite the seriousness of the situation, this was exactly the type of split he had been trying to create between Jamie and Scott. Now perhaps one of Ashton's men could move in as Jamie's new mate and consolidate power between the two campuses, and the normal way of doing things would be restored.

Jamie's latest antics were getting everyone on both campuses riled up. He had disbanded the recruiting committee and was insisting that each country choose their students themselves. Now, money didn't mean much in Tarragon society, at least the part of Tarragon society that had dragons, because all of their needs were taken care of out of a vast pool of resources that stretched the globe and was carefully watched and protected by human and dragon alike, but many individuals enjoyed having an excess of wealth. It was simply human nature. And without the enormous income from the recruiting committee, those council members had nowhere to turn to satiate their exotic needs. It was only a matter of time before Jamie found himself in a world of trouble as council members began demanding things that he just couldn't provide. At least most of the council members had legal tastes, but some were heavily into human and drug trafficking and there was going to be an ugly day very soon when Jamie discovered how some of the council members really spent their time.

Naturally Chris didn't approve of those activities, but it was part of the society and it had its place. Every system had corruption, it just needed to be controlled. That was something Ashton frequently said. He was a master of controlling corruption. Derek had the strength of will to do the same, but Jamie was weak and idealistic. He wouldn't be able to handle a system based in such things. He would try to fix it, change people's minds, and he would refuse to see that there were some things beyond fixing. That was why Jettie needed to be the primary Queen, why Derek needed his strength. That was why it was so important that the relationship between Jamie and Scott be shaky.

If Jamie and Scott showed a strong, unified front as they had up to this point, then they would be powerful enough to force a change. But if they wavered, then everything they were trying to do would come crashing down and only Derek and Chris would be left in the rubble, ready to pick everyone back up and rebuild. It was their destiny.

He glanced over at Derek who was staring out the dark window with a hint of color in his cheeks. No doubt thinking of the morning's activities. Good. Let him keep that in mind. Let him drive a wedge between Jamie and Scott that this kidnapping only strengthened. Chris wondered what Scott was thinking about, if he was regretting the threesome or if he were feeling rebelliously proud of his actions. Probably regretting it. He wasn't the type to jump into life and accept whatever she threw at you. He was a thinker, and wherever he was imprisoned would give him lots of time to think.

Chris was grateful that Scott wasn't being tortured or anything, though. He and Scott shared a bond after this morning, one that couldn't be forgotten. But the dragons had assured him that Scott was fine, would be fine, until they figured out what to do.

He hid a shiver. The killer wanted permission to be in Derek's mating flight. If it were up to Chris, he would let Scott die and surround the area with fighters and guards to ensure that the killer didn't get into the mating flight. But he knew it wasn't that easy. Even if Scott died, there was a good chance that the powerful dragon would win the mating flight despite Derek's strong preference for Chris. The only way around that would be for a quick flight so that Chris and Derek could pair off before the great dragon even appeared. But quick flights led to fewer eggs and a less convincing mating flight, making his victory hollow in some regards. He would have to rely on luck and Derek's love to get him through this mating flight.

If they allowed the killer into the mating flight – Chris couldn't even finish the thought. Giving that bastard permission to rape Derek was unthinkable. Derek was terrified of the man and letting him have sex with Chris's love was simply out of the question. There had to be a solution. Hopefully a solution that didn't involve Scott's death because as much as he wanted Scott and Jamie at odds with each other, he also needed Scott to be alive. If Scott died, the entire campus would side with Jamie in sympathy and Jamie would be unstoppable.

Besides, though he hesitated to admit it, he rather liked Scott. It was odd, but he admired the man in many ways. Scott had fought hard to be with Jamie and had succeeded and even while Chris was working to undermine that, he had to acknowledge and admire it. He just hoped Scott wouldn't give up now. They would need his fighting spirit more than ever now that Scott was being held by the killer.

CHAPTER FIFTEEN

First Kiss

J amie stared at the calendar before scrawling an X through another day. Scott had been gone for a full week. Marisol was keeping a careful watch on him and he was fine, just bored and frustrated and depressed. His wounded wrist was healing nicely and the Elder was even taking care of it. Jamie, meanwhile, was faced with the impossible choice of what to do. Tareq, or TK as he preferred to be called, had been spending a lot of time with him as he tried to cope with the decision, and probably knew more of the situation than he wanted. But TK was a good listener and Jamie needed someone to talk to.

TK was with him now, watching him mark off another day with a strange, closed expression on his face. But that expression cleared when Jamie turned to face him. TK smiled and held out his hand and Jamie took it. Once, he would have been too shy for such casual physical contact but living at Tarragon Academy had changed that.

"Your friend is still alright?" TK inquired. That was how he referred to Scott, even though he knew Scott was Jamie's mate and boyfriend. Sort of boyfriend. Actually, Jamie hadn't mentioned to TK that Scott was his boyfriend, now that he thought of it. He had avoided saying the word for fear of the bad memories it would conjure. Better to rescue Scott first and then deal with their relationship second.

"Marisol says he's fine."

TK nodded and squeezed his hand. "The other one, Derek, he still doesn't know?"

"Not yet."

"It is better that way. You are doing the right thing."

Jamie smiled. It was nice hearing someone reassure him, even if TK didn't fully understand the situation. Reassurance was exactly what he needed. TK had been doing the right thing a lot lately, and had quickly become one of Jamie's best friends in this difficult time. Amar was still his favorite, of course, but Amar and Nikki were going through another rough patch and Amar needed Jamie's support as much as Jamie needed his right now, so TK was the only one who could fully support Jamie the way he really needed.

Jamie stretched. He was so tense, and had been tense ever since this situation began. He still couldn't believe Scott had been foolish enough to get captured in the first place and inwardly he blamed Scott's actions on the threesome. It seemed just punishment in some ways, though he scolded himself for thinking it. But now that Scott was captured, they had a whole new host of problems to work out and none of the solutions were good. Jamie couldn't lose Scott, he knew that, but he couldn't agree to let the Elder into the mating flight either. Right now they were just killing time, hoping for a miracle like when Mike had freed Jamie from Ashton's care. Surely there was someone close to the Elder who could help Scott. Scott said that sometimes he heard the Elder talking to someone, so someone knew where the Elder was. They just needed to identify and find that person before the mating flight.

TK's hands landed on Jamie's shoulders and he jumped. Then TK started massaging him.

"Let me help," he said in that gorgeous accent of his.

"I guess," Jamie said, unused to anyone but Scott touching him this way.

But he relaxed into the hands on his shoulders and had to

admit that TK was slowly working out the knots as those wonderful hands ground up and down. He closed his eyes. The hands moved to his shoulder blades and he relaxed further.

"You're so tense," TK said. "Why don't you lie down and I can give you a proper massage?"

Jamie opened his eyes hesitantly but there was no deception or ulterior motives in TK's face. Jamie nodded and they went to the couch, where Jamie laid down on his belly and relaxed again. TK's hands were immediately on him and they felt incredible. They were focused on his shoulder blades now, tracing the contours and pulling against the muscles in an incredibly relaxing way. He could feel the tension draining from his body as TK worked. He shut his eyes and wondered why Scott never gave him massages. They would have to start, because this was incredible.

TK's hands drifted to his lower back and skimmed along the outsides of his spine, pressing and releasing the muscles and the tension at the same time. Jamie melted into him. He wondered what TK would feel like as a lover and blushed at the thought, but he couldn't help it. The massage was so thorough and so relaxing, and so intimate as TK's hands stroked his lower back, that the thought sprang into his mind unbidden.

He couldn't help the stereotypes that filled his mind first. He knew that black men were said to be well-endowed and he wondered if it was true. He knew that Scott was large; would TK be larger? What would that feel like? Would it be even more pleasure, or would there be pain? Maybe the pain would be pleasurable, he considered. TK certainly wouldn't hurt him intentionally. His soft hands on Jamie's back – firm in all the right places, gentle in all the delicate spots – told him that. He would be a good lover.

"Why don't you take off your shirt so I can rub you better?" TK murmured next to his ear.

Jamie was taking off his shirt before he even thought of the consequences. He hesitated with the shirt halfway off. This was a definite step in the direction of intimacy. Did he want that? Did he want to encourage TK? But TK must have thought that the shirt had gotten stuck on something because he helped Jamie take it the rest of the way off and the decision was out of Jamie's hands. As TK's warm, soft hands returned to Jamie's body and his bare flesh, he knew he had made the right call. But what would the consequences be? Was he really ready for intimacy with someone besides Scott?

TK knew exactly how to give a body-soothing back rub and in minutes Jamie was barely able to move, let alone think or talk. He felt completely safe in TK's hands, something that didn't always happen with Scott. Sometimes with Scott he felt like he was walking on a tightrope, never knowing how Scott felt about him, but with TK it was clear that he was completely safe, that TK cared about him deeply. Maybe even romantically. Oh, who was Jamie kidding, of course TK cared for him romantically, there was no other way to interpret this. Jamie was a fool if he didn't read this as the seduction technique it was. And Jamie was giving in to it without a fight.

He thought of Scott, alone in the Elder's care, and felt a brief flash of sorrow and guilt. But then he thought of Scott with Derek and Chris and the guilt lessened. He had every right in the world to be with other men. Scott was with other men; why couldn't Jamie be with them as well? And TK was such a sweet young man. So sincere and generous. Not forward at all, but definitely willing to push ahead and get what he wanted. And clearly what he wanted was Jamie.

It also reassured Jamie that TK hadn't seen Jamie in the mating flight. He was the only person on campus who had no instinctive lust for Jamie, so his feelings for Jamie were genuine. Jamie thought of Amar introducing the two of them and suggesting that Jamie consider TK, and wondered whether or not TK had asked Amar to introduce them. Perhaps TK had been crushing on Jamie since before they met. That would be rather sweet, too.

He felt the pressure change and TK's hands went to his arms as the man levered himself down and planted a kiss on the back of Jamie's neck. Jamie's breath caught and his eyes snapped open. He stared at TK and saw a warm, hopefully dreamy look in the younger man's gaze. Jamie smiled hesitantly and turned his body enough to draw one arm out and pull TK towards him. He lifted his face for a real kiss and felt TK's lips land on his. At first the kiss was simple, lips touching lips with a hesitancy that spoke of the newness of this relationship, then Jamie took charge and allowed his lips to open just enough to suck on TK's lower lip. TK let out a small moan and the kiss deepened further. Jamie let his tongue run along the contours of TK's lips until he was met with TK's tongue, and he followed TK's tongue into TK's mouth and passionately kissed him. He felt a flicker of guilt, but mostly happiness and joy and lust as he felt TK respond to his kiss.

They broke apart gasping for air and TK watched him cautiously, nearly as cautiously as Jamie was watching him. This was such a new thing, after all. It had to be nurtured carefully and Jamie still wasn't sure how to treat it. Jamie smiled and that seemed to reassure TK, who smiled in relief.

"Thank you for the rub," Jamie said. "I feel great now."

TK ducked his head in an endearing manner. "You're welcome. I'm glad."

As Jamie sat up, he was aware of TK examining his scars and he felt the familiar instinct to hide. Even though he knew scars were status symbols in Tarragon society, he still felt that they ought to be hidden after his childhood experiences with cutting himself. Besides, TK didn't know that scars were signs of victory and was staring at them in shock.

"You got those from your dragon?" he asked, reaching out to trace a hand along the deep scar ridging along Jamie's belly. It was the scar that had nearly killed Jamie and it would always be with him, a rough edge of flesh while his other scars were mere stripes of discoloration.

"Yes," Jamie said. "She was a Queen dragon and they fight more than other dragons. She had been in her shell for a very long time."

He knew the explanation likely didn't make sense to TK but the man nodded anyway as if it did and Jamie wondered again how much the African students knew about Tarragon secrets. It was dangerous to teach people without dragons about dragons, but surely it would lead to less deaths during the first year exam. Although now that Amar and Mike were working with the exam, the casualties should be very, very few, especially if the students went to Marisol and Jettie's sites and not to the older sites.

TK's eyes targeted the scars on Jamie's arms, thin white lines in perfect succession. Jamie blushed.

"Those can't be from a dragon," he said.

Jamie fingered the scars. It was true, they were perfectly parallel and no dragon could achieve that level of precision. Only a human could do it, a human at the end of his rope, searching for meaning in pain since life didn't offer any other solutions.

"I did that," Jamie said in a small voice.

He had only ever talked about this with Scott. Scott knew he had a history of cutting, and Scott accepted him. Would TK be able to do the same? Or would TK laugh at him or turn him away despite the kiss they had just shared? Or worse, would TK announce it to the world so everyone would know how unstable Jamie was?

TK nodded. "I had a very rough childhood too. My parents died when I was young and I was taken in by Akwa, the African representative. That is how I know so much about dragons – most students are not so well-informed."

Jamie nodded. That was a small relief, that not all students would know everything about dragons. His heart went out to TK for losing his parents, however, since Jamie knew exactly how that felt. He still had nightmares about his parents' deaths and without Scott here, there was no one to calm him when he woke up.

"I experimented with drugs for a while, but then I realized that life could be more. I had to keep myself ready for a dragon, for life begins when we find our dragon brothers, at least for us. That is what Akwa always tells me and I have to believe it. It keeps me going."

Jamie nodded again. He had found courage in his relationship with Scott and if he had known that he would someday find Marisol, that would have given him courage to keep going as well. He was glad that TK knew about the dragons and that dragons had given TK the incentive to keep going, but it brought up a worrying point. TK had to become a student. There was no question of that. Jamie would personally ensure that he did. But what about the other Africans? He had to be fair to all countries. Having two campuses would help bring in more people, but still, hundreds of people in Tarragon society died each year because they didn't have the opportunity to bond with dragons. He couldn't give them all dragons – there weren't enough dragons and besides, that many dragons would surely draw attention to their society – but it hurt knowing that his decisions on who to accept led to the deaths of others.

"I'm glad you're here, TK," Jamie said. "I'll do my best to make sure the right people end up here, too."

"I know you will," TK said with a smile.

Jamie also smiled, and leaned forward for another kiss. Just as their lips touched, however, he backed away. Marisol was contacting him with disturbing news. Derek had found out about Scott, and he was pissed.

CHAPTER SIXTEEN

Discovery

D erek went to take a nap in a bad mood. Such a bad mood that he didn't bother with his usual routine of protecting his dreams from the Elder. Maybe it wouldn't be such a bad thing if he ran into the Elder, he thought to himself. Maybe he could learn valuable information that would help bring Scott back.

Scott was the reason for his bad mood. Scott had vanished a week ago on a mission so secret that only a few people were allowed to know about it. Derek was not one of those people. Chris knew where he was, but avoided Derek's questions like the plague and Derek had gotten nothing out of him, just that Scott would be gone for a while until he figured more out about the Elder and Chris was in charge of Derek's safety until then. As much as Derek loved Chris, he couldn't help but take his frustration out on the man and he opened one eye to glare at him now as he settled into his nap.

"Remember to protect yourself," Chris said. He must have noticed the glare.

"I will," Derek said, but in his heart he wondered if he could learn something valuable if he faced the Elder again. Scott had been gone for a week; surely he must have learned what he needed to learn. What if Scott were staying away because of what had happened between them? Well, Derek would face the Elder and get more information, and then Scott would have no choice but to return. Derek would force the issue. He shut his eyes and fell asleep.

Sure enough, the feeling of traveling through mist soon overtook his dreams and he found himself in an underground lair or cave of some sort, facing the Elder, who looked as if he had been expecting Derek. The man's handsome face was twisted into a smile and he stretched a hand out to Derek in greeting.

"I'm surprised it's taken this long, Queen. You are welcome here."

Derek was about to speak when a second voice interrupted them, a familiar voice.

"No," the voice cried. It sounded muffled, as if it were coming from behind a thick wall or door. Derek frowned. He couldn't quite identify it. "Derek, leave now. Whatever deal you're going to make, it isn't worth it."

Scott. That's who the voice was. Scott.

Derek felt all the blood rush from his head and he felt dizzy all of a sudden. What was Scott doing here? Was this reality or a nightmare? What deal did Scott expect him to make, and why did Scott want him to leave? What was going on?

The Elder was watching carefully and placed a hand on Derek's shoulder to steady him.

"You were unaware that the Queen's mate was here, weren't you?"

Derek nodded, stunned. He heard muffled cursing from wherever Scott was being kept. Had Scott been kidnapped? Was that the secret mission that no one could know about? Did Chris know the truth? And why had no one told him? He could have come here and rescued Scott! Or at least found out more about where here was. Why had no one told him? He knew Jamie was probably mad at Scott for cheating on him, but leaving him here for a week? What was going on?

"I am petitioning to be a part of your mating flight," the Elder explained gently, stroking Derek's shoulder. "If I am allowed into your flight, I will release the Queen's mate and I will abide by all of Tarragon's rules and treat you well. If I am not allowed into your flight, however, this man will die and I will still win the flight, only I will not follow Tarragon protocol and it will be quite… unpleasant for you."

Derek swallowed hard and met the Elder's gaze. The other man was extremely calm, no emotion showing. He meant every word that he said. He wasn't threatening Derek, exactly, he was just stating the facts as he saw them. Derek now saw why Scott hadn't been rescued, and why he hadn't been told. It was a far more complex situation than he had imagined, but even so there was only one solution. Scott had to live, and the man had to be allowed into the mating flight. It was the only way to control him. Queen's mates were subordinate to their Queens, so if the Elder became Derek's mate and he followed Tarragon law, as he said he would, then he would have to obey Derek. It would be unpleasant, to be sure, but it certainly didn't require a week's worth of thought.

"You have already decided, I see," the Elder said. "That is good. Perhaps you will persuade the others. They are beginning to try my patience. If you agree to allow me into the mating flight, I will also, as a gift to you, allow the flight to occur naturally and without coercion. I will not seduce you into a premature flight. But only if you agree."

Derek nodded. Another reason why this deal needed to happen. He would be devastated if Jettie didn't develop fully because her mating flight was too early.

"Derek, don't listen to him," he could hear Scott say. "Don't make any agreements."

"He is right on the last," the Elder said with a toss of his shoulders. "You shouldn't make any agreements because you are not qualified to make any decisions. The only person unable to voice any opinion in the matter of the mating flight is the Queen being flown. Her preferences can be taken into account, but the council ultimately decides who will fly. But I think if you voice a strong enough opinion, this matter can be taken care of rapidly, don't you?"

Derek nodded. "You won't hurt Scott?"

"The Queen's mate? I have no intention of hurting him if I am allowed in the mating flight."

"And you understand that being allowed in the mating flight is not a guarantee that you'll win, right?"

The Elder chuckled. "I see. You have a lover and you think your love will be stronger than my dragon's wings? We'll find out, won't we?"

Derek thought of Chris. He knew that Chris would win the flight, so it wouldn't really matter if they allowed the Elder into the flight. But if they didn't allow the Elder in, then the Elder would be chasing Jettie without following the protocols of the race and he could potentially kill his rivals in the sky, so he would almost certainly win. And Chris's dragon would almost certainly be killed, and probably Chris as well. His whole world would be destroyed – Scott dead, Chris dead, and bound to be the Elder's slave. No, he would not let that happen. The Elder could be in his mating flight. It wouldn't matter and it would ensure everyone's survival.

"I don't want you to hurt Scott before a decision is made," Derek threatened, knowing he had nothing to back up his threats.

But the Elder, surprisingly, shrugged and nodded. "I have no intention of harming him. I need his support, after all. I will do as you say."

Derek studied him. He seemed honest enough. "What is your dragon's name?" Derek asked, hoping to get some more honesty and some information for Marisol.

The Elder chuckled. "You may call him the Elder dragon, I suppose, since I am the Elder. We no longer have names. They are so restricting, after all, and so easy to trace."

The last was said with warning and Derek blinked. So the

Elder knew why he was searching for their names, to trace them and identify them. He probably shouldn't have been so straight-forward. The Elder was hard to read, though, sometimes honest and sometimes elusive. An impossible puzzle.

"I suspect you will wish to leave soon, to discuss this situation with your friends," the Elder said. "But there is one more thing before you go."

"What?"

The Elder leaned close to him. Intimately close. Then the Elder's lips pressed upon his and he was so surprised he didn't pull away. The kiss was sweet, then deepened into something fiery and passionate as Derek moaned and opened his mouth under the Elder's insistent tongue. Their lips locked and their tongues danced together and Derek's knees went weak just as the Elder's arms wrapped around him to hold him up. Derek's head fell backward and the Elder let his kisses trail down his throat, exciting and arousing him as he panted for breath before those exciting lips met his again in sizzling decadence. When the Elder finally pulled away, Derek was dizzy and weak and con-fused. It had felt so incredibly good, better than any kiss of his life. He stared at the Elder in shock.

"That will be yours when I am allowed into your mating flight," the Elder murmured. "Now you may leave."

Derek stared at him a long moment, then mentally pulled at the mist surrounding him and found himself lying in bed again, half-hard. What an incredible kiss. Pure lust. There had been no romance or love in it, just lust and physical arousal, but even so it was seared into his mind and he knew he would always think of it whenever he kissed from now on, mentally comparing every kiss to that incredible experience. He took a few deep breaths to calm himself down.

Chris was at the window staring out at the campus and Derek made sure his partial erection was completely gone before he stood up and went to Chris's side. Some of his anger at Chris had dissipated thanks to the kiss, but as he approached Chris he felt it building again. When Chris turned to him and smiled, Derek couldn't muster a smile in return and just scowled.

"Why didn't you tell me about Scott?"

"What are you talking about?"

"I mean that the Elder kidnapped him and has him as a prisoner!"

Chris's eyes snapped open.

"You didn't go there. You couldn't. You protected yourself before you took a nap."

"I didn't. I thought I could find something useful and I did," Derek said. "I'm not an infant you can just hide things from. I deserve your trust and respect. Why didn't anyone tell me? Why didn't you trust me?"

Chris took a deep breath. "We were afraid you would go try to rescue Scott on your own."

"Maybe I should have. What are you planning on doing? It's a pretty clear offer."

Chris winced. "No, it's not. There are so many things you don't understand, Derek. We can't be seen to give him permission to be in your mating flight."

"Why not? He's not going to win. You are."

A glitter of love shone in Chris's eyes and a gentle smile curved his lips. "In a perfect world, it would work like that, and perhaps this world has a little perfection in it somewhere. But his dragon is so much larger and stronger than mine, he could easily outfly me."

"Ashton's dragon was stronger than Scott's, but Scott won the mating flight twice," Derek pointed out.

"It's not exactly the same," Chris said, "But perhaps you are right and there's no need to worry about that. But still, if we accept him into the mating flight, we're accepting him despite his past crimes. We know he kills dragons and we would be sending the message that this behavior is acceptable, that you can kill dragons and still be a part of Tarragon society."

"But he would stop killing them," Derek pointed out. "He says if he's accepted he'll follow Tarragon law, which forbids killing dragons. But if he's not accepted he'll win the flight and keep killing dragons whenever he wants. We would be saving dragon lives by accepting him, don't you see?"

"Perhaps you should talk to Jamie about this," Chris said slowly. "Jamie is the only one with the power to make this decision. The council has been notified and many of them have reached their own decisions, but they all decided to obey whatever Jamie decides, and he hasn't decided yet."

"Then I will talk to him. Hell, I'll even go to Portland to talk to him. It's a weekend and I don't have classes, and this is important. Besides, it'll get me away from here for a while."

"You know I'll come with you," Chris said.

"I know," Derek said with a smile. "I want you to. That will leave Mike in charge of this campus. Have someone find him and bring him here, and I'll explain the situation. Er, does he know about Scott?"

"He knows."

Derek scowled. "Does everyone know?"

Chris shook his head but didn't specify, which was probably a good idea since Derek was feeling increasingly out of the loop. Still, a trip to Portland was exactly what he needed. And if Jettie somehow went into her mating flight while they were gone, then the situation would resolve itself, he thought. Or maybe it wouldn't, he realized. The Elder would likely see that as a rejection and kill Scott, then wreak havoc until Jettie's next mating flight when the offer would be extended again. Derek shivered. Well, it was highly unlikely she would enter her mating flight for at least two months, so he should be safe.

Derek sent a cautious message to Marisol, trying to conceal his anger that once again Jamie was in charge, only this time Jamie was in charge of his future. It was completely unfair that the man who Derek resented the most was the one who held his fate in his hands. Jamie had far too much power, Derek thought, but unfortunately there was no way to change it. Maybe after Jettie had mated and was a more official Queen he would have more authority and be more equal to Jamie, but until then he would have to go before Jamie and beg for scraps just to have a future that he wouldn't mind living in.

CHAPTER SEVENTEEN

Journey

C hris could tell that his lover and boyfriend was pissed as Derek packed his things for a weekend excursion to the main campus in Portland. The boy's eyes flashed fire and his beautiful full lips were tight and thin, and even the skin on his face looked stretched with the attempt to hide his anger. Chris didn't know why Derek was hiding his anger now, when only Chris could see, but maybe if Derek let go of his emotions he wouldn't be able to control them again. Derek had found out about Scott, and had reached his own conclusion about the Elder's deal.

He had hoped against hope that Derek wanted to leave Scott there and forbid the Elder from being in his mating flight, and the boy was furious because Jamie was even considering allowing a dragon-killer into his flight. But Chris knew that the opposite was true, that Derek was furious because Jamie had left Scott there so long without even consulting Derek about his own mating flight, that Jamie hadn't thought Derek could handle the decision or would make a poor decision. They had all betrayed Derek to some extent, in Derek's eyes, and while Chris longed to explain, he couldn't.

He couldn't explain that Derek's reaction right now was exactly what they had all feared, that Derek would be so moved by his feelings for Scott that he would act without thinking and allow the Elder into the mating flight without a second thought.

Although to be fair, Derek had seemed to think through his decision far more than Chris would have thought. But Derek's dismissal of the idea of the Elder winning the mating flight was disturbing. Yes, Chris was his lover and his first choice, but the Elder was far larger, stronger, faster, and more ruthless. Chris would be hard pressed to win and while he would obviously do everything in his power to win his love in Derek's first mating flight, there were no guarantees as Derek seemed to think.

Chris was frankly impressed that Jamie had managed to put his emotions aside for so long and look at the situation rationally instead of immediately giving in to the Elder's demands, as Chris would have thought and as the Elder must have guessed would happen. If nothing else, it would give the Elder respect for Jamie and the decision that the council ultimately reached. Theirs was no rash decision, made in the heat of a lover's disappearance, but a well thought-out decision that would be honored because the consequences had been considered in advance.

Derek finished packing with a silent snarl and took Chris's arm, practically dragging him to their dragons. It would take several hours to reach Portland. Dragonflight was fast, but the two cities were still a sizeable distance apart. They climbed on their dragons and Chris wished he could ride with Derek and hold the boy as they flew, and comfort him somehow. Derek was going to be wrapped up in his own thoughts the whole time, with nothing to distract him from his anger. There was little Chris could do except squeeze his hand before they parted and watch him from the back of his dragon. The wind and mist made it impossible to talk, and soon, as they left the protection of the mountain, the mist thickened and he could barely see Derek, just the Queen's tail in front of him.

Jettie would lead them to Portland with unerring accuracy – all dragons had excellent senses of direction and could fly almost anywhere. Besides, she was undoubtedly targeting Marisol and heading in the larger Queen's direction. Marisol was like a beacon for the dragons. They all knew where all other dragons were at all times but they rarely cared; Marisol, on the other hand, they all tracked scrupulously. He had never considered how that affected Jamie's life, if Jamie ever felt that it was an invasion of his privacy. He wondered if the dragons tracked Jamie too.

Many of them do, Yaris said as they flew. *The human Queen is like a dragon and is visible to us just as we are visible.*

How does he feel about that? Chris asked.

He has gotten used to it, Yaris responded with a mental shrug. *There is nothing he can do about it. Derek is lucky to have some privacy. Only Jettie is watched carefully. Many dragons will be wondering about this flight, though most will understand the reason behind it.*

Do all the dragons know about Scott, or just us? Chris asked, curious about how secrets were shared among dragons.

We all know, but we do not all communicate this knowledge with our partners. Only a few of us are allowed to share the knowledge. I am one of them, Yaris added unnecessarily, but with a certain amount of smug pride.

Chris wondered how much of an honor it was to be singled out by Marisol in the way that Yaris was being singled out right now, and figured it was quite an honor by Yaris's tone. He smiled, pleased that his connection to Derek was making his dragon happy as well.

Derek makes me very happy, Yaris said. *Even if he bonded with a different dragon. But being bonded with a female, and a Queen, with give both of us great pleasure.*

The dragon rumbled underneath Chris's fingers and Chris grinned, for the moment thinking of the mating flight without fear, as it should be, with Chris easily taking the lead. He would chase his Queen for miles in the sky to exhaust her before finally laying his stake to her and claiming her, snatching her from the sky like a giraffe plucks a leaf from a tall tree, elegant and sure of himself despite the stretch. Then they would enmesh together, becoming one, and in the bedroom down below Chris would enter his beautiful lover and the doubled sensations would envelop them and increase their pleasure beyond anything either of them could imagine.

Or so the stories went. Scott and Jamie were the only ones who had experienced a Queen's flight, and they didn't talk about it. The previous Queen, decades ago, had fought the flight and resisted the pleasure, so his experiences weren't reliable but even he had admitted – before he killed himself – that it was better than anything he had ever felt before. Chris couldn't even begin to imagine how good it would feel with Derek, a man he loved and cherished, on their first time together as men and dragons. And then the Elder came and ruined it.

His face settled into a scowl that he suspected was present on Derek's face as well, though for different reasons. Chris was furious that someone dared interfere with the mating flight that Ashton had all but assured him, that he had worked so hard to achieve, with the boy – no, man – that he was now in love with. But if they forbid the Elder from participating, then the Elder would still enter the mating flight only he wouldn't follow the rules, and he would likely see Yaris as his main target and kill him first. As much as it hurt Chris, he had to agree with Derek that it was better to let the Elder into the flight provided he follow the rules than risk losing both the flight and his dragon's life. He sighed and shook his head. If even he had come around to Derek's way of thinking, the council would be sure to follow, and Jamie would as well. The decision was all but made, and the only real choice now was in how to tell the Elder.

They arrived faster than Chris would have expected and before long were circling down to the dragon canyon as the mist shed from them and Derek was fully visible again, his beautiful face set in hard lines. Chris's heart ached for his lover and he wished he could have been with him on the flight once again. But Derek wouldn't have allowed it, he was sure. He hadn't even dared to ask. And Yaris wouldn't have wanted to fly alone. Chris had to consider his dragon's feelings as well.

There was a landing field at the bottom of the dragon canyon and they landed gently. Derek slid off quickly and Chris followed suit. Jamie was striding towards them with a wide, forced smile on his face. He was flanked by Margot and another council member, Gerald, that was acting leader of the council until Scott could take over. Margot practically glided across the ground and Chris stifled a shiver, wondering where her dragon was. The ability to erase memories was not to be taken lightly, even though she claimed not to be able to erase memories from someone bonded with a dragon.

Marisol landed behind Jamie with a thump, excitement in her clear, young eyes. She was looking at Jettie with pride and joy and reached out her snout to nuzzle the younger dragon. For a second Chris thought Jettie would refuse but there was no hesitation on Jettie's part – the daughter reached out to her mother despite her partner's anger at the other. They nuzzled each other and Marisol settled back down, but her eyes still glowed. Jettie looked somber, however, despite the warm greeting, as befit her partner's mood.

"Queen Derek and Jettie," Jamie said, extending his hand.

"Queen Jamie and Marisol," Derek said, probably glad that Jamie had spoken first because Chris realized that Derek hadn't been drilled on proper protocol yet. He had learned the basics, but this was a formal meeting and Derek was out of his depth.

"What brings you to my campus?"

Derek just stared at him for a second and Chris shut his eyes, silently pleading with Derek to be civil and give the proper response. Margot and Gerald shifted and glanced at Jamie, as if wondering why Jamie was asking instead of welcoming Derek without reservation or doing one of the many other things within Jamie's power that wouldn't require knowledge of protocol. Derek started speaking and Chris's eyes snapped open.

"I am here to discuss a certain situation with you and with the council. I believe the details are better left to be discussed in private."

Jamie nodded. "You are welcome here. Please take the visiting Queen's chambers with your lover. I will meet with you later today to discuss the situation."

Derek nodded regally and Margot and Gerald relaxed slightly, as did Chris. There was a lot of tension between the two Queens and protocol wasn't doing much to defuse it. Then they left, and a few students came to help lead Chris and Derek to their rooms, which were lavishly decorated and enormous, with more than enough room for Jettie and Yaris in the dragon chamber. As soon as they were alone again, Derek flopped into the couch and sighed, resting one arm over his eyes.

"Why does he make it so hard?" he asked.

"It's all right," Chris said, leaning in close to him and kissing his lips. "You're here now, and he'll listen to you. You're doing everything right."

Derek's lips curved into a smile, his eyes still hidden. Then his arm lowered and his eyes were sparkling.

"I love you, Chris."

Chris's heart swelled again, just as it had the first time he had heard the words.

"I love you, Derek, and I'll be with you every step of the way."

CHAPTER EIGHTEEN

Preparation

J amie snuggled into TK's arms. It was a brief respite, but a needed one. Derek was so infuriating. Jamie couldn't look at the man without remembering that Scott had slept with Derek, had chosen Derek, had wanted Derek. He had tried to slip up Derek in the introduction, as much as he was able with Margot and Gerald there, but Derek, the jerk, had managed to get through everything with poise. And now everyone felt sorry for Derek because Jamie had been hard on him! TK stroked his arm. At least TK was on his side. TK would always be on his side, because he didn't understand this conflict and only knew what little Jamie had told him, and Jamie had been sure to tell him a one-sided version of events.

"Why does he make everything so hard for me?" Jamie asked.

TK snuggled closer. "He may not even mean to," TK said. "Perhaps he doesn't realize what he's doing is hurting you."

Jamie buried his head. That was likely. Derek didn't understand that the mere sight of him was enough to make Jamie burn with jealousy. Derek had been the last one to see Scott, to sleep with Scott, not Jamie. It wasn't fair. But Derek had no clue and was probably confused as to his cold reception. After all, Derek had far more reason to be mad at Jamie than Jamie had reason to be mad at Derek. But it sure didn't feel that way.

He took comfort in TK's arms and wished he could do more and level the field a little, but he knew he couldn't sleep with TK.

Not without Scott's permission, and he wasn't going to ask for Scott's permission while Scott was in captivity. That would destroy Scott's ability to survive, most likely, and as much as Jamie wanted revenge, he also wanted his boyfriend back. He had tried to explain to TK why they couldn't sleep together. The reasons were fairly simply, but hard for someone not bonded to a dragon to understand.

Dragon law forbade the Queen from sleeping with anyone besides her mate without her mate's explicit permission. Her mate could sleep with anyone, Jamie thought darkly, imagining Derek and Scott together once more, but Jamie couldn't sleep with anyone else. It was law. It was also an excuse. He wasn't sure he could bring himself to take that final step. Snuggling with TK was one thing, but actually having sex with someone besides Scott was a final, irreversible step that he wasn't ready to take yet. Perhaps he would never be ready to take it. It probably wasn't fair to TK to tease him like this, offering some intimacy but denying him sex, but he had explained the rules to TK and TK was still here. Maybe TK knew he needed a friend and a friendly shoulder, or maybe he thought he could win the next mating flight, who knew, but Jamie was grateful either way. Still, he was extremely limited in the things he could tell TK about the current situation and he longed for the day when he had Scott at his side again and had someone he could be open with.

He stayed in TK's arms for a long time, then asked TK to leave. He needed to prepare for his meeting with Derek and he needed to finish calming himself. There was a knock at the door and he called for TK to come back in, wondering what he had forgotten. He was shocked when Margot appeared in his doorway, raising one eyebrow at his state of half-undress. He leapt out of the bed he and TK had been cuddling in and whipped on a shirt, feeling her eyes on him the whole time. He couldn't tell if she were judging or not.

"You need to be careful, Jamie," she said. "You know the rules as well as I about your activities."

He glared. "I know exactly what I am and am not allowed to do, and so does he."

"He may know, but he may try to take advantage of you and be barred from this campus if you encourage him enough."

Jamie's eyes widened. He hadn't thought of that. If TK tried to force himself on Jamie – which he didn't think would happen – then TK would be banned from the campus permanently, dragon or no, and he would be doomed to die young. Jamie would not allow that to happen.

"It's not serious," Jamie whispered.

"For you, perhaps, but make sure he sees it the same way," Margot said. "Often these trysts end badly. You are a Queen, and can command the heart of anyone on campus. For you to choose someone without a dragon is unusual and dangerous to both of you. Your mate is unlikely to approve."

"Well he's not here, is he?" Jamie snapped, unable to stop himself. "He had other people to worry about and now he's gone!"

Margot took his arm and led him to the living room, sitting down with him and squeezing his shoulder.

"You should not take your anger out on Derek, or on Scott. It will only lead to poor decision-making, and right now we need your mind clear. You are making your first major decision as Queen. You have our support, if you need it, but in the end this will be your decision and we will all have to live with the result. What result are you willing to live with? Tell me, Jamie, have you already made up your mind? Are you stalling for other reasons?"

Jamie looked away. "I know what I'm doing. It seems too easy, doesn't it? If we could have demanded something from him, this is what we would have demanded: that he obey Tarragon law. There's some catch I haven't seen yet, some consequence I haven't figured out. I'm going to deal with him, but not until I know what I'm walking into. The mating flight isn't for a couple of months, so I have a few weeks at least. Scott isn't being hurt and the Elder shows no signs of changing that – if he threatens

Scott, I'll act, but I want to understand this first. Don't you?"

Margot nodded slowly, though a glint from the light hid her eyes. Jamie wondered how much she knew, and if she had information she wasn't sharing. Did she know why the Elder was agreeing to obey Tarragon law so readily? Tarragon law forbade dragon killing; why would he agree to it? What loopholes did he know about from his centuries of life in Tarragon society that Jamie, brand new to the life, didn't know about? Margot had to know something but if she did she choose not to share.

"It is curious," she said. "And I agree that Scott is safe enough for now, though if you delay too long that will change, I have no doubt. The Elder will only wait so long. But we must also talk about Derek, Jamie."

Jamie shrugged uncomfortably. He had known this was coming. Of course she was here to scold him for his actions earlier. Of course she took Derek's side without even considering Jamie's.

"I know I should have been more courteous," Jamie acknowledged, though the words stuck in his mouth like a burr.

"And I fully understand why it is difficult for you," she said, surprising him with the compassion in her voice and eyes. "But you cannot alienate him. Already his loyalty to you is loose, at best, and primarily due to Scott's influence. You need to secure his loyalty and embarrassing him isn't the way to do it."

"He'll never be loyal to me," Jamie said, inwardly puzzled.

Derek could be a lot of things, he knew, but loyal was never one of them. He had never even imagined that Derek could be loyal to him, or that there could be anything other than jealousy and resentment between them. He couldn't imagine a world where such a thing existed. It couldn't.

"He could, if he were handled correctly," Margot said. "But if you continue on this path, then he is likely to welcome the Elder rather than fight him as we all hope will happen. Is that really what you want? Aren't you aware that Derek might side with the Elder against you if you don't handle this the proper way?"

"Of course I'm aware!" Jamie snapped. "Why else do you think I allowed Scott to- to-"

He stumbled to a halt. He hadn't meant to say that, to admit that the only reason Scott had slept with Derek was to prevent that possible future. But Margot's eyes widened and she nodded in sudden understanding.

"I see now why you're so angry, Jamie," she said. "You sacrificed something very dear to you to prevent the Elder from gaining a hold on Derek, and now the Elder has outmaneuvered you despite your efforts. But you cannot take it out on Derek, or your sacrifice will be in vain."

"I know," Jamie said helplessly. "It's just so hard. Every time I look at him, all I see is Scott, trapped somewhere without me, because of me, because of him, because of the Elder. I hate all of this. I just want the Elder to know that his antics won't be tolerated, that I'll accept him on my terms, not because he threatens me."

"He'll respect you," Margot said. "I'm sure he already does. But don't try the Elder's patience, and don't mistreat Derek. You'll regret both decisions."

"Thank you, Margot," Jamie said, trying to sound as humble as possible.

It must have worked because she looked satisfied and stood up. He escorted her to the door and she let herself out, then a few minutes later there was yet another knock and the sound of someone letting himself or herself into Jamie's rooms. Jamie groaned. He was truly tired of visitors and didn't want another scolding from Gerald, or whoever else it was. He turned to see TK enter the room.

"TK, what are you doing here?"

"The woman who was just here asked me to wait while she talked to you. She said you might be upset after she left, but that I shouldn't ask you questions about what you talked about."

Jamie glowered. He was in a lousy mood and TK was exactly

the person to cheer him up, but how dare Margot direct TK like this? She didn't control him, and didn't have the right to tell him what to do and where to go.

"Jamie, I'm tired of this," TK said, and Jamie caught the edge of anger in his voice. "Not being allowed to know what you're talking about all the time. It's frustrating and I'm done with it."

Jamie sighed. "You know I can't tell you until you have a dragon. It's Tarragon business."

"I don't care. No one would know. Only we would know and I won't tell anyone."

"The dragons would know, don't you understand? They know everything I do, everything I say. They follow me all the time and they wouldn't approve. I have to follow protocol more than anyone else because the dragons watch my every move."

"They can't watch you all the time. There aren't any dragons here now, after all. I know you're connected to your dragon but she wouldn't tell anyone either, would she?"

"You don't understand dragons," Jamie said dryly, thinking of how freely they shared information between themselves, "And you don't understand how easily they can see and sense me."

"I think you're exaggerating a little," TK said. "Surely they can't see you all the time. They can't know everything you do and say. You'd have no privacy."

"I'm used to it," Jamie said. "And I don't have any privacy. Not since I bonded with Marisol. I didn't realize it at first, but lately I've begun to realize how much access the other dragons have. They don't talk about me to their humans, luckily, they consider that privileged knowledge, but they all know and they would never allow it."

"So I can't sleep with you and I can't even know what you talk about during the day?"

Jamie stared at TK, standing with his hands on his hips in front of him, and thought of Margot's words. Maybe it would be better to break things off with him. Maybe he was a fool for thinking things would work with an outsider. Maybe everyone was right and he shouldn't be seeing someone who wasn't bonded with a dragon. TK's angry, sullen expression shifted to one of concern.

"What are you thinking?"

"How difficult this is," Jamie said. "Maybe... maybe she was right."

"She?"

"Margot. The woman who was in here."

TK stared at him, then a hint of a smile crossed his lips. "She told you to break up with me, didn't she? She said it was too difficult to date someone without a dragon. And then she sent me in here, deliberately telling me not to ask about what you talked about because she knew it would force a fight and you would break things off. Well, it's not going to work. I care about you more than I care about whatever you talk about. This is just a minor fight, Jamie, not something to end our relationship over. You understand the difference, right?"

"But why?" Jamie asked, honestly curious. "What is it about me that you're willing to put up with all this? You know there's probably no future for us."

"Perhaps," he said with a wider smile. "Perhaps. And as for why, well, you'll just have to find out."

CHAPTER NINETEEN

Confrontation

Derek straightened his hair and his navy blue sports jacket. He was dressed up to see Jamie, a show of respect that Chris had insisted on, even though he was wearing jeans to offset the formality a little. He wondered if Jamie would even notice. Probably not. Jamie was too stuck up to notice anything. How could Scott love him?

He emerged into the hallway and Chris flanked him as he walked to Jamie's quarters, mentally preparing himself for conflict. Margot and Gerard were waiting outside the room as well, no doubt to make sure that the meeting started smoothly, even though they couldn't be present for the meeting itself. Only the Queens were to be a part of the actual meeting. Jamie left his room, eyes darting in surprise to the crowd in the hallway before settling on Derek.

He was dressed in dark slacks and a tailored white shirt, matching Derek's level of dress. Derek was glad Chris had insisted on the jacket. He would hate to be outdressed in the silent competition they had going. There was less anger in Jamie's eyes but he was stiff as he gestured for Derek to come in, and his hand gesture ended abruptly as his eyes snapped to the crowd as if to ensure they knew they were not welcome. Chris nodded and left, and Margot and Gerald lingered for a moment, looking to Derek. Derek started to enter the room and heard them leave. Then he was alone with Jamie, in Jamie's personal quarters.

Jamie led him to a comfortable sitting room populated with several overplush chairs and Derek gingerly sat in one. Jamie took a seat opposite him in the room and offered him a drink of water or juice. They were both too young to drink alcohol, because Derek knew the traditional offering was wine. Derek accepted water, and Jamie stood up and got them both shimmering glasses of water, wet with condensation, that Derek took a nervous gulp from and set on his coaster. Jamie took a smoother drink but also set his down. His hands were trembling, Derek noticed. But Jamie had no right to be angry, he reminded himself. Jamie had been the one keeping secrets. Derek was the one with the right to be angry.

"You shouldn't have lied to me," Derek said, but he knew his anger rang false. The atmosphere was wrong, everything was wrong about this scenario. Jamie was following protocol exactly now and just as it was intended to do, it was defusing the situation and making it difficult for Derek's anger to find a place to light. "I had the right to know about the Elder's demands. They involved my mating flight, after all."

"You're probably right," Jamie said after a moment, much to Derek's surprise. Jamie turned away from him, shadowing his face so that his eyes were nearly invisible at the angle he was at. "It was selfish. I was angry at you. I'm sorry."

"You're – sorry?"

Derek's mind spun. He wasn't expecting this turn of events. Never in a million years had he expected an apology from Jamie. It wasn't any of the possibilities in his head of where this conversation could go. He hadn't even realized Jamie had anything to apologize for, to be honest. In his heart he believed that Jamie had the right to keep information from him, as unfair as it may be. But Jamie was acknowledging a mistake, acknowledging that his emotions got in the way of his judgment. What an unexpected turn of events, and he had no idea what to make of it.

"I was angry at you because you were the last one with him,

with Scott," Jamie continued, his face still hidden. "I didn't want you to know about Scott and be the one to rescue him."

"Then why didn't you rescue Scott?"

"Because I needed to wait. I needed to understand, and to show the Elder that I'm not ruled by emotion or fear. But now that I'm ready to deal with him, you come along and it'll seem like you're the one to rescue him after all."

"Jamie, I don't think it matters who rescues him as long as someone does," Derek said, surprised at Jamie's reasoning.

He had never put himself in Jamie's shoes, he realized, this entire time. He had been so focused on himself and his own worries that he hadn't realized that Jamie had been going through an even harder time than him and was having to make an impossible decision in a very difficult situation. Derek's interference was unwelcome and unnecessary – Jamie had already made up his mind but was waiting for his own reasons. Of course. Of course Jamie wouldn't leave Scott there. Derek had been so caught up in the thought of Scott in danger that he had forgotten how much Jamie loved him.

"But the mating flight," Derek said. "You would still have needed my permission. You would have had to tell me sometime."

"I don't technically need your permission," Jamie said, keeping his eyes averted. "You have no say in who is in your mating flight. We will accommodate your requests, provided they are reasonable, but the council – and I – have the final say in your mating flight."

"You would have gotten it, though," Derek said with some conviction.

He remembered the stories of Jamie's previous two mating flights, especially his first one when Scott had fought to be in it and only won by a hair. Jamie would have been devastated if anyone but Scott had won. He wouldn't force someone else into a mating flight with a stranger, Derek was certain. Now that he was thinking clearly and remembering who Jamie was, he was certain.

"I would have," Jamie acknowledged, and finally looked over at Derek.

Derek was stunned at the pain and suffering in those shadowed depths. Jamie sniffled and his eyes shone with unshed tears. To Derek's surprise, he found himself standing up and walking over to the other man, extending his arm to Jamie, who took it and stood as well. Jamie wrapped his arms around Derek's shoulders and shook with repressed sobs.

"I miss him so much," Jamie whispered.

Something broke down inside of Derek and all of his fear and pain began to leak to the surface as well. He sniffed and buried his head against Jamie's auburn one.

"I miss him too," he whispered, realizing how very true the words were. He missed Scott with a sharp pang that filled his entire being. And the thought of Scott in the hands of a dragon killer was a sharper pain, with a twinge of horror that the same man might someday be Derek's mate.

"What will I do if he wins the flight?" Derek whispered, giving voice to a fear he would never acknowledge in front of Chris. He shuddered.

"You'll survive," Jamie said, squeezing his shoulders. "He is forbidden from hurting you and I think he will be very gentle with you. He needs you."

"You sound afraid that he'll be gentle with me," Derek said.

"He may try to brainwash you, to persuade you to follow his ways," Jamie said. "If you agree to let him kill dragons again-"

"I never would, no matter what," Derek said firmly.

The very thought sickened him. But he could see why Jamie was afraid. Maybe Jamie's previous anger was even somewhat justified since he had so much fear inside of him. But this was one fear that was completely unfounded, Derek was glad to say. He would never support the old ways. He had heard about Ashton and how he had drunk dragon's blood when killing dragons before their riders, gaining additional life and youth that way, and he would never tolerate that in his campus. Anyone who took a dragon's life without cause and without the previous death of the rider would find themselves facing the full force of the dragon's justice system. And dragons had little in the way of mercy, as Derek's father had found out.

Jamie hugged him tightly. "Thank you, Derek," he said softly. "I'm so sorry I've been hard on you."

"It's okay. I'm sorry I've been hard on you. I know you're doing your best. But please, let's get Scott back, okay? I'm so worried about him and I know you are, too."

"I think it's time," Jamie said. "There are some things I need to do first, but let's get him back."

Derek hesitated, knowing he ought to say something but not wanting to say the words. Then, finally, he said it.

"I know he's yours."

There was a silence as Jamie stiffened in his arms. Jamie leaned back to meet his eyes and Derek saw surprise and hurt there.

"He's yours, too," Jamie said bitterly.

"No," Derek said. "I mean, maybe a little," he acknowledged, thinking of Scott's sweet kisses and his surrender during sex. "But he's yours, Jamie, through and through. He always will be."

"Thank you," Jamie whispered.

There was a silence between them and Derek could practically feel a relationship forming between them. He wasn't sure how he felt about that. He had resented Jamie for so long he wasn't sure he was ready to forgive Jamie yet, but Jamie had made himself so vulnerable that he couldn't help but rethink his views of the man. It was a strange feeling. He was starting to like Jamie. He had always admired Jamie, to some extent, and felt sympathy for him for the things that Jamie had been through, but he had never felt a personal connection to the man before but in their love of Scott there was a connection and he hadn't expected that it would draw them together – he had assumed it could only push them apart. He could tell that Jettie was pleased by this turn of events, since she didn't like having to be angry at her mother and her superior.

"How do we get him back?" Derek asked. "Do we tell the council or go directly to the Elder? Do I need to do anything? I'll do anything you want, just tell me."

"I'll address the council, but they should already know my decision by now. You can address them if you want, but it won't matter much other than to reassure a few of them who wouldn't matter in the voting anyways. Still, it would show solidarity, which might be important at this time. I'll arrange the meeting for tonight. Can you prepare a brief statement of support? You'll just need to get up and say you agree with my decision. Can you do that?"

"Of course," Derek said. "And then I'll take that decision to the Elder?"

"No," Jamie said sharply. "We're not risking you with him any more than we have to. He might kidnap you now that Scott will be freed. You have to be extra careful about your own protection until your mating flight – he cannot get an advantage. No, I'll convey the message to Scott and the Elder will dictate how to proceed. I hate leaving it up to him, but we have no other choice other than using you and I will not put you at risk."

"Thank you, Jamie," Derek said. "I'll be careful, too. I don't want him winning any more than you do, trust me. So we put this in the Elder's hands and trust him? Can we do that?"

"We don't really have a choice," Jamie said. "It'll be a test of his sincerity. But Margot seems to believe him. I do too. He just wants in the mating flight."

"Because he knows he'll win it," Derek said bitterly. "I keep telling myself Chris will win, but he won't, will he?"

"Doubt will weaken your chances," Jamie warned. "You have to believe if you want to have a chance."

Derek sniffed, tears filling his eyes once more. He was terrified of the thought of the Elder winning the flight but he knew he needed to be strong for Chris, and Jamie's words confirmed it. For now, all they could do was get Scott back. He needed to worry about the flight when it happened. He had some time, after all.

"All right. Let's go tell the council."

CHAPTER TWENTY

Freedom

Scott paced his cell and cradled his now-healed right wrist. He had quickly grown accustomed to the sparse living conditions, a task made easier by the fact that the Elder was also living with the same limitations. There was no plumbing, no running water, nothing in this dark cave that had been hollowed out and made into a series of rooms divided by large, heavy wooden doors that Scott was unable to budge. He was treated well, considering the circumstances, but he was always aware that he was a prisoner.

As far as he could tell, the Elder never left the cave even though the dragon left regularly. And, as far as he could tell, there was someone else on occasion. He sometimes heard voices talking in the distance, though he couldn't make them out. But he doubted the Elder would talk to himself – the man was twisted but fully sane – and he couldn't help but wonder who it could be. Who in their right mind would want to converse with a man who killed dragons? Scott had no idea, and the voices were mere echoes by the time they reached him, faint reflections of voices without any substance.

The days blurred into each other, helped by the fact that sunlight never reached him. He had torches on the wall, but that was it for light. He was groggy and disoriented at all times, and it didn't help that the Elder only gave him food twice a day, and at what seemed like arbitrary hours. He knew what time it was through his connection with Narné, but somehow hearing that it was morning or night had little meaning when his reality was a dimly lit cave. He was ready to escape, but no opportunities presented themselves and besides, if he did escape he was afraid what kind of reaction the Elder would have. Better to let Jamie deal with the Elder and not throw a wrench in Jamie's plans.

But even though he didn't want to ruin Jamie's plans, he wasn't prepared for Marisol's command. Her voice, normally so comforting, appeared in his mind but was unusually stern and commanding, as if she knew he wouldn't like what she was about to say. And he didn't. Jamie had acquiesced to the Elder's demands. The Elder would be allowed into Derek's mating flight provided the Elder obey all Tarragon laws and Scott be freed. The council had met without Scott present and agreed unanimously, and a unanimous vote overrode the Queen's mate. And Scott would have protested.

Not that he didn't trust the Elder to keep his word – the Elder had been honest enough in his treatment of Scott – but he didn't want to put Derek through having the man as a mate. Jamie didn't seem to realize how much power a Queen's mate truly had. The Queen's mate was completely in charge of the Queen's bed, and that kind of leverage would give the Elder a powerful weapon over Derek, who was in love with both Scott and Chris. And if Derek decided to change Tarragon law according to the Elder's whims, then the Elder would still be obeying Tarragon law even while killing dragons. Was Derek really strong enough to stand up to the Elder, day after month after year?

Scott stood up. He was angry at the decision, but Marisol was firm. The decision had been made and there was literally nothing he could do about it. He could keep the decision from the Elder, of course, and not tell the man, but that would only worsen matters as Derek would have to return to tell him. No, he could do this. It would hurt, but he could do it. Scott went to the heavy door and banged against it.

"Elder," he called.

There was a silence, then the sound of footsteps drawing near. Chains rattled the way they did before the Elder brought him food and Scott knew he was undoing the locks on the door intended to keep Scott captive. Finally, the door opened and a little more light shimmered into the room. Scott eyed the man.

He was handsome enough, Scott figured, but evil to his core. How was Derek going to handle him?

"The council has reached a verdict," Scott said without preamble. "They've agreed to let you into Derek's mating flight provided you obey all Tarragon laws and you release me immediately."

A pleased smile crossed the Elder's face. He was quite handsome.

"Very well," the Elder said, and took a step back, gesturing for Scott to leave the little room. "I will see you returned to the campus. I expect to be welcomed in the mating flight. Should there be any resistance to my presence, the mating flight will not end well for the other suitors."

Scott shivered. The Elder was threatening to kill the other dragons in the mating flight, when they would be operating based on instinct and blind to danger. The mating flight was always a vulnerable time for dragons. At least the man wasn't threatening the Queen, but something about the way he was smiling made it clear that if he wasn't welcomed, the Queen would be in danger as well.

"You will be welcomed, as much as any other dragon," Scott said.

The Elder nodded and led him into the room he first entered, a room dwarfed by the enormous grey-green dragon curled up at one end. The dragon stretched and reached out a taloned hand towards Scott, who withdrew instinctively.

"My dragon will carry you back. You will not be injured this time," the Elder said, glancing at his dragon as he said it as if to scold his dragon and reassure Scott at the same time.

Scott hesitantly walked forward and the dragon grabbed him, then leapt out of a hole in the room into the brisk air outside. The light was blinding after being inside in the dark for so long and he shut his eyes, feeling the mist cling to his cheeks and eyelids. They traveled for about twenty minutes and then suddenly there was land beneath his feet and the talons released him. When he opened his eyes the dragon was gone. He was alone in the woods, disoriented and lost. He had no idea where the campus was or where he was, and it was still so bright out.

Scott started walking in one direction rather aimlessly. The mountain was crisscrossed with paths and he ought to find one no matter where he went, and then things ought to look familiar. After walking for about ten minutes, he heard voices. Many voices. His pace quickened. The voices grew more distinct and he heard males and females, though he couldn't make out their words. Suddenly a building appeared before him, then another, and he nearly sobbed in relief. He was back at campus. He was safe.

He arrived at the stables and as soon as the stablemaster spotted him, the man gasped and ran towards him, enveloping him in a hug.

"We were preparing to send out a search party for you," the man said. "Derek told us that you would be released sometime today or tomorrow. Are you alright?"

"Yes," Scott said, biting back his tears of joy at being around good people again. "I'm fine. Where is Narné?"

He felt Narné's presence before he saw him as the great dragon landed in front of the stables and let out a resonating cry of joy and relief. Scott sprinted forward to embrace his dragon, inhaling the clove scent of the great beast. Narné arched his neck until he was cradling Scott as well and the two of them stayed together for several long minutes, their minds entirely open to each other, luxuriating in each other's physical presence that they had missed for so long.

They would have stayed that way for hours except for a cough from someone nearby, clearly meant to interrupt their moment. Scott pulled away, a little angry, to see Mike and the Spokane council. Scott's anger welled. These people had agreed to let the Elder into the flight as well, even Mike. How could Mike do something like that to Derek? But Mike's eyes were sad, and Scott guessed that it had been a hard decision for the man and not one he should judge lightly. Until he knew all of Mike's motives, he should keep his anger to himself. The rest of the council, however...

"How could you?" Scott snapped at them.

"We knew you wouldn't approve," one of the women said. "But it did save your life. Jamie informed us that this was the only option, and besides, we were obeying Derek's direct request."

Scott scowled. He had worried that when Derek found out, the boy would volunteer for opening his mating flight just to save Scott's life. He couldn't really blame the council. They had acted according to their superiors' wishes and probably in the most logical manner. And Scott hadn't wanted to die. He had just hoped – without cause – that another pathway would be found. And one wasn't, so now he was angry. He took a deep breath.

"You did what you had to do. Let's just hope he doesn't win the mating flight. Where is Derek now?"

"He's on his way back here," Mike said. "He was just in Portland. Which is where you need to return, as soon as possible."

Scott nodded. He needed to get back to Jamie. He had missed Jamie sorely, with all of his being, and he just wanted to hold Jamie in his arms and know that everything was all right again. He was more than ready to go back to Portland and the main campus. Besides, he had caught an odd thought from Narné – one that Narné had quickly hidden – about Jamie hanging out with someone new, someone the dragons didn't approve of, and Scott wanted to see what that was about. The dragons had refused to be more specific or even talk about it with him. Now he could finally figure out why the dragons, who usually adored Jamie, were mildly irritated with him and who this stranger was.

"We'll leave immediately," Scott said. "Let me get my things and I'll be off."

Mike nodded. "I'll go with you."

They went to Scott's room in silence, but once they were alone Mike placed his hand on Scott's arm. Scott shivered, remembering when that touch had once promised more. He had gotten over his hatred of Mike now and could look back at what Mike had done to him impartially, even with a little warmth now that he knew that Mike had indeed felt something for him. Mike had been through so much lately and lost so much, he sometimes seemed like a shell instead of a man and it hurt Scott to see him like this. But today he looked strong and in control of himself, and Scott was relieved. Perhaps Mike would recover from Ashton.

"Scott, there's nothing you could have done differently. The Elder outplayed us. But I can assure you that I will do my best to ensure that the Elder does not abuse Derek. We value our Queen too much, and we all know the danger posed by an abusive mate."

Scott let out a sigh. "I wish it didn't have to happen like this. I wish there were another solution. Mike, if the Elder overpowers Derek, if he forces Derek to change the law, he could kill dragons legally!"

"We're all aware of that possibility but you're forgetting that the mate is not allowed to cause any physical harm to the Queen. We'll have doctors checking Derek for injury every day if we have to. We will not let him overpower our Queen."

"And what of Chris? There are ways of overpowering besides physical."

"Let's just hope Chris wins the flight," Mike said darkly. "If the Elder wins, Chris may have to go to Portland to be safe, and I don't want to have to do that to Derek. Or the Elder may be kind to Derek, you know, and woo him. There is that option as well."

"There's so much danger, and I just don't know if he's strong enough."

"He will be," Mike assured him. "We're all going to be training Derek these next few weeks and preparing him for the worst even while hoping for the best. Whatever happens, Derek will be ready."

Scott let out another sigh. "Thank you, Mike. That helps."

Mike smiled a lopsided smile and clasped his arm again. There was a moment of warmth between them that hadn't been there since before the forceful encounter in the hallway shattered Scott's trust in the man. Then it was gone. But the memory remained.

CHAPTER TWENTY-ONE

Intimate Accident

There was a nervous energy in the air when Derek and Chris returned to Spokane. They must have passed Scott midflight, but hadn't seen him. He was returning to Portland to be with Jamie and help get things back to normal, and Derek was in charge of doing the same here. Getting things back to normal. Derek scoffed. When had things ever been normal? Ever since he had bonded with Jettie things had been chaotic, with the campus dividing and everyone turning against Ashton, and now the appearance of the Elder.

Jettie nudged him mentally and he reassured her. He hadn't meant to imply that she was the cause. But the timing was exact, and it wasn't by accident. Bonding with Jettie had given him access to the real Tarragon world, and it was a mess. He could hardly believe it had lasted as long as it had. But he supposed with a strong leader like Ashton in place and no rebellions, perhaps it had worked well for hundreds of years. Not anymore, though.

Chris helped him unpack and moved his things back into their shared room, though Derek noticed he didn't move everything back in. He wondered at that for a moment, then realized Chris must be afraid that he would lose the mating flight and have to move out again. He was, consciously or not, preparing for failure and that would doom their chances.

"Move everything back in," Derek ordered.

Chris looked up at him, then around as if surprised to see that he hadn't been moving everything back. It must have been an unconscious impulse, then. That was more dangerous than a conscious one. If Chris held back at all during the mating flight, they would be lost.

Derek smiled encouragingly, realizing his command might have seemed harsh. He and Chris had been a little wary of each other lately, ever since Derek found out that Chris had lied to him, and this was a good time to mend that fence. He helped Chris move the rest of his belongings back into their room and then took Chris's hand shyly, stroking the palm with his thumb. A wicked smile bloomed on Chris's face at the subtle invitation and he placed Derek's hands on his waist before tilting Derek's face up towards his and kissing his nose playfully.

"You're being so sweet," Chris murmured, nuzzling his nose against Derek's cheek as Derek nuzzled back happily. The tip of Chris's nose was cold and Derek longed to warm it up through close contact, and he knew soon Chris's blood would be pumping and nothing in the man would be cold at all.

"I know how much you love sweet things," Derek said, then boldly kissed Chris on the lips.

Chris locked on quickly and pulled Derek flush against him, curving his body back as the man leaned into him. Derek went limp in his arms willingly, allowing himself to be tilted backwards in the romantic kiss like a girl from a movie. Chris ran his hand from Derek's waist up his chest to his cheek, all the while kissing him passionately, and Derek was willing to bet his nose wasn't cold anymore given the heat pouring off their bodies from the intensity of the kiss. He was already hot and getting hard, and it was just a kiss. How he had missed this!

He let himself be led into the bedroom and they broke away from their kiss for short moments as they undressed, keeping their lips locked as much as possible between unzipping and peeling off and stripping down to their skin until finally their nude bodies were flush against each other, the kiss still going hotter than ever. Derek's heart was beating erratically and he was gasping for breath between kisses, dizzy with passion as Chris held him up. Then the back of his knees hit the bed and he tumbled backwards as Chris stood over him with that same wicked smile on his face.

Derek stretched out on the bed, showing off his body for Chris to enjoy, seeing in the older man's eyes the pleasure as he took his fill of Derek's lithe body sprawled and hard. They were both aroused and Derek knew it pleased Chris to see him so turned on from their kiss, so he spread his legs to show off his arousal and gestured for Chris to come get him.

Chris didn't hesitate, pouncing on him and sweeping him into another mind-numbing kiss. Derek's fingers and toes tingled as his body somehow leapt into an even higher level of arousal and Chris's hand made contact with his cock, stroking it in long, steady pulses. Derek moaned and clawed at Chris's chest, wanting more speed, wanting the other man to skip the preliminaries and plunge inside of him. He was so hot, and he was dripping precum; Chris's hand was slick with it as he continued to stroke slowly up and down. He wanted Chris so badly.

Chris nibbled his ear and it felt as though something dropped out from under him, as if his pleasure were somehow all that existed in the world. He was vaguely aware of Jettie in the new plane of pleasure and he sensed her curiosity. Then Chris slid his hand along Derek's thighs and the pleasure consumed him. Everything became pleasure and the world vanished from around him. He was no longer aware of Chris or anything Chris was doing – except that Chris was touching him, and touching was good – and all he could feel was Jettie stirring in her chamber, confused and empowered by the new feeling of arousal.

Jettie trumpeted once, then went to the exit and launched herself into the air. She needed to fly, needed air against her body to cool the sensations filling her. The air tingled her scales and she let out another trumpet. She wanted a dragon to fill her the way Derek was being filled. But not just any dragon. She would test them, race them, and choose only the best to be her mate. Male dragons appeared around her and she snapped her teeth at them. They all had potential, but she couldn't tell if any were truly worthy of her. She knew there was one she was supposed to look for but she wasn't sure why. She would have to see if he passed her test. She began flying, the air brushing against her scales sensuously.

The males soared after her and she went higher and higher, the males dropping off one by one as their smaller lungs couldn't handle the elevation. Finally, she sank back down to see that only four dragons still chased her. She slowed to examine them and one of them grabbed her. She struggled and was about to bite him when he licked her neck and a strange warmth flooded through her veins. He released her and she quickly recovered, flying back up into the clouds to escape them. He could have won the flight, she thought, he had captured her, but instead he had done something to her that made the air tingle against her body even more. Every gust of wind heightened her pleasure and she found that all she wanted was the dragon to lick her again.

She soared back down and two of the dragons lunged at her. Startled, she picked up speed but the larger dragon caught her and again licked her neck, lingering near her vein this time in an irresistible manner. She struggled to escape and he let her go, but as she flew away she knew her mind was set. She wanted that dragon. He made her feel alive and he was her choice. When she looked back, two of the dragons, including the one she preferred, were fighting. There was a splatter of blood and then the dragons she preferred suddenly charged at her and rammed into her, entangling himself firmly in her body. She gasped.

Suddenly Derek was back in his body just as something enormous was being thrust into him. His head spun and his eyes were tightly shut from the pain, but just like the dragon had seduced Jettie, the man was seducing him and he knew it was Chris, kissing him on the shoulders and cheek to reassure him as the man entered him. Derek moaned at the penetration, far more painful than usual, and the man's mouth descended to his nipples. Derek moaned again and shifted as streaks of pleasure mingled with pain as the man's cock pressed into his body, further and further, until he was deeply seated inside of him.

Chris was always good about waiting for him to be comfortable before starting to thrust and this was no exception; even though Derek's eyes were still tightly shut and his mind was spinning and he didn't think he could see even if he opened his eyes, he knew it was his lover because the man kissed him passionately before moving inside of him. It hurt more than usual but Derek was so sensitive and tender right now it was no surprise.

He could feel the dragons making love as well and the sensation was doubled, the thrusts coming in waves that swept Derek off his mental feet and bowled him over with their intensity. He could barely remain conscious it felt so good, and every thrust sent him closer and closer to an orgasm unlike any he had ever known. Every moment now was like an ordinary orgasm; he couldn't imagine what it would be like when he came with Jettie.

The man, Chris, licked his neck the same way his dragon had licked Jettie, and Derek trembled. His entire body felt limp and out of his control but he managed to lift one hand to grasp the man closer to him. He kissed back passionately when Chris kissed him again on the lips. Their lovemaking had been interrupted by the dragons in the most beautiful way. Chris was different now, not holding back. His tongue plundered Derek's mouth in a way that Chris had never done before and Derek found it made him breathless and even more weak than he already was.

His touches too were different, more intense than usual. There was more pressure and Derek squirmed as Chris squeezed his nipple firmly. Chris had never done this to him before but he found he liked it immensely. His cock, sandwiched between their bodies, was near to exploding and he knew that even with the mating flight and the dragons extending his pleasure, there was no way he was going to be able to last.

"Do you want me?" Chris asked, in a husky voice that didn't sound like his usual voice. He must be turned on by the mating flight as well.

"Yes," Derek cried. "I want you."

Derek gasped in surprise as the pace of thrusts picked up and his body hummed in unbelievable pleasure. He couldn't think, couldn't feel, everything was fuzzy and so damn hot and sexy. He wanted to cum, ached to cum, but for some reason his body wouldn't obey. Jettie wasn't at her peak yet, he sensed, and they had to cum together in the mating flight. But she was rapidly approaching it, since her arousal was directly influenced by his and vice versa. He almost wasn't ready when she suddenly tipped over the edge, the sudden inundation of emotion too much for him to bear. He screamed at the shock of pleasure swamping his senses. He was aware of nothing except his own body exploding outward into a million pieces, dividing and dividing until nothing was left and everything was darkness. Just before he slipped into a deep unconsciousness, he heard Chris's voice calling his name and was comforted.

CHAPTER TWENTY-TWO

Mating Flight

C hris pushed Derek into the bed gently and Derek allowed it. He was in a docile mood tonight and Chris loved it. Derek was always unpredictable in bed, sometimes taking charge, sometime allowing Chris to take charge, and Chris loved trying to guess what mood he would be in and loved the variety it brought to their sex life. Tonight, though, he could tell that Derek just wanted to be carried away in pleasure and Chris could easily provide that.

He fixed his lips on Derek's and stroked their tongues together in a way that had Derek squirming underneath him and panting when they finally broke apart. He was panting too, and they were both already hard. Derek's nude body against his was like a rod of iron in more ways than one and he wanted to feel Derek grow even harder when he slipped inside that silky interior.

Chris let his breath ghost over Derek's face, then he nibbled on Derek's ear in a way that he knew Derek loved. Derek let out a moan and shifted under him. Then Derek went still and Chris wondered if he were trying to hold everything in and keep from cumming. Perhaps the stimulation was too much. He pulled back to examine his lover and Derek's eyes were shut, a look of concentration on his face.

Chris kissed him again and stroked his body. He was hard, but not at the point where he should be overly concerned about cumming. None of the signs were there: his cock was dripping precum but it wasn't quaking or turning slightly purple at the tip as it usually did just before he came. Derek let out a sigh and Chris heard movement in the adjacent dragon chamber. His heart skipped a beat and he drew back from Derek as if he had been burned. It couldn't be. Not this early, not like this. It couldn't be the mating flight.

Jettie let out a piercing cry and Chris let out a whimper, then placed his hands back on Derek. He knew that touch was important and the one touching the Queen had the greatest chance of persuading her to mate with him. He shouldn't be afraid. He was in the ideal situation. He took a deep breath. Yaris was already waiting outside to pursue the Queen. The Elder was who knew how far away. They would make this a quick flight and Chris would be the victor.

Jettie cried again and then there was the sound of wings as she launched herself into the air. Yaris was after her in an instant. He was strong enough to chase her no matter where she went, Chris knew. Chris had to focus on keeping Derek anchored until others arrived. As much as he didn't want others here, it was vital to the mating flight to have people touching Derek or else Derek would lose contact with his body completely while he was flying with Jettie during the mating flight.

It was easier for the males: Chris was aware of what Yaris was doing but not completely swept up in it. But for Queens and other females in their mating flights, he knew that they ceased to exist in their real bodies and existed entirely with their dragon for the majority of the flight. It could be very dangerous, especially if not enough people participated in the flight to keep the female grounded.

Derek writhed sinuously under him and without warning, five men from the council showed up. Chris maintained his primary position over the body while allowing them to touch Derek. They didn't challenge his authority. One of them was Mike, he was interested to see. He hadn't thought that Mike was up for a mating flight with everything that had happened to him, but perhaps he was making an exception. His dragon was strong and large, so perhaps he was figuring he would rather participate than risk the Elder.

Over the next few minutes, more people came pouring in. In the sky above, Jettie was stretching them to the limit by flying into the clouds, something relatively few dragons could do. But Yaris could, and he wasn't going to let her get away. Then a strange dragon appeared, a large dragon whose green scales were so muted they were almost grey, and Chris knew without a doubt that it was the Elder. He quelled the panic in his heart. He was winning, he would win. Derek loved him.

The Elder strode into the room and Chris couldn't deny him a position at Derek's body, as much as he wanted to. The Elder had a hand on Derek's arm but Chris was still straddling the boy, giving him far more claim over the body. The Elder's lips quirked but he said nothing.

In the skies above, Jettie returned to lower altitudes and the Elder's dragon made his move. Chris gasped as – without warning – the Queen was in the dragon's clutches. But the dragon didn't mate with her, he simply licked her in precisely the way that aroused dragons. Chris glared at the Elder.

"How dare you," he hissed. "Is this a joke to you?"

"I intend on a long mating flight," the Elder said. "The longer the flight, the better."

"You can't treat her like that."

"I'm in this mating flight the same as you."

"Well maybe you shouldn't be," Chris snapped, then shut his mouth, appalled. It was the truth, but he couldn't just say it like this. He and the other council members had agreed to let the Elder into the flight, after all. He couldn't go back on his word.

The Elder smirked. "You don't have a chance of winning and you know it. Why don't you just give up now?"

Something inside Chris snapped. Maybe it was his fear of losing finally getting the better of him, but all of his self-control vanished and Yaris's hatred and anger flooded over him. He whirled and flung out his fist, landing it squarely on the Elder's cheek. The Elder reacted instantly, leaping up and shoving Chris violently off Derek and taking up his position straddling the boy. Chris lunged at him but two men caught him and held him back.

"Chris, you can't fight with another member of the mating flight," they hissed. "You'll get yourself killed."

"Let me get to him, to Derek," Chris begged, realizing that this was the Elder's intent in baiting him. The Elder had played him too well. Now the Elder had primary position and Chris would likely be thrown out of the mating flight altogether. "Please, I won't fight, just let me touch him."

The two men holding him let go and he rushed to Derek's side and clutched his arm, stroking it and kissing it. His chances of winning had just dropped dramatically all because he couldn't control his anger. The Elder's dragon continued to seduce Jettie, despite Chris's best efforts to stop it, and as Chris looked on in horror, the large mottled dragon finally moved in for the kill, so to speak, and Chris and the others touching Derek were dragged away so that the Elder could have sole custody of Derek's body during the final stage of the mating flight.

The Elder was gentle, Chris had to give him that. He didn't hurt Derek, and he was careful not to move too fast, something important as the Elder had the biggest cock Chris had ever seen. When he first exposed himself, two men had grabbed Chris as if knowing that Chris was going to try something stupid. And he would have. It was forbidden to interrupt the mating flight but Chris would have done something if those two men hadn't been holding him back. It was torture watching his Derek being taken by another man. It wasn't like their threesome at all – this was an enemy, a hated foe, taking advantage of Derek's clueless state to have sex with him without Derek's knowledge. Derek probably thought he was making love to Chris.

Their rhythm quickened after what seemed like ages and then the Elder looked straight at Chris and smirked again, his cheek starting to purple a little from where Chris had hit him.

"Do you want me?" he asked quietly.

Two more men rushed to grab Chris as Chris lunged forward and growled.

"Yes," Derek cried. "I want you."

It was like a knife in Chris's heart. Never mind that Derek likely didn't know what he was saying. Derek wanted someone else, someone besides his true love. Derek wanted the Elder. Derek was going to be crushed when he finally came to his senses and realized what had happened. Chris went limp against his acting guards and tried not to cry, knowing the Elder was watching him for tears, that tears would mean victory for the cruel Elder. But he would not cry.

The mating flight ended quickly after that, with the two men on the bed, the hated Elder and the innocent Derek, cumming at almost the same time. Once the Elder was off Derek, Chris knew the mating flight rules were weakened.

"Derek," he cried, hoping the young man would answer and would have returned to his senses. But there was silence as Derek seemed to slip into a deep sleep. Not surprising, given everything he had just been through. But dangerous, as it meant he would return to his senses later, without people he loved surrounding him.

The Elder stretched, then pointed at Chris.

"I want that man executed for interfering with the mating flight."

There was a stir at his words. Most of the council was in the room and Chris gulped as he realized that it was within the Elder's rights to ask for such a thing. Only the Queen could override such a request, and the Queen was currently unconscious.

Mike stepped forward and Chris looked at him curiously, not knowing which side he would take in this issue. Mike tended to follow rules, but he had also lost a loved one and wouldn't want Derek to lose a loved one as well.

"We will consider your request, but won't make any final decisions until the Queen has added his input," Mike said. Chris let out a sigh of relief.

"He attacked me during the mating flight," the Elder said. "That is a capital offense."

"Of course," Mike said. "And he will be punished. But we no longer execute without the Queen's permission, and we always wait until we have it, no matter how long that takes. You agreed to follow Tarragon laws and that is a Tarragon law now."

The Elder scowled but nodded. His eyes flickered to Chris and were utterly dismissive. In his mind, Chris was already dead and it chilled Chris to the bone. What would happen when Derek decided not to kill Chris? Would the Elder punish Derek for refusing to side with him on this issue? Would the Elder forbid Derek from ever seeing Chris again? The latter at least seemed likely, and Chris felt tears once again fill his eyes. He needed Derek in his life. He loved Derek, and Derek loved him. Surely there was a way to persuade the Elder to keep Chris in Derek's life. He just needed to find it.

"At the least I want him removed from the council," the Elder said. "He has no right being on it, even if he is allowed to live."

Mike turned to look at Chris as if in apology, then looked at the other council members who grudgingly nodded. Kicking someone out of the council was rarely done. But given his actions in attacking someone during a sacred mating flight, he was lucky if that was all that happened to him. Maybe the Elder would be mollified and not insist on removing Chris from Derek's life altogether.

"Very well," Mike said. "We will need to have a full council meeting for the final decision, but until that time, Chris is no longer part of the council."

A heavy weight sunk in Chris's chest. If only he hadn't reacted so rashly, but he hadn't been thinking of anything besides Derek and protecting Derek. And his hatred of the Elder. He nodded slowly, accepting the decision and wishing again that this was the extent of the Elder's vengeance.

Then the other council members grabbed his arms and started leading him from the room. He dug his heels in.

"No, we have to wait until he wakes up, to make sure he's okay," Chris protested.

"Is that also a new law?" the Elder asked scornfully. "In my time we gave the new mate privacy with his Queen."

"We do now too," Mike responded, placing a hand on Chris's shoulder and tugging him towards the door. "Come on, Chris. It's over."

The words were like a death knell and tears welled up in his eyes, but he wouldn't let the Elder see him cry. He dashed from the room as the others filed out as well. Once he was out of Derek's rooms – his rooms – he let the tears flow. He had blown it. He had lost his one chance to save Derek and save the campus.

Mike pulled him off the wall he had collapsed against and started leading him to the rooms he stayed in when he didn't live with Derek. They were empty, because he had just finished moving his things into Derek's room again. He wondered if the Elder would let him collect his things. Probably not, and there were several sentimental objects he had moved into Derek's room. But Derek would probably return them. He had to remember that Derek wasn't being erased in this relationship; he would still have authority to do what he wanted.

"It'll be fine, Chris," Mike murmured. "We didn't have time to prepare him for this, but he's still a student, and we'll still have plenty of excuses to teach him what he needs to know to be strong against the Elder."

"But when he wakes up, he's going to be alone with that – monster. He doesn't know it was the Elder, I know it."

"I don't doubt it," Mike said grimly. "But there's nothing we can do at the moment. We can only protect him in the future and make sure this doesn't get worse. Can you be strong, Chris, or will you let your emotions get in the way again?"

Chris flushed at the implied insult. But it was true, he had let his emotions get in the way and now they had lost Derek.

"I'll behave," he said. "Anything to get Derek back."

"Good," Mike said. "Because this is going to be more difficult than we originally planned, and we're going to need your help every step of the way. For now, let's focus on keeping you alive. I doubt Derek will allow you to be killed, but if enough of the council is persuaded then his opinion won't matter. Let's go talk to some council members."

CHAPTER TWENTY-THREE

Voyeur

J amie sprawled in his bed, waiting for Scott to arrive. He wasn't sure how to greet Scott. His conversation with Derek lingered in his mind. Despite their budding friendship and Derek's words about Scott being his, there was still some hesitation in his feelings for Scott. Plus there was TK. How was he supposed to explain his fling with TK to Scott, especially since it hadn't ended and, to be honest, he didn't want it to end? He still had feelings for TK; after all, TK had been there for him when Scott was gone and TK was such a great guy. Not to mention the fluttering sensation he felt when TK held him. It was like when he and Scott had first met – an innocent, loving sensation unsoiled by death and outsiders. He missed it.

As he lay there, he felt a stirring among the dragons and his attention centered automatically on the dragon who was causing the stir: Jettie. Something was happening to her. It almost felt as if she were expanding in his consciousness to envelop the nearby dragons and invite them to do – what? Then a shudder of pleasure slammed through Jamie's body and he gasped, his eyes opening with a start. It was her mating flight. She was entering her mating flight too soon, and he was caught up in it.

He closed his eyes again and focused on her. He could read her emotions easily and it was almost as if he were experiencing Marisol's mating flight, though the sensations were much lessened. But he could trace her movements and – more import-

151

antly – he could tell who was chasing her and who was winning. Perhaps he could push her into choosing the right dragon if she started to falter. Just then two hands landed on his shoulders and he hissed as the sensation grounded him in his body and removed him from Jettie.

"Let me go," Jamie cried. "I have to follow her."

"Jamie, what's happening?"

It was Scott. Jamie whined. He would need Scott in this, but not now, not yet. Not until Jettie had chosen her mate.

"It's Jettie," he managed, knowing he ought to say something to his lover. "She's in her mating flight. Please don't touch me until I tell you to."

He heard a gasp but the hands were released so he ignored Scott's reaction and instead zeroed back on Jettie. Something had changed in the flight, something was wrong. There was a dragon chasing her closely, only it seemed that she was pursuing him, not the other way around. The dragon came close and licked her and Jettie shivered and the bond between the two dragons solidified. That wasn't good, Jamie thought with panic, because he couldn't sense this other dragon at all and that meant it had to be the Elder's. The Elder was seducing Jettie, not chasing her, and it was working.

He tried to focus Jettie's mind on the other dragons but it was too late and the Elder had too tight a hold on her. Plus, he couldn't even sense Yaris who should have been battling for control. Chris ought to have had an advantage in this flight but he was nowhere to be found, it seemed, and without his presence there was almost no choice but for Jettie to fall into the Elder's clutches.

The Elder toyed with her a little longer before catching her and taking her, hard. Jamie tried to wrench his mind away before the Elder and Derek's minds melded together but he was caught for one blinding instant and he saw the Elder. The Elder seemed surprised to see him, but smirked and sent a wave of seduction towards him that had his already inflamed body blazing with pent-up passion. Then Jamie managed to free himself and his mind was clear except for the lust filling him. Scott was leaning over him, naked, just as he was naked. Even though Jamie was desperate for Scott to plunge into him immediately, Scott hadn't been properly aroused yet.

"Who won?" Scott asked.

Jamie didn't answer. If he answered, Scott would be unable to perform and he desperately needed Scott. Instead, he ducked his head to the furry patch between Scott's legs, causing Scott to moan in surprise. Scott laid down on the bed and allowed Jamie to access his body freely as Jamie's tongue worked its way up and down his stiffening shaft. Jamie barely even thought about his inexperience or whether he was doing this right, he just knew he needed Scott inside him and this would get him there the fastest.

As soon as Scott was hard, Jamie straddled him.

"Jamie, who won?" Scott insisted, putting his hands on Jamie's waist to prevent him from thrusting down.

"Please, Scott, please, I need this."

Scott didn't answer but gently guided Jamie down his shaft as Jamie moaned. He wanted to go quick but Scott forced him to go slow and it was delightful torture. Once they were together, the magical melding that always happened took place and suddenly Jamie was in Scott's mind. He was careful to hide the knowledge of the mating flight within his own mind even though he knew it would frustrate Scott. He wanted Scott first, then they could discuss the future. He needed Scott so bad.

Scott began to thrust into him and Jamie arched his back. He had never been this turned on, at least not when he was fully conscious of his actions. The mating flights were different. This was just like a mating flight only he was aware and completely awake, and it shocked him how desperate he was for his lover's body to fill his. It was totally unlike him but he craved Scott as he lifted his hips and slammed them back down, tucking his legs closer to Scott's thighs as he straddled his lover. Scott whined and Jamie could feel the building pressure inside him and knew that he was starting to feel as desperate as Jamie felt.

Jamie leaned down and kissed him again and again, strings of saliva connecting this lips when they broke apart for short breaths before kissing again. They were desperate for each other now, for a love that only the other could fulfill. Jamie shifted position and cried out as it struck something deep inside him, something wonderful and fiery and incredibly sexy. Scott grabbed his hips to hold him in place and thrust violently, hitting that same spot repeatedly as Jamie cried out again and again. His cock swelled and precum dripped from the tip. He knew he couldn't last but luckily, neither could Scott. He felt the growing orgasm in his lover's mind and rode the sensation to its brink, then a well-timed thrust of his hips thrust Scott over the edge.

Scott moaned Jamie's name and began kissing him as he came, and then Jamie's own orgasm couldn't wait any longer. He exploded between them but just as he did, he thought he felt a flicker of the Elder's cold laughter and was chilled. He collapsed onto Scott and they lay there for just a few minutes, exhausted, before Scott finally demanded answers.

"Who won, Jamie? No more delays. Tell me it was Chris."

"No," Jamie whispered, still wondering if the Elder's laughter had been imagined or some remnant of the link that had formed in their brief encounter during the mating flight. "I'm sorry, Scott, it was the Elder."

Scott went still in his arms, then shoved him away and stood up, pacing.

"It was the Elder, but you still- You didn't tell me and you made me- How could you make me do that when you knew it was the Elder?"

Scott looked at him and his eyes were full of rage, helplessness, and betrayal. Jamie swallowed. He hadn't expected Scott to react like this. Oh, he knew Scott would be horrified by the outcome – who wouldn't be? – but the accusation in his voice and eyes was shocking. Jamie hadn't realized that making Scott have sex while Derek was having sex with the Elder would be a violation in some ways, but clearly it was. Jamie had taken from Scott's body without Scott's full informed consent and now, with a mind clear from the haze of the mating flight, he realized what a huge mistake he had made.

"I'm so sorry, Scott, I didn't think-"

"No, you didn't think. You just took. You left me to rot with the Elder for weeks and then I get back and the first thing you do is make me betray my friend. And he is my friend, nothing more," Scott said, as if he knew he were getting into dangerous territory and wanted to take the offensive early. "I can't believe you could do that while he was- while that poor boy was getting raped."

"You know the council would never allow a rape," Jamie said, though he knew it wouldn't help.

"Derek loves Chris. No one else should have won."

"I know. I don't know what happened. When you touched me I lost contact and when I came back everything had changed and the Elder had the advantage."

"Oh, so now this is my fault?"

"Of course not," Jamie snapped.

He and Scott had never had a real fight, he realized. This was their first, and it might be their last if Jamie couldn't somehow explain himself.

"I think," Jamie said, encouraged when Scott didn't bite his head off immediately, "I think Derek didn't know who he was with. You don't know what it's like during the mating flight. You lose all control and all inhibitions, you just want to be satisfied."

"And I suppose that explains your actions as well."

Jamie blushed. "I'm so sorry, Scott. I should have controlled myself better but I wanted you so much. I needed you. The mating flight was already decided and I was so- turned on."

"By the Elder."

"Yes," Jamie said, anguished. "How do you think that makes me feel? And how do you think Derek will feel when he wakes up and realizes it wasn't Chris he slept with? We have to protect Chris and somehow I have to contact Derek before he fully wakes up, to try to cushion his knowledge."

"Then what are you doing talking to me? Talk to him, now, and make sure he's all right."

Jamie opened his mouth, then shut it. Scott was right. He should be talking to Derek, not Scott. And if Scott was willing to put his anger aside in order to protect Derek, then perhaps they would get past this bump in their relationship.

"But I won't forget what you made me do," Scott said, erasing that hope.

No, there was a definite crack in their relationship that would take time and effort to seal. But with TK waiting in the sidelines and the friction that already existed between them, was it really worth the effort? Jamie looked at Scott through the corner of his eye as he laid down. Yes, he decided. No matter what, he loved Scott and he would do anything for the man, and he knew Scott would do anything for him as well.

Jamie shut his eyes and prepared to make contact with Derek. Well, with Jettie. She felt glutted and self-satisfied, entirely unaware of the chaos her choice was about to create. Already had created, to some extent. Jettie was excited to hear from him, her ruling Queen, and proudly introduced him to her mate. It was the first time Jamie got a good look at the dragon through a psychic lens and he was stunned at the magnificent, enormous dragon. No wonder Chris had lost. This dragon was ancient. Luckily, now that Jamie had a connection with the dragon, he could contact him at will and locate the dragon anywhere he went. The dragon, oddly, didn't give a name nor was a name associated with his psychic scent as it was with most dragons. He was unnamed, simply the Elder's dragon.

At Jamie's command, Jettie gently woke Derek up and brought him into contact with Jamie. It was dangerous for Jamie to directly reach out to another human like this, but necessary in this case. He could contact other dragons with ease and they him, but humans were another case altogether. He could only do it with Derek, since Derek was also a Queen, and he had never tried it before because of the danger.

Derek, he said softly, hoping to wake Derek up slowly.

Derek rumbled in his mind, a sleepy sound that seemed surprised to hear Jamie.

Jamie?

Derek, your flight is over.

I know! Chris and I will be together now.

No, Derek, Jamie said with a heavy heart. It was as he had thought: Derek assumed he had slept with Chris during the mating flight. *You ended up with the Elder.*

That's impossible, Derek said.

Jamie gently connected him to Jettie, who showed him a brief glimpse of the Elder's dragon at her side. Derek was immediately alert and Jamie groaned. He knew Derek had just woken up and was probably talking to the Elder now. He had wanted to control the conversation. Who knew what the immature and rash young man would say to the Elder?

Derek, you must be calm, Jamie insisted.

Shut up, Derek said in a near yell. *How could this happen? And I am not letting anyone kill Chris! My word is the law, right? Well, it's my word that he lives.*

No, Derek, Jamie said, mind whirling. He didn't understand what was happening but Derek was already falling into the Elder's trap. *Your word cannot become the law. Tell the Elder that you follow Tarragon law and Tarragon law prohibits Chris's death. Tell him that now.*

Jamie wondered what had possibly happened to put Chris's life at risk but this was vital. If Derek's word became law, then the Elder would just have to brainwash Derek and then everything Derek said would become law. They had to ensure that the Elder followed Tarragon law, not Derek's words. Derek's words were too easily swayed.

I don't have to do what you say, Derek said in a silent snarl.

Jamie winced. If only there was a greater friendship between them, as Margot had suggested. Then Derek would obey him out of friendship, not only out of responsibility. But he had to be firm in this. The fate of the Tarragon world relied on him, right now, reigning in the stubborn Queen in the aftermath of a disastrous mating flight.

Derek, you must obey me, he commanded, and Marisol echoed the command in his mind. He could feel Derek's anger and refusal to listen fade away slightly in the face of the double assault of Jamie's words and Marisol's command. Reluctantly, Derek acquiesced.

Several moments passed as Jamie waited anxiously. He knew Derek and the Elder were speaking to each other, setting the tone for their entire relationship and the relationship between the Elder and the entire Tarragon world. He wished he could be present, or have more impact, but he was trapped. Finally, Derek's voice appeared as though at the end of a long tunnel. The connection between them was fading fast, but not before Derek's final words were heard.

I did it, Jamie. I told him my decision but that we had to obey Tarragon law. He understands.

Thank you, Derek, Jamie managed before communication between them became too difficult and the link between them snapped. He felt Marisol easing Derek's mind back to its body, then turning to him to ease him back into a body that at first felt alien. His arms felt too long and without a protective sheath that would allow him to soar through the skies, and his body far too skinny. Then Marisol pushed him out of her mind completely and he was Jamie again, looking up at Scott who watched him with worry and love. Jamie was relieved to see the love there; he had worried it had been lost forever through his actions.

"Derek is all right," Jamie managed, "And the relationship is developing as well as we could hope."

"The Elder isn't hurting him?"

"Of course not," Jamie said, though in truth that thought had never crossed his mind. No, the Elder wouldn't do anything to violate Tarragon law and it was forbidden for the Queen's mate to leave a mark on the Queen's body. He might manipulate Derek, but he wouldn't abuse him. That much was certain.

"You don't know how callous the Elder can be," Scott said, "How carelessly cruel. He doesn't do it intentionally, but everything he does is designed to hurt others. I know, I've been with him for weeks now."

"He'll be careful with Derek," Jamie said. "Derek is his only chance to regain power. He's probably the safest person in all of Tarragon society right now. I'm worried about Chris."

"We have to get Chris out of his reach. When he finds out that Chris and Derek are in love, he'll kill him."

"I think he already knows," Jamie said. "Derek said something about not letting Chris be killed. Don't worry, Tarragon law requires the Queen's permission before killing anyone and Derek will never agree to Chris's death. But it might be a good idea to bring Chris here, just until things have settled down. I'm sure we'll receive a full report of the mating flight soon and we can discuss Chris's future then."

Scott nodded. He looked torn, as if he didn't want Chris in Portland but didn't want Chris killed either. Which was probably the case, Jamie reflected. He tried to stifle the jealousy that rose in his mind at the thought of what Derek, Scott, and Chris had shared. It was over, and would never happen again. He could only hope their sacrifice was worth it and Derek would stand strong against the Elder.

"We'll wait and then decide," Scott repeated, sighing. "In the meantime, you and I need to talk. About a lot of things."

Jamie gulped and nodded, extending his arm as Scott scooted closer to him. There was a distance between them, a psychological distance, that he was afraid to bridge, but physically they were as close as ever. It was time to bridge that gap.

CHAPTER TWENTY-FOUR

A New Partner

Derek awoke to Jamie in his mind, and when Jamie's words made sense to him he snapped awake to find the Elder leaning over him, about to kiss him. He flinched and would have screamed but the Elder quickly covered his mouth as if he had just been waiting for Derek to open it.

"Quiet, little one," he murmured. "Your friends are all outside and you don't want to upset them, do you?"

Derek thought of Chris waiting outside and shut up. This must be hard enough on Chris; he didn't need to hear Derek screaming on top of everything else.

"One of your friends attacked me during the mating flight," the Elder continued. "I need your permission to carry out the standard punishment, which is death."

Derek did let out a cry at that, noticing now the bruise starting to darken the Elder's cheek. Who had done it? Who had been foolish enough to fight during the mating flight? The sanctity of the mating flight was drilled into all of them from the time they partnered with their dragons; no one would dare violate that rule. Then he thought of Chris and how desperate Chris must have been when he saw that the Elder would win. Yes, Chris would break that sanctity if he thought it would win him Derek. Derek felt tears fill his eyes.

"No," he said. "No one will be killed, because I won't allow it."

Immediately Jamie started chiming in his head about his

wording and he shut his eyes to block out the insistent babble. What did it matter how he phrased things? No one was going to kill Chris, that was that. But Jamie was insistent and Marisol was commanding him as well, so he reluctantly opened his eyes again.

"I misspoke," he said. "Tarragon law prevents anyone from being killed, and I follow Tarragon law. So do you," he pointed out.

The Elder seemed amused. Derek sent a reassurance to Jamie and then felt Marisol pushing him fully into his body. Instantly he was absorbed in a world of pain and he gasped. His body ached from the thorough pounding it had received and he felt as though he had been split in half and sewn back together. Looking down at the Elder's massive member he knew why. It was no wonder he had fallen unconscious afterward.

"Was our dear Queen in Portland conversing with you?" the Elder asked.

"Yes," Derek said, immediately defensive.

"He had a taste of our mating flight as well. His abilities are quite useful."

"I have abilities too, you know," Derek said, even more defensive.

As much as he hated the Elder, the Elder was now his mate and ought to take his side in matters, not be impressed by Jamie the way everyone else was. What was it about Jamie that had everyone swarming to him?

The Elder laughed. "Your abilities are quite impressive, and just as useful. Traveling through the mist is a very valuable gift and I hope to show you many ways to use it, if you let me."

Derek frowned at him. Aside from the ache in his body left over from the mating flight, the Elder hadn't hurt him at all and wasn't doing anything to him that was especially evil. In fact, he was being quite nice. He had always been nice to Derek, he reflected, even in the dreams where they had seen each other.

Maybe the Elder wasn't as bad as everyone made him out to be. But he wasn't Chris, Derek thought sadly. And Chris was the only mate he wanted. Tears filled his eyes.

Instantly the Elder was leaning towards him, cradling Derek's face in his hands and wiping the tears away with his thumbs. Derek sniffled but the tears wouldn't stop. His panic was gone, but the cold sickening realization that he wasn't with Chris was beginning to sink in. The Queen's mate controlled the Queen's bed. Would the Elder ever let him see Chris again? Or would he be trapped with the Elder forever, apart from the one man who had truly earned his love? The tears came faster and the Elder pulled him into a hug, letting him cry against his shoulder as the Elder stroked his back in a surprisingly gentle manner.

"It's all right, little one," the Elder murmured. "You're safe now. I'll protect you, I won't let anything happen to you."

"Chris," he managed between sobs. "I want Chris."

The Elder's body stiffened for a moment, then the Elder began running his hands through Derek's hair.

"I'll let him live, sweetheart. I'll let his transgressions go. But you must remember that I am doing this for you, and repay me in the future."

Derek shuddered. As nice as he was being, the Elder was still a cold monster, he realized, who didn't value human life at all. And trying to exchange Chris's life for a future favor when Chris's life wasn't even at stake? Derek wasn't going to let him get away with that.

"No," Derek said, pushing back from the Elder and meeting his gaze squarely. "His life will be spared because that's Tarragon law, not because of any favors from you."

The Elder blinked as though surprised, then the hint of a smile crossed his lips. He was quite handsome, especially when he smiled.

"Naturally," the Elder said. "You know, you remind me of a student I once had. He was bright, beautiful, and precocious as well. I loved him quite a bit."

"What happened to him?"

A shadow crossed the Elder's face. "He died recently. I wish I could have been there to stop it."

Seeing the Elder like this humanized him and again Derek felt himself softening towards the man. He wasn't all evil, after all. He just had different values.

"What was his name?" Derek asked.

"Peter Ashton," the Elder replied.

"What?"

Derek was stunned. Peter Ashton was his father. How could his father be a student of his mate's? But the Elder was ancient, he remembered, stealing youth and life from other dragons through their blood. No one knew how old the Elder was. Ashton had been centuries old; the Elder was likely centuries older than that. Curiosity welled up inside Derek. He had never gotten a chance to get to know his father. He had grown up apart from his father and by the time he came to Tarragon Academy – and especially after he partnered with Jettie – there were so many other things going on that Ashton hadn't been able to pay full attention to him. And Derek had been a disappointment in some ways, he had to admit. He still didn't know if Ashton had ordered Alan to kill him or if Alan had acted on his own, but either way he had nearly died because his bond with Jettie was insufficient for their needs.

But now he could learn about his father from the very person who helped his father become who he was. A sudden, desperate desire to become his father filled Derek and he wondered if the Elder would teach him the way he had taught Ashton. Not the dragon killing, he would never do that, but everything else. Everything that had made his father who he was.

"Speak, little one," the Elder said.

Derek realized he had been staring off into space for several long moments and he gulped and turned his attention to the

Elder's almond eyes.

"Ashton was my father," he said simply.

The Elder's eyes widened, then he began to laugh. He hugged Derek to his chest as he laughed and the sound was enticing. The Elder stroked his hair again and kissed his forehead.

"No wonder you are so beautiful," he said. "Your name is Derek, is it not? Well, Derek, I am honored to be the mate of Ashton's son."

Derek blushed. He had hardly noticed that the Elder hadn't referred to him by name before this moment but he knew he had suddenly gone considerably up in his estimation. The Elder accepted him as a person now, not just as a Queen to be dominated. It was an unusual realization and he was glad that he wouldn't be treated like an object, but now he wondered what the Elder expected from him. Did the Elder expect him to know what Ashton had known? Ashton had barely been in his life except as an aching absence. He didn't know how to explain that, though, so he remained silent and accepted the Elder's embrace. At least they weren't fighting, and at least it seemed like the relationship between them would be friendly. He knew the Elder killed dragons, but it was hard to link that reality with the flesh and blood person holding him right now.

"Are you prepared to go and tell the others that you are all right?" the Elder asked, cupping Derek's cheek in his hand and wiping away the last remnants of tears.

Derek took a deep breath. The loss of Chris was like a knife in his gut and he didn't think he could face Chris right now, but Chris probably wouldn't be waiting for him – they would have taken Chris away if Chris really had attacked the Elder. And he could deal with the other council members. He nodded and the Elder helped him stand. He wobbled a little, his body was so sore, and the Elder ran his hand down Derek's nude back possessively.

"It won't always be that rough," he said. "I can make it so you don't feel a thing afterwards."

"Then why didn't you this time?"

"The mating flight is always different," he said, though Derek had the feeling he was hiding something. "It's harder to maintain control."

Derek remembered the enormous dragon seducing Jettie rather than rushing in for the kill. That had been a controlled, deliberate action. Had the Elder wanted him unconscious for some reason? He didn't know, and it hurt his head to wonder. He would likely never know, but at least this wouldn't ever happen again.

Derek collected his clothes from around the room and dressed shyly, aware of the Elder donning dark robes that almost looked like the council's robes, without the sigil. Once they were both dressed, the Elder's hand was back at the base of his spine possessively and the Elder led him to the door, pushing it open and escorting him out to the hallway where three council members waited.

Not Chris, Derek was pleased to see, but not Mike either, which surprised him. The three council members pulled Derek away from the Elder and one of them took his head in his hand and tilted it from side to side as if looking for injuries.

"Are you all right, Derek?" he asked.

"I'm fine," Derek replied, pulling out of the man's unwelcome grasp.

If it were Mike, he wouldn't have minded the touch but this man felt foreign and invasive. As if he didn't really care about Derek, and just wanted to get the required inspection out of the way. Which was probably the case, Derek reflected. These men didn't know him, and didn't care about him other than as their Queen. Why wasn't Mike here? The Elder reappeared at his side and for some reason his presence was reassuring. At least the Elder cared what happened to him. And the Elder seemed to have taken a personal interest in him as Ashton's son, so it was more than just a liking as his mate.

"As you can see," the Elder said, "Derek is fine. He will alert you if he needs you. Until then, he and I would like some more privacy."

Derek nodded his agreement, though he had no idea why he and the Elder would need more privacy. Instantly he thought of what the Elder had said about their sex not hurting and he blushed slightly. Was that what the Elder intended? He wasn't sure he was up for that, but his body sent a tingle through his limbs that let him know that it that were the case, he would certainly try his best to perform. He had thoroughly enjoyed the mating flight despite having a partner besides Chris. A flash of sadness cooled his body down and he looked around again.

"Where's Chris?" he asked as the council members started to leave.

One of them turned back. "He's with Mike. Are you carrying out the execution?"

"No, of course not. I just wanted to make sure he was... okay."

The council member stared at him as if to say that of course he wasn't okay, and Derek ought to know it. Derek shrank slightly from that gaze.

"I just wanted to make sure," he repeated softly, then turned to the Elder, who wrapped an arm around his shoulders and led him back into his room – their room – and shut the door firmly.

CHAPTER TWENTY-FIVE

Persuasion

C hris followed Mike around for hours talking to various council members. All had heard about what Chris had done – news traveled fast among dragons, especially with a transgression such as his – and most seemed satisfied that being kicked off the council was punishment enough. There were a few that eyed him as if longing to demand more, but Mike's presence put a stop to anything.

He and Mike started with the easy to persuade members and then worked their way through the ranks of council members loyal to Ashton who would be harder to persuade, until they had only one left: Carys. Chris was especially wary of him, because the two of them had a history that he suspected Carys wouldn't be ready to forget so easily. But with Mike at his side, he felt confident.

He took a deep breath before they knocked on Carys's door and Mike looked at him questioningly.

"It's all right," Chris assured him. "I'm just glad we're almost done."

Mike nodded, not looking reassured at all. But he knocked and the door opened immediately. Carys was on the other side. The man's eyes went straight to Chris and his stomach dropped. No, Carys was not going to let him off easy.

"I know why you're here," Carys said, "And if you want my help, I'll need to speak to Chris alone. It may take some time."

Chris fought to hide a tremble that ran through his body. He felt confident enough with Mike at his side but without Mike, who knew what would happen? But Mike didn't know anything – Mike had only been in Ashton's circle a short time – and so Mike agreed and gestured for Chris to enter on his own. He would be waiting outside, which was some comfort, but a very small one. Chris gathered his courage and went inside, feeling some of his hope vanish as Carys shut the door behind them and then turned to Chris with a wicked smile.

"How the tables have turned," he murmured. "Once, I was desperate to enter the inner circle and you took advantage of me. Now you're desperate for my help to survive. I believe in fair play, don't you?"

"It was Ashton's policy and you know it," Chris snapped, then wished he hadn't risen to the bait so quickly.

But it was true. He hadn't quite taken advantage of Carys, or at least not in the way Carys was implying. Ashton required every member of his inner circle to prove their loyalty by sleeping with at least one current member of the inner circle as well as Ashton himself, and Chris had simply been the council member that Carys had approached. Sure, Chris had been a little forceful and hadn't explained all the rules or explained why he was doing it, but the end result had been exactly what Carys had wanted. But now it put him in a very uncomfortable situation because Carys could demand anything from him in exchange for his life, and they both knew he would have to give it.

Carys laughed and reached out to stroke Chris's cheek. Chris flinched.

"So sensitive. No wonder, since you just lost the mating flight."

Chris flinched again, the pain going straight to his gut. He had managed to push that out of his mind, pretend it hadn't happened, that they were doing this for some other reason and he would be reunited with Derek at the end. But he wouldn't.

Chances were good that he would never see Derek again.

Carys's eyes gleamed victoriously as he must have realized his advantage.

"Ashton would be disappointed in you. After all, he trained all of us in the inner circle to seduce Derek and win the boy's mating flight. You came the closest, and you failed. You failed Ashton, and yourself."

At least Carys didn't understand the real pain of his loss, Chris reflected. But hearing Carys's word brought up a new fear. What if Carys – or any of the council members – told Derek that they had all been assigned to seduce Derek and Derek assumed that Chris didn't love him? If Chris weren't allowed anywhere near him, how could Chris possibly explain that though it had started that way, he had quickly fallen hard for the boy and loved him with every fiber of his being?

"All that pent up sexual energy from the flight," Carys mused. "I bet none of the others were brave enough to ask to speak to you alone, and no one would dare lay a hand on you in front of Mike. That boy's been through enough," he added with a surprisingly gentle tone. "But now that we're alone, I require a little more to persuade me. After all, the Elder wants what Ashton wanted: a return to the old ways. Why wouldn't I want him in power? Why shouldn't I support him instead of you?"

Chris glared but his heart was cold. That was the real fear here, that the Ashton supporters would line up behind the Elder because they foolishly thought they were the same person. They didn't understand how drastically different the two men were; how ruthless the Elder was.

"If you support Ashton, you should support his son," Chris said. "And Derek doesn't want me killed."

News of Derek's decision had already reached them, but it hadn't made their job any easier. Under Tarragon law, a council member could still oppose the Queen's will and demand a vote on the matter and if Ashton's supporters sided with the Elder,

Chris's life was still at stake. That was why every vote was important, why they hadn't stopped when they heard the news. Even though everyone had already agreed not to oppose Derek, if Carys did, he might be able to re-persuade enough members to put Chris's life at risk.

"Oh, I support Derek," Carys said with a wave of his hand. "But what does Derek see in you? I think it's about time I found out."

Another wicked smile crossed his face.

"Get on your knees, Chris," he commanded.

Chris considered disobeying, but he knew his life was on the line. He had to do exactly what Carys told him or risk his life, and he knew if he were killed it would devastate Derek and he would do anything to protect Derek. He got on his knees, already knowing what was coming next.

He wasn't surprised when Carys parted his robes to reveal a swelling cock, or when Carys grabbed his hair and forced his head upwards so his lips were level with that cock. But he wasn't going to volunteer for this. He would wait until ordered to open his mouth and humiliate himself. Carys tightened his grip in Chris's hair and forced his head up until their eyes met.

"Just think of all that energy from the mating flight, Chris, and release it on me," he urged. "I know you're aroused still. You can't avoid it. I want you to satisfy me and yourself. Take off your pants."

Chris blinked in surprise. What was Carys doing? But he had to obey, so he removed his jeans. He was still not used to wearing clothes other than robes, but Mike had insisted that he remove his council member robes immediately and given him a pair of jeans and a shirt to wear instead. Now his jeans were around his knees, along with his briefs, and he was exposed in the cool air. Carys was right; he was a little turned on still from the after effects of the mating flight. Coming so close to completion was tantalizing and not satisfying himself afterwards meant he would be on edge for hours, which Carys knew, of course.

"I want you to cum while you suck me off," Carys said in a husky voice. "I want to know how much you enjoy being my slut."

Chris's eyes darted back up to him. So Carys wasn't doing this for any kind reason, he was doing it to increase Chris's shame. He should have known. But he would do it. He would do anything for Derek. He placed one hand on his own cock and one on Carys's, then extended his tongue and let Carys's cock slide into his mouth while he jerked himself off with his other hand. At least Carys was attractive and had a nice cock, he reflected. It was one of the reasons Chris had taken advantage of Carys in the first place when the young man had come asking how to become a part of Ashton's inner circle.

Chris had not been kind to him, he thought as his tongue massaged Carys's sensitive member. Chris had taken him to the bedroom and stripped him, then fucked him while he tried to resist. It had been an intense and pleasurable experience and eventually Carys had given in to the pleasure and enjoyed himself, but it had started as rape and even after joining the inner circle, Carys and Chris had always been at odds. Now, as Carys's hand in his hair tightened and Carys slammed down the back of Chris's throat, he knew that Carys was finally getting payback.

As Chris played with himself, he tried to picture that this was Derek forcing himself onto Chris and immediately got harder. Derek could be forceful, after all, and Chris could imagine him taking charge like this. It would have to be a very specific situation, but it might happen. He imagined Derek's hand in his hair, Derek's cock in his mouth and he pushed forward, taking as much of the cock as he could into his throat.

"That's it, slut," he heard in a voice he pretended was Derek's. Would Derek ever call him slut? It didn't matter.

His hand stroked faster and his lips moved on their own, his tongue working small circles as he alternated thrusts and massage in a way that had his pretend-Derek moaning and grasping his hair desperately. Finally, he felt a tightening in the base of the cock in his mouth and he knew the end was coming. He pulled out slightly but the hand on his head kept him locked in place as pretend-Derek cried out and exploded into his mouth. The taste was wrong but he clung to his illusion as he jerked his hand back and forth on his own cock and felt a wave crash over him as his orgasm hit.

The moment his orgasm reached its peak, it evaporated as he realized that not only was this someone besides Derek, it would never be Derek again. Derek was gone, forever out of reach because the Elder had won the mating flight. Because Chris had let his anger get the better of him and had attacked, giving up his prime position on Derek and losing the flight in the process. Chris had done this to himself and now Derek was gone. A tear ran down his cheek unbidden.

"Why are you crying, slut? I can see it was good for you, too," a cruel voice said and Chris returned to reality abruptly.

He sniffed and held back the other tears that threatened to fall. Carys was already getting cleaned up. There was a dark taste in Chris's mouth from the man's cum but when he tried to head to the bathroom Carys stopped him.

"I'm sure your friend outside is wondering where you are," he said. "I'll let you live, but don't do anything stupid again, Chris. I might demand more next time."

Chris nodded his thanks and backed out of the room into the hall. Mike stared at him but said nothing as the two of them walked to Mike's quarters. As soon as the door shut and it was just the two of them, Chris let some of his tears fall. He knew Mike wouldn't judge him for his emotions.

"What did he do to you, Chris?" Mike asked. "You look horrible."

"Nothing, he did nothing I didn't expect but I realized that Derek... he's gone, isn't he? The Elder will never let me see him again. Everything we've just done is for nothing. I won't be going home to Derek tonight, or any night. He's lost to me."

Chris trembled and collapsed into a couch. Mike sat beside him and stroked his arm.

"He's alive and as long as he's alive there's still hope. We don't know what the Elder plans to do but it's safe to say that you won't be allowed to see Derek for a long time, it's true. But come next mating flight, we all hope you'll try again to win."

Chris shook with suppressed emotion. Even Mike was acknowledging that he probably wouldn't see Derek again, and Mike was comforting him.

"I might as well be dead," he whispered.

"No," Mike said sharply. "For Derek's sake, you need to stay alive. Trust me, I know what it's like to lose a loved one."

Chris instantly regretted his words, remembering too late how Ashton had murdered Mike's lover Kale right in front of him before Ashton was executed. Mike was still recovering from the incident and everyone – including Carys, it seemed – tread carefully around him. No one wanted to lose Mike, and everyone knew how delicate he still was psychologically.

"But if I can't be with him, how will I survive? I can't be on this campus and not be with him."

"No, you can't. That's why Jamie and Scott have offered to have you stay in Portland for the time being. They'll make sure you return in time for the next mating flight, of course. But it'll be easier for everyone involved if you aren't here and aren't as easy a target for the Elder."

"You want me to abandon Derek to that monster?" Chris asked in shock.

"The Elder has so far treated Derek with kindness and courtesy, as a mate should, and I don't expect him to violate any rules," Mike said. "He won't be in any danger but you will be. The Elder will undoubtedly target you if you remain. Directly or indirectly, you'll be in great danger."

"I won't leave Derek."

"Do this for Derek. Think how hard it is for him, always worrying about your safety. If he knows you're in Portland, he doesn't have to worry about you. But if you're here, he'll have to keep an eye on everything the Elder does."

"Which he should be doing anyways," Chris pointed out.

"But not because it might hurt you," Mike said.

Chris sighed. It made sense, but he didn't want to leave. Still, it would be torture being so close to Derek and not being able to see him. If he were in Portland he could pretend he was merely on a trip and he could see Derek again when he returned, which might even be the case depending on the next mating flight.

"All right," he said. "I'll go to Portland. When should I leave?"

CHAPTER TWENTY-SIX

Reunion

Jamie stared at Scott and wondered how to start the conversation. There was so much to say, so many secrets between them. He took a deep breath and then jumped when Janna, his cat, leaped between them. Scott leapt as well, and seemed confused when she nuzzled against him.

"You got a cat?" he asked.

"Yeah," Jamie said, realizing he hadn't mentioned Janna a single time. "Her name's Janna. She's been keeping me company while you've been gone."

A smile softened Scott's face. "I'm glad you've had someone to cuddle. She seems sweet."

Jamie took a few steps so that he could scratch between Janna's ears as Scott stroked her back.

"She is a sweetie. I'm glad you like her. You aren't allergic or anything, are you?"

"No, I love cats."

Jamie grinned. Scott looked peaceful petting the cat, and she purred loudly. He was delighted that this introduction was going so well. He didn't want to tell Scott about the other person he'd been cuddling while Scott was gone. He still wasn't sure how to bring up TK in the conversation, but they needed to talk about him so Scott and TK didn't run into each other and start a fight or something.

"So what else have you been up to while I've been gone?" Scott asked in a seemingly innocent voice, though with an undertone as if he knew about Jamie's infidelities.

Jamie took a deep breath. "I've been seeing someone."

Scott straightened, the cat forgotten for the moment. His face was completely impassive.

"What does that mean?"

"I mean, we've gone on a few dates and hugged and stuff. But you're still my boyfriend, my mate," he hastened to add.

"And stuff," Scott repeated in a dull voice. "What does 'stuff' entail?"

Jamie blushed. "We haven't had sex, if that's what you're asking. I wouldn't sleep with anyone besides you," he added in a bitter tone, reminding Scott that Scott couldn't get too mad at Jamie because Scott had a 'friend' on the side as well.

Scott had the decency to blush, at least, but his face was still impassive. It was so difficult to figure out if he was mad, or upset, or sad, or what. He was like a blank wall and it was beginning to worry Jamie. Jamie licked his lips nervously and continued.

"You know I can't have sex with anyone without your permission," he said. "Not that I wanted to. Well, I guess I kind of did when I was mad at you, but- Well, I was so mad at you, Scott. I was so afraid and jealous and then scared when you left and scared the whole time you were gone and I needed someone to comfort me. Someone to listen to me and reassure me and you know as well as I do that there's no one here who could do it, everyone here has ulterior motives."

"Right," Scott said. "So who was it?"

"His name's TK. He's a student from Africa, he won't enter the university until next year. He doesn't have a dragon yet, but he knows about them."

Scott's jaw dropped. "He's not even a student? How young is

he? Is he even eighteen yet? Jamie, have you completely lost your mind? Going after a kid like that? And without a dragon? No wonder the dragons are so mad at you right now! Jamie, you can't see him anymore. You can't risk someone without a dragon learning too much about our society. What if he doesn't bond with a dragon? What then?"

"Amar says he will," Jamie said.

He was a little embarrassed at how young TK was. He had never given it much thought before, because TK always acted older than he was and seemed so mature, but he was just a kid. Not even in college yet; a high school student. And he was surprised to hear that the dragons were mad at him. He'd noticed some of them being snippy with him lately but they had hidden any anger very well. Thinking about it, though, he could see why they would be mad. They wouldn't want him getting together with an unpartnered person because they wouldn't be able to communicate with his boyfriend's dragon. They were quite snoopy after all, plus they were very attached to the idea of him and Scott staying together so any interference with that was frowned upon.

"If he doesn't bond with a dragon, then he'll die young, you know that, right? And what if he ends up at the Spokane campus?"

"I'll make sure he goes here," Jamie said without thinking, then knew he made a mistake when Scott's eyes narrowed.

"Maybe it's best if he goes to Spokane."

Jamie hesitated. He cared for TK, but he also had to honor his boyfriend and mate. If Scott felt threatened by TK, which he shouldn't but Jamie could see how he would, then maybe TK should be in Spokane. After all, Jamie had made sure that Derek ended up in Spokane. How was this any different?

"I guess that's one possibility," Jamie finally said. "I haven't decided where the students from Africa will go yet. Maybe Spokane is the best place for them."

"I think it is," Scott said.

Scott turned his back to Jamie and looked out the window. His shoulders hunched up.

"I can't believe it," he whispered. "I waited so long to get out of that place, knowing that once I did I would come back here and you would be waiting for me. And when I finally get out, you greet me by tricking me into sex and betraying Derek, then telling me you've been seeing someone else this whole time. You can't imagine what it was like being a prisoner, Jamie. Having nothing to do all day but think about you and what I would do when I finally got free. Sometimes the Elder talked to me but he mostly just left me alone. I talked to the dragons a lot, but I wanted you. So badly. Those messages you sent me through Marisol every day were the only things keeping me going. And they were lies."

"No they weren't," Jamie said, coming up behind Scott and wrapping his arms around his boyfriend. "I meant every word. I do love you, and I thought of you all the time. I can't even begin to imagine what it was like for you." He closed his eyes and winced. "I'm so sorry you came home to this. I didn't mean to hurt you, I hope you know that. I never want to hurt you."

"You've ripped my heart out, Jamie," Scott whispered. "How can you not see it?"

Jamie leaned his cheek against Scott's shoulder. Tears were rapidly filling his eyes and he suspected Scott was crying as well. It would be so easy to just send TK to Spokane and never think of him again, but he cared about TK. He wanted to be with TK still, and with Scott. Scott first, of course, but wasn't there room for both of them? For romance with Scott and friendship with TK?

And he had no idea how to heal the rift caused by Derek's mating flight. He hoped time would work on that. Scott had entered the room at just the wrong time and caught Jamie in the midst of a mating flight passion, and Jamie would have done anything to satisfy himself even though it meant hiding the results of that mating flight from his partner until after he had cum.

"We're going to be okay, aren't we?" Jamie asked in a shaky voice. "I mean, we'll get through this, right? I still love you more than anything."

"I still love you, Jamie, but it hurts so much right now," Scott replied. "But I don't want to leave you. I can't leave you. I want to be at your side, but I don't want you to ever keep a secret from me again. I think that hurt more than anything – when our minds were joined but you were hiding from me."

Jamie nodded and moved until he was in front of Scott, gazing into his eyes. There were unfallen tears in Scott's eyes.

"I won't lie to you ever again," Jamie promised. "You won't either, will you?"

"No, I won't lie to you," Scott said.

Then Scott tilted his head down and their lips met in a chaste kiss. Jamie tried to end the kiss almost immediately but Scott kept his lips pressed against Jamie's so Jamie held still, and after a moment Scott's lips opened and Jamie hesitantly opened his lips as well to let their tongues dance together. It was a quiet kiss, reminiscent of some of their first kisses when they were just getting to know each other, and it felt as though they were just getting to know each other again. They had both been hurt and were recovering, and this was their fresh start. Jamie wondered what TK would think and how he would explain this to the man, but he pushed that out of his mind. This was about Scott, not TK.

Finally, the kiss ended and Scott opened his eyes to gaze at Jamie. Jamie couldn't keep back a smile at that beautiful face that was his again. They were together and nothing could stop them. A loud meow interrupted their gaze and they looked down at Janna simultaneously as she threaded her way through their legs. They started laughing together and the laughter erased some of tension in the room. But Scott sobered quickly and took Jamie's hand.

"There are a lot of questions still. What are we going to do about the Elder? And about Chris?"

"Chris will come here," Jamie said. "I've already talked to his dragon. He's leaving immediately. He spoke with the council and they've agreed not to challenge Derek's decision to spare his life."

Scott nodded. "He won't be happy here," Scott warned.

"He won't be happy anywhere," Jamie said with a shrug. "At least here he'll be safe."

"You know he's one of Ashton's men."

"I know. Marisol checked him out when he first started dating Derek. But I think his intentions toward Derek are pure enough, and with the Elder, I think Ashton's men will side with Derek over the Elder. That seems to be what they're signaling by letting Chris live."

"And if Derek is corrupted…"

"Then we have bigger problems to worry about," Jamie said darkly. "We have to do everything in our power to prevent that from happening. From what the council has said, the Elder is already trying to take control of Derek. When Derek appeared to the council for them to examine him for injuries, the Elder controlled the situation and Derek let him. But Derek was probably in a state of shock and not his usual self. I think the Elder will have his hands full trying to tame Derek, for a while at least, and in that time we can teach Derek how to resist the Elder even better."

"You think we can fully teach him to resist?"

"We have to. But yes, I think we can. Derek hates being below anyone in terms of rank, so it shouldn't be too hard for him to want to remain the dominant one in the relationship."

Scott blushed and Jamie realized his words had a sexual overtone to them, with talk of being below people and domination. He wondered briefly what Derek was like in bed. He had thought – briefly, and not too seriously – of asking Scott to be in a threesome with him to level the playing field and had thought – again, briefly – of having Derek be the other partner, since Derek was quite attractive, but he knew he would never have the guts to actually go through with it. Derek would probably turn him down, anyway. Derek had very few good feelings for Jamie and Jamie needed to nurture those feelings, not risk them all for sex. But he still couldn't help but wonder what the arrogant, domineering Derek was like in bed, if he carried on his dominant personality or if he allowed himself to be dominated.

"I think Derek can learn, yes," Jamie repeated, and Scott nodded.

"I just hope he learns in time. He only has to mess up once and the Elder takes control. The Elder can wait as long as it takes for that mistake. He's not in a rush."

Jamie agreed. The Elder was playing a waiting game. He just had to be on the lookout for a single slip up from Derek and he won. Derek, on the other hand, had to be constantly vigilant to never take a false step or speak a wrong word. It was going to be exhausting for Derek and he hoped Derek had the stamina for it. Hopefully it would only last until the next mating flight when Yaris and Chris would win, but there was a chance – a real chance – that the Elder would continue to win the mating flight for years to come. After all, the Elder's dragon was enormous and so powerful. It was awe-inspiring in a lot of ways. What dragon wouldn't want such a beast for a mate? But unfortunately that beast was paired with the Elder and the dragon, like the partner, was completely corrupt and was almost entirely reliant on dragon blood to survive.

Jamie wasn't sure how long the Elder could survive without dragon blood but the instant the Elder broke Tarragon law, he would find the full force of Tarragon society ranged against him. He suspected it wouldn't happen for years, perhaps even decades. Hopefully the Elder would still be seen as an outsider at that point. The fear, of course, was that the Elder, like Ashton, would worm his way into the society and there would be another civil war between dragons. Jamie would do anything to prevent that, and keeping Derek strong and on his side was the key. If Derek turned, the cause was lost. They had to make sure Derek continued to hate the Elder even as Derek learned to live with the Elder and tolerate him. A tricky balance, and Jamie was grateful that he wasn't being asked to do such a difficult task.

CHAPTER TWENTY-SEVEN

Coming to Terms

Derek allowed himself to be led back into his room by the Elder but as soon as the door was closed he shook off the Elder's possessive hand. The Elder let him go after caressing his shoulder, and let him retreat to the other side of the room. Derek felt as though reality were crashing in on him all of a sudden and he didn't know what to do. He just remembered the council member's look when he had asked about Chris. Chris must be in terrible shape. He needed Chris, needed to hold him and be with him and assure him that everything would be the same. But would it? What would the Elder allow?

"I want to see Chris," he said in a half-commanding, half-pleading voice.

"I don't think that would be a good idea," the Elder said.

"Why not?" Derek cried.

"It might give you false hope," the Elder said in a gentle voice. "You aren't going to be allowed to see him again."

Derek's lip quivered. That was not an option. He couldn't not see Chris. Chris was his love.

"You have to let me see him. I order it!"

The Elder reached out and caressed his shoulder again, but Derek twisted out of his grasp.

"You can't order this, Derek. I have control over who you see, and your bedroom. You know that. And I don't want you seeing him."

"Why not?" Derek demanded again. "I'll still love him even if I can't see him."

The Elder smiled and shook his head. "Someday you'll understand."

A pout formed on Derek's lips and he couldn't make it go away. So he was too young to understand, but not too young to take in a mating flight. Well, he would show the Elder. If the Elder wouldn't let him have Chris, then the Elder wouldn't have Derek either. Derek would simply refuse to sleep with him. He headed towards the door.

"Where do you think you're going?" the Elder asked, appearing between him and the door with lightning speed.

"Out."

"Not yet you aren't. I control your bedroom, remember? You can't leave without my permission. And I'm not giving it."

"Well you're not getting anything from me," Derek warned. "Not until I can see Chris."

A blank look crossed the Elder's face, then he smiled and seemed to return to the present. "Chris has just left the campus. Ask Jettie if you don't believe me."

"He wouldn't leave me here," Derek said, but he reached out to Jettie at the same time. Jettie confirmed that Chris had just left to go to the Portland campus to live there until the next mating flight. She sounded sad, but her sadness was nothing compared to Derek's. He felt as though he were wading through shifting sand and suddenly it had become quicksand. He wobbled a little and held a hand out to grab a chair and steady himself. Chris was abandoning him. Leaving him alone to deal with the Elder. Chris hadn't even tried to say goodbye. Tears welled up in his eyes. Why would Chris do such a thing?

"You see?" the Elder asked gently. "Now please, sit down."

Derek sank into the chair the Elder held out for him without protest. The Elder started rubbing his shoulders. It felt wonderful, even though it wasn't as good as when Chris did it. But Chris was gone now. At least Chris was safe, he reflected. If Chris had stayed, the Elder would surely try to seek revenge on him for trying to interfere in the mating flight. Maybe it was best that Chris go to Portland. But leaving without saying goodbye? Without even telling Jettie to tell Derek? It was just so abrupt. A few hours ago he had been with Chris and everything had been fine, and now he was with the Elder and Chris was essentially banished. How had everything changed so rapidly?

Derek looked up at the Elder.

"Why are you doing this?"

"It was Chris's choice to leave," the Elder said. "All I've done is played by the rules and won your mating flight, and I intend to be a good and loyal mate for you."

Derek sniffled. If Chris were truly gone, and it seemed that he was, then Derek had to find some way to tolerate the Elder and starting with hatred was no way to do it. And there was something they had in common, something he was dying to ask about even as he mourned Chris's absence.

"You said you knew my father," he began, hoping the Elder would let him change the subject.

The Elder nodded. "Ashton was my best student. I loved him dearly."

"Can you tell me about him?"

With a smile, the Elder sat down in a chair next to Derek. He reached out to take Derek's hand and Derek allowed the contact.

"What do you want to know?"

Derek licked his lips. What didn't he want to know? He wanted to know everything about his father, the man he never knew, the man he'd been trying his entire life to impress. If he impressed the Elder, would it be the same as impressing his father? He wasn't sure. If that were true then sleeping with the Elder would be like sleeping with his father, which he was definitely not okay with. No, the Elder was a different person and he couldn't make up lost time, but he could learn, perhaps.

"Did he love me?" Derek asked, then blushed.

The Elder probably had no way of knowing whether or not Ashton loved his son, but it was the only question he really cared about, the one question that still burned deep inside of him. He fingered the scars on his belly from where Alan had stabbed him, before Marisol had saved his life. Had Alan acted alone, as everyone claimed, or had Ashton known about it and silently given Alan permission, as Alan claimed? Only Alan knew for sure, but he had vanished after Ashton's death and was hiding out with the other survivors who refused to acknowledge Jamie as their Queen.

Jamie knew about the survivors and said they were stationed near Spokane, probably because Derek was there and Jamie wasn't, but Jamie wasn't able to track Alan's dragon due to the dragon's gift. They were harmless for the moment, everyone knew, but they could be dangerous if given a leader and that was one reason the Elder was so dangerous. And it was Derek's job to contain the leader even though he didn't know how.

He snapped back to reality and saw the Elder considering him very carefully.

"I have no doubt that he loved you, in his own way," the Elder said. "But I also have no doubt that he showed his love in ways other than the usual ones. He was not the type of man to be a good husband or father, but he would take pride in your accomplishments and love you for those."

Derek's heart swelled. It was a good answer. The Elder was acknowledging Ashton's limitations and not trying to insist that his father had done all of the fatherly things he hadn't, but he was still sure that Ashton had loved him despite his absence. The Elder, as Ashton's teacher, probably knew Ashton well and if he said that Ashton loved him despite the usual displays of emotion that most fathers would show their sons, then there had to be an element of truth to it. Unexpected tears filled his eyes and the Elder stood and approached him, once again wiping the tears from his eyes.

"You are a beautiful, intelligent, willful boy who bonded with a Queen," he said, tilting Derek's head to look up at him. "That is everything Ashton could have dreamed of."

"My- my bond wasn't good enough," Derek stuttered. "Ashton wanted me to bond the way Jamie and Marisol are bonded."

The Elder's brows creased for a moment and the vacant look crossed his face again. It must be his expression when he communicated with his dragon, Derek realized. In an instant the Elder was studying him again.

"Your bond is a true reflection of you, and doesn't need to be changed. I imagine Ashton would have realized that in time. You are a true Queen, no matter what anyone says."

Derek nodded, pleased that the Elder at least was satisfied with the level of his bond with Jettie. At least he wouldn't have to worry about that. He had hated feeling inadequate and he still felt that way when compared to Jamie sometimes. Even though Jamie had shown a more human and compassionate side towards him, he still felt jealous of the other man. More jealous now, because Jamie got Scott and Chris while Derek was left with the Elder.

"Thank you," Derek whispered.

The Elder stroked his cheeks and leaned forward for a kiss. Derek didn't protest. His emotions were in a jumble and everything was confusing and he just wanted to feel something he understood. A kiss was something he understood. He would have preferred a kiss with someone besides the Elder, but the Elder was being kind, had been kind other than the situation with Chris, and Derek badly wanted to be on good terms with his mate. He couldn't imagine surviving if it were constant arguing and essentially war between him and the Elder. He would watch the Elder, and prevent the Elder from doing anything against

Tarragon law, but that didn't mean they had to be enemies, did it? No, he decided. They could make this work. Maybe it was better that Chris wasn't here to stir up Derek's aching heart. Instead, he could just deaden the pain and embrace the Elder.

The kiss was slow – a brief touch of the lips, then another, this time with the lips a little further apart, then another, more open still. Soon the Elder gently entered his mouth and Derek let him. A shiver ran through his body but he couldn't tell if it was arousal or fear, or some odd combination. The Elder pulled back from the kiss and stroked his cheek again.

"I won't hurt you," the Elder said. "You know that, don't you?"

"I know," Derek said in a shaky voice.

Tarragon law prevented the mate from leaving a mark on his queen's body. If the Elder so much as bruised him, the Elder could, if Derek complained or anyone noticed, be removed as the mate. No, the Elder would be careful not to injure Derek at all. But there were other kinds of hurt, Derek knew, and robbing him of Chris was one of them. He wasn't thinking of that now, though, Derek reminded himself. He was deadening the pain and accepting the present. It was fine, he would survive. He would thrive. He would show Jamie that he was fully capable of handling the Elder.

Derek stood up and took the Elder's hand, then hesitantly placed the Elder's hand over his heart. The Elder smiled and wrapped his other hand around Derek's waist, pulling him close. He kissed Derek again, passionately this time, and Derek responded as best he could. It wasn't Chris, but the Elder knew what he was doing and in just a few moments Derek let out a low moan as his body began kicking into gear.

He hadn't expected this. He had expected it to be a challenge to be aroused by the Elder, but it wasn't. The Elder was extremely attractive, for starters, and very skilled. Derek felt like a fly caught in a venus fly trap, except this trap was sweet and wouldn't hurt him. At least he didn't think it would.

A knock at the door interrupted their kiss and the Elder looked angry as he reluctantly let go of Derek and answered the door.

"I asked for some privacy," he snapped as the door opened.

Mike was on the other side.

"I'm so sorry, but Derek has classes to attend. You know that you can't keep him from his classes, even on the same day as his mating flight."

"In my day dragons were given their mating day off," the Elder said, narrowing his eyes.

Mike looked surprised. "Well, I'm sorry, but that law changed long ago. As long as the partner and dragon are able to attend, they are required to. I do apologize."

"He'll be out in a minute," the Elder said, then shut the door with a little more force than necessary.

Derek went to his backpack, which was already packed as he had already finished his homework the night before. He had planned on spending the morning with Chris before his afternoon classes but the mating flight had gotten in the way. It would be strange going back to class now that his world had changed.

"How long are your classes?" the Elder asked.

"I have two, and they get out at five."

"Come straight here afterwards. I'll prepare something for us to eat," the Elder added as if to soften the command.

"Thanks," Derek said. "I guess I'll see you then."

He slung his backpack over one shoulder and walked out the door, looking back once to see the Elder where Chris should have been.

CHAPTER TWENTY-EIGHT

Arranging the Details

After Jamie left for his classes, Scott leaned back on the sofa and let out a sigh. Everything was in pieces, including his heart. He felt as though he couldn't trust Jamie, but he knew that he just needed time for his heart to recover. He had been away for too long, punished for too long, and now that he was back everything would go back to normal. Jamie had been through a great ordeal as well and they both needed time for their relationship to snap back.

Scott felt betrayed and angry and horribly sad at the same time, and he covered his face and fought the urge to cry. Now that Jamie was at classes and Derek's mating flight had ended so terribly, Scott needed to call the council to a meeting and sort out their plan. It was his responsibility as the Queen's mate, even though he had just returned. He couldn't put it off even though his heart was breaking.

He was just gathering his courage to face the council when there was a knock at the door. He frowned. It was too soon for Chris to arrive and everyone else knew that Jamie would be at class. So someone wanted to see him, but the council would wait for his move. Who was it?

He opened the door and stared at the handsome black man on the other side. The man had a beautifully sculpted face and body, and carried himself with grace and confidence. It was almost shocking to see his chocolate skin, since there was so little diversity on campus, and Scott immediately remembered Jamie telling him that his crush was a student from Africa. But surely this man wasn't a student, not even old enough for university. He seemed mature, not like a high schooler at all. But it had to be him. TK.

"You must be TK," Scott said as way of warning the man that he knew about his and Jamie's relationship.

"And you must be Scott," the man said as if warning him in return.

Scott fought a scowl. So TK wouldn't back down easily. Well, two could play that game. He would see what kind of grip TK really had on Jamie because he knew that in the end, Jamie would choose Scott over everyone else.

TK extended his hand. "I've heard a lot about you."

Scott did scowl now, though he took TK's hand. He didn't respond, though, because there was nothing he could say. He couldn't say that he'd heard a lot about TK because it would be a lie, but he also couldn't say that he hadn't heard of the man because it would reveal the weakness in his and Jamie's relationship right now. At least TK was being courteous, he thought. That boded well. Maybe TK would respect their relationship and back off.

"I'm glad you're safe," TK continued. "I know Jamie's been worried about you."

Scott's hands clenched into fists at the subtle reminder that TK had been with Jamie while Scott was away, that TK had been the one to comfort Scott's lover. How was he supposed to respond to any of this? What was he supposed to say? He was drawing a complete blank.

"How are you doing?" TK asked with what had to be false sincerity.

"As well as can be expected," Scott snapped. "I'm surprised you know anything about this, since you don't have a dragon."

It was the only weakness in the man he could find, and he

wanted to hurt TK so badly.

"Oh, Jamie only told me the basics," TK said carelessly. "I know he can't discuss Tarragon matters until I bond with a dragon."

"If you bond with a dragon," Scott said.

TK smiled. "If," he repeated. "You're right. Nothing is certain. Everything can change, can't it?"

Scott realized TK was talking about his relationship with Jamie and the scowl settled on his features again.

"I don't think you should be spending as much time with Jamie," Scott said, skipping all of the negotiations and getting straight to the meat of the matter.

"You can't do anything to stop me," TK warned, the smile dropping from his face.

"Actually, I can. As the Queen's mate I control who Jamie spends his time with, and I've decided you are not one of the people he should be seeing."

"What will Jamie think of this decision? Do you think he'll appreciate you dictating his life like this?"

"He'll accept it."

At least Scott hoped he would. Jamie had been okay with sending TK to Spokane, so hopefully he wouldn't mind too much if his contact with TK were cut off immediately. But he worried that Jamie would view this as an attack on his freedom and resent Scott as a result, sending yet another crack in their relationship. In fact, now that he thought about it he was almost positive Jamie wouldn't react well to this, but he'd already said it and he couldn't back out now. He set his jaw and stared at TK threateningly.

"Unless you can prove your worth and your innocent intentions to me, you are no longer allowed to see Jamie," he said, lessening the harshness of his command and giving TK a chance to redeem himself. Hopefully that would help with Jamie; if TK made the effort, he could see Jamie but if he didn't, then it would be TK's fault and not Scott's. That was better.

"So be it," TK said with a shrug. "But I don't think this will go well for you. I'll be seeing you, Scott, and I will prove my worth."

He left the room and shut the door and Scott sank into the nearest chair. That had not gone well, but it could have gone worse. He wasn't quite sure how, but it could have. They could have physically fought, after all – that would have been catastrophic. Instead, they had talked and reached an agreement, which was a reasonably good outcome for a meeting between Jamie's lover and Jamie's new crush. Of course, now Scott had to ready himself for the council meeting and he already felt drained. This meeting would not go well, but he had to do it.

Scott took a breath and left, then headed to the council room. He sent a message to Narné to invite the council member's dragons on both the male and female campuses and prepared to wait for everyone to arrive. Chris would arrive around nightfall and when he did, Scott wanted the campus to have a plan for helping Derek and winning the next mating flight.

It took nearly an hour before the council members began arriving. They had talked to each other via the dragons and arranged the time, so Scott had known to expect the delay, but he still waited in the council room because he didn't want to run into TK and this was the one place TK would never be allowed. Margot arrived first, then Gerald, head of the men on the council until Scott learned his duties. The others arrived soon after while Margot and Gerald approached Scott and shook his hand.

"It's good to have you back," Margot said. "We've been worried about you."

"The campus can go back to normal now, I hope," Gerald said in a questioning voice.

Scott knew he was talking about Jamie, not Derek, since he knew that everyone knew the Elder had won the mating flight. Gerald was wondering if he and Jamie were back to normal. Did he know about TK, Scott wondered. Did everyone know?

"I hope so too," Scott said, shaking his hand firmly.

The other members had arrived and soon everyone waited for the three leaders to speak from their position on the dais. Scott took a deep breath as neither Margot nor Gerald looked about to speak. This was his meeting and he had to lead it.

"As you know, Derek's mating flight was won by the Elder," he began. "We need to build a plan to protect Derek and the two campuses until the position of the Queen's mate can be reclaimed."

"What is to be done with Chris?" someone demanded. "I heard he attacked during the mating flight."

"He's been removed from the council and is travelling here until the next mating flight," Scott said.

"But he attacked," the person repeated. "What's to stop other people from attacking if he's barely punished?"

Scott stared at the man objecting. "He's been banned from the council, and essentially banned from the Spokane campus. That's enough of a punishment for him. You know we haven't killed anyone for that offense in almost a hundred years. We're not going to start with him."

The man grumbled but was silent.

"What are we doing about the Elder?" a woman asked.

"That's the question," Scott said. "I need your input on how to handle this situation."

Margot stepped forward. "This is a dangerous time for our campus, and the strength of our campuses relies on the councils. Any suggestions are welcome."

There was silence, and then low talking. After several minutes people starting giving the more obvious suggestions, such as killing the Elder or banning him from the campus, but soon they were getting better suggestions about how to educate Derek to handle the Elder properly. Scott made sure Narné listened and took notes, since dragons remembered everything they heard when they wanted to, and soon they had a plan of attack that Scott could take to the other council in Spokane to help guide Derek. He knew Derek, like Jamie, would be at class a lot of the day and that would make it easier to teach him what he needed to know, and there was nothing the Elder could do about that. Queens still in school were required to attend classes and the Elder could be removed as the mate if he tried to stop Derek.

Scott almost hoped he'd try, as that would make everything easier. But he knew that if they had to remove the Elder from power, the Elder would retaliate – brutally. No, he was accepting their leash and following their laws, and until they were strong enough to destroy him, they needed to keep him as Derek's mate, no matter how much it hurt. As much as he hated it, it was probably better for Tarragon society that the Elder had won the flight or else the Elder would have slaughtered the rest of the mating flight, probably even Jettie as well. Scott shivered. The thought of killing a Queen was shocking, but he wouldn't put it past the Elder.

The meeting ended quickly and everyone but Margot filed out. She lingered and when everyone else was gone, she turned to Scott.

"I know you're having problems with Jamie," she said. "You need to resolve them quickly, for the sake of Tarragon society. Jamie was... distracted while you were gone, but now that you're back you need to recapture his interest."

"You mean TK," Scott said, flushing with embarrassment that she knew about it.

"Yes," she said. "Even the dragons disapprove. They nly approve of people with dragons for their Queen, and Jamie risks alienating them if he insists on flirting with this child."

"He's hardly a child," Scott said dryly, thinking of the mature TK.

"He doesn't have a dragon," Margot said with a shrug. "In Tarragon terms, he is a child and Jamie shouldn't be seeing him.

I expect you to take care of this, quickly. We can't afford any friction between you and Jamie, or between Jamie and the dragons. They've tolerated it so far because you have been gone, but now that you're back any continued contact will frustrate and confuse the dragons. This is a bigger issue than your pride or your heart," she added. "This could have consequences for all of us. Even if he joins the academy, he won't bond with a dragon until next fall. That's too long. So you need to end it, now."

Scott nodded. "I am. I will. I already spoke with TK and I made it clear he can't see Jamie again."

"He'll disobey," Margot warned. "He doesn't respect Tarragon law because he doesn't have a dragon. Be prepared for that."

Scott nodded. "I will. Thank you, Margot."

She smiled and left the council room, leaving him alone with his worries. How was he supposed to get rid of TK without hurting Jamie? Well, if it was alienating Jamie from the dragons then he would find a way. He'd had no idea TK was causing a rift between Jamie and the dragons as well as Jamie and Scott. That was far more dangerous and something that needed to be prevented.

It was his job as the Queen's mate to protect his Queen from such things, and it just happened to also be something that would help him personally. But even if it meant that Jamie hated him forever, he would get rid of TK to protect Jamie's relationship with the dragons. He would rather have Jamie on good terms with the dragons than on good terms with Scott, because that was his duty as Queen's mate. It would hurt, perhaps, but eventually Jamie would forgive him.

Scott sighed and left the room. If he ran into TK again, so be it. Maybe it would be a good thing, because he and TK needed to have another, more serious chat and hopefully TK cared enough about Jamie to understand that his relationship was hurting Jamie. Scott could only hope.

CHAPTER TWENTY-NINE

Romantic Dinner

Derek trudged out of his last class, his heart heavy. He had to return to the Elder now. There was no way around it. He was especially nervous now that his teachers had spent the past three hours telling him about how to handle the Elder, how to not let the Elder take control, how to remain a strong Queen despite a man who had the makings to be a stronger mate. His head was spinning and he wished they would just leave him alone and let him work it out on his own. He was capable, after all, and besides, all their advice was just puddling into a pool of fear in his belly.

He hadn't been afraid of the Elder before, but now he was. He had been so sure that the Elder couldn't hurt him, but his teachers had filled his head with all the ways the Elder could legally hurt him, ways that wouldn't leave a mark physically but certainly would psychologically. He was afraid now and he shouldn't be. No one should be afraid of their mate, no matter who that mate was. But above all they had stressed that if the Elder was kind to him, to be especially on guard because it meant the Elder was planning something. So now he couldn't even relax if the Elder didn't hurt him, because being kind was another way of hurting him.

He shifted his bag on his shoulders. Chris wouldn't even be in Portland yet, he thought as he gazed at the sun sinking on the horizon. It was still cold and the sun still set fairly early here, but the days were getting longer now and spring was in the air. It was only a matter of time before summer hit and classes ended. What was Derek supposed to do then? He would be with the Elder full time. He had been looking forward to spending the time with Chris and enjoying his first summer of college lounging about with his new lover. Instead, he would be spending it with a man who was as cold-blooded as people used to think the dragons were.

Or at least that's what everyone was telling him. The Elder hadn't seemed that bad to him. Which was the danger, according to some of them. He appeared kind but was scheming the whole time. He was a serpent in sheep's clothing, far worse than a wolf.

Derek sighed. He was nearly back at his rooms. The Elder had all but ordered him back here after class and he had no reason to disobey, and the teachers had told him to obey any simple requests to prevent the Elder from breaking his agreement with them. It was a horribly scrambled mess. Obey him, but disobey him. Humor him, but resist him. Derek didn't know what to do anymore; he just wanted to be himself and figure it out himself. So he would ignore their advice, he decided, and form this relationship based on his own experiences. He wouldn't let the teachers instill fear in him, and he wouldn't let the Elder lull him into complacency. He would be himself, and that would be that.

He reached the door and opened it. A heavenly aroma greeted him as he stepped into the chambers and he dropped his bag onto the floor as usual and wandered towards the kitchen, where the smell emanated from. He and Chris rarely cooked but he knew the smell of home cooking and this was exquisite. He was expecting to find a maid or servant or someone, anyone, doing the cooking, but the Elder himself was at the stove stirring a pot. He looked up at Derek and smiled gently.

"You said you'd be getting home around now," he explained, gesturing to the meal. "I thought I'd have something ready for you."

"I- this is great," Derek said, feeling a little speechless. There were noodles in a large casserole dish and as he watched, the Elder finished stirring his pot and poured a beautiful marinara sauce filled with fresh peppers and chopped up sausage over the noodles.

"Do you like spaghetti? This was an exotic food back when I was here, but now I hear Italian food is quite common," he said, sprinkling a little parsley on the top as a garnish.

"I love spaghetti. My mom used to make this, though I'm sure it's not as good as this," he said.

"Please, sit down," the Elder said, gesturing towards the table. "I'll get you a plate. Do you want bread and salad?"

Derek nodded mutely. This was so completely unexpected, and ran contrary to everything his teachers had just been telling him. The Elder wasn't a monster at all. He wasn't trying to hurt Derek. But he might still be trying to manipulate Derek, so he needed to be wary even as he enjoyed this scrumptious feast. Derek sat at the table and the Elder placed a plate in front of him heaped with noodles and sauce, with a generous slice of garlic bread and salad. He sat down across from Derek with a similarly full plate and gestured for Derek to start eating before digging in himself. Derek didn't wait. The food smelled delicious, and as he took his first steaming bite, it tasted delicious too.

The spices were perfectly blended, and he realized he had never really appreciated spaghetti before. His mother just bought a jar of sauce, but Derek was willing to bet this was entirely homemade, or else a very local brand. He couldn't believe how good it was and before long his plate was empty and he went to get seconds while a bemused Elder looked on. The Elder ate at a more leisurely pace, but still ate everything on his plate. But Derek scarfed his food and had two plates for the Elder's one, and was heading for a third when the Elder finished. The Elder stopped him from his third dish with a simple question.

"Are you going to have room for dessert?"

Derek set his plate down and looked back at the Elder.

"What's for dessert?"

"Italian cream cake," the Elder said in a mildly smug voice, as if he knew how much Derek adored that dessert.

"That's my favorite," Derek said.

"I know," the Elder said with a smile. "I asked Jettie."

Derek smiled, a purely happy smile that his mate would think to ask his dragon about his favorite dessert and then go through the trouble to make it for him. No, he didn't need a third helping of spaghetti, not with his favorite dessert on the way. There was just one question.

"Why are you being so nice?"

"Shouldn't I be? You're my mate, and I haven't gotten a chance to properly woo you," he said. "Normally I would have time before the mating flight to do these things for you, but circumstances prevented it. I want to make up for lost time and get to know you now, and show you how our relationship can be."

"I would like our relationship to be like this," Derek said honestly.

"And it can be," the Elder said, standing and approaching him. "There don't have to be hard feelings between us. I know the circumstances of our mating flight weren't the best, but we can move forward together and recover from this. I would like to move forward from this, with you at my side. Is that what you want, too?"

Derek shied away. His words sounded so good but all of his teachers' warnings were screaming in his head. There was something wrong here, some motive he wasn't seeing. And he couldn't forget Chris.

"You made Chris leave," Derek said in a shaky voice. "I want to move on, but I can't, not yet. Just give me time."

The Elder nodded. "Time is something I can give you. Until then, can we be on friendly terms?"

"Of course," Derek said. "I don't want to be enemies."

The Elder stroked his shoulder. "Neither do I. Let's get you your dessert."

The Elder went into the kitchen and reappeared with two plates of the yummy dessert, setting down Derek's with a flourish. Derek dove into it. It was perfect.

"Did you make this yourself?"

"I got some help from one of the council members," he replied. "She's an expert baker."

Derek nodded. A baker. That meant that the Elder had likely cooked the spaghetti by himself. He was quite an accomplished chef, though of course he had lived for centuries so it wasn't too surprising that he had learned to feed himself well. Derek would learn to cook too if he had to live that long. He wondered what the appeal of such a long life was. It seemed so hard to imagine, but then again, he was so young. Perhaps as one got older life seemed more valuable.

"It's wonderful," Derek said, returning his attention to the cake.

When he was finished with his second helping of the cake, he helped the Elder do the dishes and felt a sense of peace as they worked together to clean the remnants of their meal. When they were finished, the Elder turned to him and pinned him to the counter, his body pressing against Derek's in a way that took Derek's breath away. It wasn't constricting or controlling, but rather inviting and welcoming.

"How was your day, Derek?" the Elder asked. "Did your classes go well?"

Derek was distracted by the feel of the Elder's body against his and nearly missed the questions, and was surprised when they finally made sense to him. The Elder was being such a good mate. Would he always be like this?

"They were good," Derek said. "A little boring. The teachers think they know so much, you know?"

The Elder smiled. "They always do."

Derek placed one hand on the Elder's chest, startled by his own boldness.

"Would you ever hurt me?"

"No," the Elder said simply, then placed his own hand over Derek's. He brought Derek's hand to his lips and kissed it. "I would never hurt you."

Derek's heart was pounding unevenly and all he could remember was the Elder's words that it wouldn't have to hurt as much, that sex wouldn't be as painful as their first time. He wanted to feel what it would be like but it felt like it would be a betrayal of Chris. But then again, Chris had left him without saying goodbye, and besides, the Elder was his mate now and he had to get used to that. What was the harm in sleeping with his mate if that's what he was expected to do?

Derek leaned forward on his tiptoes and pressed his lips against the Elder's, who gently kissed him back. The Elder squeezed his hand and wrapped his other arm around Derek's waist, pulling him tighter and deepening the kiss. Derek melted into his skilled arms as the man's tongue began stroking his and a fire began building deep inside him.

"Let's go somewhere more comfortable," the Elder suggested, already pulling him in the direction of the bedroom.

Derek nodded dizzily, his defenses rapidly shrinking as his lust began to boil through his veins. He was on fire and they had only kissed, only embraced. The dragons had something to do with it, he knew. His teachers had warned him that for the next few days he would be vulnerable to the Elder's amorous approaches because Jettie's body was still in heat and still attuned to the Elder's dragon. But he didn't care about that. He just cared about the masculine body in his arms that promised to make him forget about everything for a few precious moments.

The Elder let go of him for a moment and Derek was disappointed, but then the Elder swooped his arm down and scooped Derek up into his arms. Derek clung to his neck and felt delicate and light in his arms, and incredibly sexy as the Elder carried him into the bedroom and then tumbled him onto the bed. The Elder grinned down at him.

"This time, it won't hurt at all," the Elder promised. "This time, only pleasure. Are you ready?"

CHAPTER THIRTY

Arrival

C hris landed in Portland and was immediately greeted by Scott, who seemed preoccupied and worried. Chris had expected no less. The mating flight no doubt had thrown everyone into disarray and he knew the blame lay squarely on his shoulders. After all, he had been the one to lose the mating flight. His anger and lack of control had cost them all dearly and it was only because of Mike's quick actions and Derek's refusal to kill him that he was even alive right now.

He deeply regretted not saying goodbye to Derek, but everyone had told him that it would be a mistake, even Jettie. Jettie had assured him that she would convey his message of love at an appropriate time, but he wasn't sure she understood what would be appropriate for humans. She was a dragon, after all, and a young one at that, plus she was still flush from her first mating flight. But there was nothing else he could do – everyone was rushing him off campus and no one was willing to let him stay until Derek left for his classes. He needed to be gone before Derek left the Elder's side or else the Elder wouldn't let Derek leave, they told him, and he had to admit that it was probably true. The Elder wouldn't risk Derek seeing Chris again. Too much potential for damage to their budding relationship.

Chris glared at the ground as he followed Scott to his new rooms. A relationship between the Elder and Derek disgusted him but he knew it would happen. Derek needed that relationship to survive. If they didn't get along it would be hell on Derek and above all else Chris wanted Derek to be comfortable, if not happy. Eventually, Derek and the Elder would need to get along. He just hoped it wouldn't be too soon. He hoped Derek put up a good fight first. He hoped the Elder learned to respect Derek.

Scott led him to a suite of rooms near the Queen's chambers and Chris dumped his small bag. Most of his belongings were still in Spokane, in Derek's rooms, after all. He had very little with him and he wondered when Derek would realize that Chris's things still haunted his quarters. Or more importantly, when the Elder realized it. But for now there was nothing Chris could do except move on and hope the Elder didn't destroy all of his things back in Spokane. His dragon was already settled in and he needed to settle in as well. He tossed his one bag on the ground and turned to Scott, who still looked preoccupied. Scott had just recently returned here as well, Chris realized. What had he returned to?

"Is everything all right?" Chris asked.

Scott seemed surprised. "I should be asking you that."

"But you're not, and that means something big must be up."

Scott sighed. "I'm surprised your dragon hasn't told you. It seems everyone else here knows."

"I've been in Spokane, not here. What's wrong?"

"Jamie's taken another lover."

Chris gasped. It was forbidden for a Queen to take a lover without her mate's permission and surely Jamie knew it. Scott waved his hand.

"No, not a lover," he quickly explained. "A- a crush. Just a flirtation. But still."

"I'm sorry," Chris said.

He tried to imagine what it must feel like to return to his lover after being imprisoned by an enemy for weeks only to find that his lover had replaced him. It couldn't feel good. No wonder Scott was preoccupied. And with Derek's mating flight on top of everything else, this was probably a disastrous time for Scott, though probably not as disastrous as it was for Chris. But it wasn't the time or place for a pity party. They needed to be coming up with solutions, not moaning about their problems.

"Well, you'll win him back," Chris said firmly. "Just like I'll win the next mating flight. I let my anger lose this flight but it won't happen again."

Scott nodded, slowly at first then faster as if coming out of a deep depression.

"You're right," he said. "This is just the beginning. I won't let anger get the better of me. I have the whole campus on my side."

"Just like I did," Chris whispered and hid his bitterness.

It was true; the entire campus had been on his side and he had blown it all in a fit of rage that left him bereft of the one thing that mattered. He would make sure it didn't happen to Scott as well. He gazed at Scott and remembered how superior he had felt to the man during their threesome, yet how connected he had felt to him. They shared something special, something that he felt with no one except Derek. He wondered if Scott felt it too. From the blush growing across Scott's cheeks at Chris's regard, he suspected that Scott knew exactly what he was thinking of. Scott cleared his throat.

"Well, I hope you feel comfortable here, Chris. If you need anything, please feel free to ask me, or Jamie, or anyone really. But try to stay away from the council members. Not all of them took kindly to what you did during the mating flight and some think that you got off easy with exile."

Chris nodded somberly. "Thank you for the warning."

Scott undoubtedly didn't realize how serious a warning that was, but Chris did. If those council members were followers of Ashton, then they could easily request more from him in exchange for their cooperation just as Carys had in Spokane. While it wouldn't be the end of the world, Chris knew that sex of any kind would be painful because it would remind him that he wasn't with Derek, and Derek was with the Elder. He would stay away from the council members like the plague, or at least the many of them who were Ashton's favorites.

Scott made his goodbyes, then vanished into the hallway while Chris closed the door and began unpacking his few clothes and other items. His rooms looked scarce and empty and he shivered as he thought of Derek, who must be with the Elder after his classes right now. What were they doing? Were they fighting? He half hoped they were, but at the same time he didn't want to wish for any more stress in Derek's life. But the other option was too horrible to imagine. Instead, he imagined that the Elder kindly allowed Derek to be alone for the night, though he suspected it wouldn't be true.

There was a knock at the door and Chris opened it to see a beautiful black man, perhaps a freshman, maybe a sophomore. He introduced himself as TK and Chris invited him in, not knowing what else to do.

"How can I help you, TK?" he asked, a little unnerved by the student's casualness in the face of one of his elders but trying hard not to show it. After all, Chris wasn't in his council robes anymore and didn't inspire the fear he was accustomed to.

"We're in a very similar situation and I thought we could help each other out," he said. "You see, the man I love more than anything has been forbidden from me unless I prove myself. I understand that you are also forbidden from the man you love until you win the next mating flight. I think we can help each other."

Chris's mind whirled. "You're the one Jamie likes," he said slowly, the pieces falling together. "But what do you mean, until you prove yourself?"

"Scott said I could see Jamie again when I proved myself."

Chris inwardly groaned. No doubt Scott had been flustered and unsure of how to handle the situation, and had unknowingly made a condition that TK was determined to exploit. Well, what TK didn't know was that their situations couldn't be more different, because what TK didn't know was that Chris and Scott had shared Derek and shared an intimacy that wouldn't be broken by a mere student.

"I'm sorry," he said. "But I don't think I can help you."

TK looked taken aback. "But I can't see him, I can't see the man I love! Doesn't that mean anything to you? Don't you have feelings?"

Chris flushed. "Of course I do. But I'm not going to help you in this. I stand with Scott in this matter and nothing will sway me. Now go back to your studies and try to forget about Jamie."

"Can you forget about Derek?"

"You're still a child, with a child's crushes. This isn't the kind of love that will last."

"How do you know? How does your love mean more than mine just because you're older? You don't know the depth of my feelings. I would do anything for Jamie."

"If you truly love Jamie, then let him be with Scott. That's what's best for our society."

"I don't care about Tarragon society. I care about Jamie."

Chris stared at him in shock. He had never heard anyone say they didn't care about Tarragon society. It was the primary drive for everyone with a dragon. He reached out to his dragon to find out more about this boy's dragon and was stunned when Yaris told him that TK didn't have a dragon. The boy wasn't even a student and was daring to court the Queen. No wonder Scott objected so strongly. This boy shouldn't even be on campus, let alone be talking to the Queen.

"You don't have a dragon," Chris said slowly.

"No, but I will."

"If you continue to see Jamie, the dragons will turn against Jamie," Chris said, checking with Yaris to ensure that what he said was true.

"Why would they do that?"

"Jamie is the Queen, and can only partner with people with dragons. Anything less is an insult to them. If you continue to see Jamie before you have a dragon, it will severely harm Jamie's standing as the Queen. And right now, with the Elder in Spokane, Jamie needs that support more than ever. If you love Jamie as you say, you should stay away from him until you have a dragon. If you still love him then, then by all means go in his mating flight but courting him without a dragon is hurting him more than you can possibly imagine."

TK's eyes grew wide. "You're not kidding, are you?"

"No," Chris said. "This is the truth. If you have a dragon, then perhaps Scott will make room for you but since you don't, there's no way he'll ever let you prove yourself."

"Then I'll have to get a dragon," TK mused. He nodded to himself. "Yes, that's the only step to take. Thank you, Chris."

"You can't get a dragon until next winter," Chris warned.

TK smiled. "I know. The first year exam. I'll be ready."

Chris nodded, wondering what was going in TK's head as the boy seemed deep in thought, and probably not the kind of thoughts anyone in Tarragon society would approve of. He wondered what he had set in motion and hoped it wasn't anything too bad. TK wished him well and left, and Chris once more turned to his empty rooms. He went to the bedroom and collapsed on the bed. His mind was racing with thoughts of Derek and the Elder and Scott and TK. Everything was chaos. Nothing made sense. He felt like everything was falling apart and he didn't know what was going on anymore. He had no control of anything; everything was slipping through his fingers. Derek was gone. The Elder had won. Scott was upset. TK was plotting something. And it was all his fault. He shut his eyes and let emotion overtake him as he wept.

CHAPTER THIRTY-ONE

Within the Dragon

J amie sighed and listened to the teacher rambling about the responsibilities of the Queen dragon and wondered if Derek was getting the same speech. Almost all of his classes were individual now; only one class was taught with other students. The council had explained it was because he was still new to his position and needed to learn so much in such a short period of time, they couldn't afford other students distracting him. But he didn't think he would be distracted any more than he already was.

"Jamie, are you paying attention?" the teacher snapped. "What did I just say?"

"The Queen dragon is responsible for the welfare of all the dragons who live in her territory and is sworn to defend them," Jamie repeated dully.

He hadn't known that before today, but it made sense and it explained why Margot had insisted on Jamie being the one to kill Ashton, an act that still haunted his dreams and had him waking in a cold sweat at least once a week. It was the Queen's duty to protect the dragons from danger, and Jamie was responsible for killing the threat. But she could have explained that to him, at least, and maybe someone else could have taken that burden from him given how young he was. He shivered just thinking about it. He knew he would regret it the rest of his life. Not the fact that Ashton was dead – as much as he valued life, he knew the world was a better place without Ashton – but being the one to kill Ashton.

He felt a stirring of emotion in the back of his mind, the area he associated with Marisol. She needed his attention. He turned his focus inward. Something was troubling her and she needed his help and his complete attention. But for his complete attention, he would have to essentially leave his body behind and the teacher would surely notice that. He eyed the stern man in front of him lecturing about yet another section of Tarragon law. Would he be willing to let Jamie speak to his Queen?

He would have to, Jamie thought as the urgency from Marisol grew stronger. Marisol really needed him.

"Excuse me," Jamie interrupted, leaving the teacher slack-jawed and wide-eyed in dismay at being cut off midsentence. "My dragon needs me. Can you leave me alone for a few minutes?"

The teacher smirked. "You think I'm going to fall for that?"

The urgency grew and Jamie clutched his head. He was going to be drawn in against his will and he didn't want that to happen while this man was in the room.

"Out. Now," he commanded, pointing to the door.

The teacher frowned and must have decided he was serious because he left, lingering in the doorway.

"If you need guidance-"

"I don't," Jamie snapped, then pushed the door shut and locked it.

He wanted to be alone for this, while his body was vulnerable. He sat at the desk again and laid his head on his arms, then shut his eyes and let himself be swept up into Marisol's mind.

Something was wrong with one of the eggs. It wasn't right. It hadn't been right since she had laid it, but now the wrongness was overwhelming. She had to get it away from the other eggs before it spread to them. She sniffed it again, hoping the wrongness would be gone, but it wasn't. It was overpowering. It wasn't a physical scent but a psychic one and she knew she would have to isolate the egg and devour it. Eating the egg would give her valuable nutrients and prevent the egg from harming the other eggs. Yes, she decided. That is what she would do.

She nuzzled the egg and it shifted and began to roll very slowly in a wobbly manner. It bumped against one of the good eggs and she flinched, expecting one of the eggs to burst open. Probably the rotten egg, but what if the good egg burst as well? She would have to be more careful. She gently straddled the eggs and maneuvered her snout between the good eggs to cautiously roll the bad egg between them until it was a fair distance from the others. Once it was isolated, she examined it.

It looked like a normal egg, though it was slightly hot to the touch. More like an egg about to hatch than the rest of the eggs which wouldn't hatch for months. Physically it was almost perfect, but that psychic scent was so alien to her, so unlike the other eggs yet oddly familiar at the same time. She had smelled it before but she couldn't place it. But it was so different than all the other eggs.

She didn't want to have to eat it but she knew she couldn't leave it here to rot. Something was wrong with it and as the mother, she had to deal with that. She shouldn't feel the flush of shame that one of her eggs was imperfect. Some people thought that eggs imprinted on students as soon as the eggs were laid, even if those students weren't on campus yet, so perhaps one of the students who would normally have imprinted on a dragon had a fatal illness or had died, and now the egg was dying too. Or perhaps she had just laid an inferior egg. There was no way to tell. But she didn't like thinking of herself as capable of creating something that felt and smelled so different from other eggs.

She opened her mouth and was about to devour the egg when her senses went on high alert and she froze, lifting her head and completely forgetting about the egg. Someone was nearby. Someone had gotten onto her island. Someone was not supposed to be here.

Her eggs were in danger. Every other thought vanished from her mind and she leapt into the sky and soared back to her eggs, landing in the center of the nest and extending her tail and wings to cover them all. In that position, all of the eggs were in the shadow of her matronly body and she could easily kill anyone who dared approach. She let out a roar of possession to alert anyone nearby that these eggs were hers and she would not hesitate in her defense of them.

Whoever was nearby did not have a dragon, or else she would have been able to sense them and warn their dragon that they were too close and needed to back off. Was it a stranger? Or a student? Were there any students who didn't have dragons? She instantly thought of the student that Jamie had been seeing, much to her and the other dragon's chagrin. It was an insult to all the dragons that he had been flirting with someone without a dragon and he had ignored her attempts to explain why he should stop. But could this be that student? Would he dare come to the hatching grounds when the eggs weren't ready to be hatched?

If he touched an egg too early, that egg would shatter and the dragon inside would be born, yes, but it would still be an embryo at this stage, incapable of surviving in the outside world. The first year exam could only take place when the eggs were fully ready to be hatched. Of course, if the boy had found his way onto one of the older hatching grounds, he could have hatched one of those dragons but they surely would have killed him, since he lacked the preparation students were given during their first semester. But if this was that student, then he hadn't found his way to an older hatching ground, he had found his way here, and her eggs were in danger.

She snarled and listened for him. He was to the east, in almost the exact spot she had rolled the rotten egg to. In exactly the same spot, she realized as the boy's scent finally reach her delicate nose. The boy and the rotten egg had to be next to each other. Would he try to hatch the egg that was so different than all the others? Would that work? She thought back to how the egg was so different, yet so familiar, and a chill went down her spine.

It was familiar because it was the scent of an egg ready to hatch. The egg had always felt wrong because it had matured faster ever since she had laid it. She had thought it was defective and maybe it was, but what if that was the dragon inside's special ability, the ability to mature faster? If this egg did successfully hatch, then she had almost devoured a creature capable of living a rich, fruitful life simply because it didn't smell like all of her other children. Her stomach roiled. That was not something she wanted to think about.

There was a sound like shattering glass; the egg broke open. Marisol held her breath, waiting to hear a voice from a new dragon. Long minutes passed and she began to relax. The dragon had been born dead. She hadn't misjudged the situation; the egg had been wrong. The boy hadn't been able to bond with the dragon.

Then, out of nowhere, she heard a chirping sound. At first she thought the student was doing something, then she realized the chirping was in her mind, not her ears. It was a baby dragon, trying out talking for the first time. Her heart sank and lifted at the same time. The dragon lived, and had imprinted on the boy.

Devon, the dragon chirped. *My name is Devon.*

I am Marisol, your Queen, she replied, and sent a brief stream of information that all new dragons were sent that filled them in on Tarragon society. Dragons didn't come into the world with a lot of knowledge, but they gained almost all of their knowledge in the first day or two of life as their elders pushed knowledge into them in concentrated chunks. Luckily, dragons understood and retained information effortlessly, so in a minute or two Devon knew everything he needed to know about Tarragon society to get along with the other dragons. The actual elders would teach him the rest.

Marisol reached out to sense the boy to see if he was indeed the one Jamie had been entranced with and wasn't too surprised to find that it was. She knew he would face severe punishment for coming to the hatching grounds this early and without permission, but she hoped she could lessen the punishment by explaining that if he hadn't come, Devon would have died. She would leave out that she would have eaten him, naturally.

She wished she could fly back to campus to watch over the little dragon as the boy started walking with Devon to campus, but she had to guard her eggs. Now that one student had found his way to her island, she was feeling especially paranoid and knew she would linger here as long as possible, probably through the first year exam if Jamie let her and didn't force her to leave as he had done last exam. She huddled over her good eggs and began to brood.

Jamie felt a slight distance opening up between himself and Marisol and jumped at it, ripping himself back into his body and consciousness with great effort. He looked around. There was banging at the door and he stood up on wobbly legs and opened it. Several council members were present and all of them looked furious, and worried.

"Jamie, what just happened? Our dragons are saying that someone just partnered with a dragon, and we find you in here communicating with Marisol, both of you completely unavailable!"

"I'm sorry, I can explain everything that just happened. I think we might need a council meeting but make it fast, okay? I want to settle the rumors before things get out of hand. Have someone waiting for TK and Devon when they return."

"TK and who?"

"The student TK and his new dragon, Devon."

"Then it's true? And how do we have a student who isn't already partnered to a dragon?"

"I'll explain everything. Just call a council meeting asap."

CHAPTER THIRTY-TWO

Submissive

Derek looked up at the Elder from where he lay on the bed. Derek felt very small, but protected at the same time. He knew he was in good, or at least skilled, hands. The Elder deftly stripped him while he lay there, silencing his protests with a kiss and every time Derek tried to help, the Elder kissed his hands and pinned them over his head before peeling off another item of clothing. Finally, Derek stopped trying to help and simply lay there, hands over his head, watching the Elder undress him. He had to admit it was quite arousing.

Then, while Derek lay naked on the bed with his hands over his head, feeling deliciously vulnerable, the Elder stood up and let his robe slide to the floor. His beautiful body was exposed and Derek licked his lips. The Elder was so gorgeous. He wanted to run his tongue along those contours and taste that cock that was already starting to jut out, much like Derek's. Those firm, powerful muscles, that beautiful creamy skin, with scars from his dragon proudly displayed across his belly and chest and one along his thigh, oh how he wanted to run a finger along those scars and kiss them until they vanished under his tongue.

When his gaze finally lifted back to the Elder's powerful face, he saw lust in the man's eyes and the Elder moved towards him quickly, grabbing his wrists, still above his head, and locking him in a dominating kiss. Derek's eyes went wide and he struggled, surprised by the sudden movement, but in a few seconds he went limp with desire as the Elder's other hand began tracing its way along his body and tickling him in the most seductive way he had ever felt. He let his eyes close and his mouth open further to give the Elder unlimited access to his body, and the Elder took it.

They kissed for what seemed like ages, the Elder taking his time to ease Derek into increasing levels of passion as his body seemed to go limper and limper – except for his cock, which was close to bursting just from this simple kiss. Finally, the Elder pulled away and Derek gasped for air. The Elder rearranged himself, drawing himself up on Derek's body until he was straddling Derek's shoulders, his cock just barely above Derek's lips.

Derek squirmed, uncomfortable by the position, but his arms were locked in place by the Elder's powerful thighs and the Elder leaned forward to massage his hands, the motion causing the man's cock to brush against his lips.

"You're not used to being a submissive, are you?" the Elder asked softly.

Derek didn't answer, afraid if he opened his mouth the Elder would slide inside of him. Instead, he shook his head. But he had to admit this situation, the helplessness of it, was turning him on.

"You want to be a master?"

Derek thought of how good it felt controlling other people in bed, the pleasure he had felt forcing Scott to submit to him during their threesome, how much he enjoyed controlling Chris's pleasure when they made love. He nodded.

The Elder leaned close, his cock pressing against Derek's lips, a drip of precum trailing. It took all of Derek's willpower not to lick it up.

"The best masters start as the best slaves," he whispered. "Do you want me to teach you?"

Derek's cock jolted. This was the man who had taught Ashton, after all, and even though Ashton was his father he had still heard about Ashton's legendary prowess in the bedroom. Could he learn to be like that? Did he want to learn to be like that? His cock ached and he knew that he did. He wanted people to submit to him. He wanted them to beg him for sex, not take it from him. Mostly, though, he wanted Chris and Scott again. And Scott would never agree until he was powerful enough to force it.

Derek nodded.

"Then open your mouth, slave, and let me show you the pleasures of being a submissive."

Derek opened his mouth slowly, extending his tongue and sliding it along the cock awaiting him. It was musky and masculine and clean, and he opened his mouth further. The Elder didn't rush him at all, letting him explore with his tongue as he slowly opened his mouth further and further and invited the cock inside. He licked and tasted and teased the Elder until finally he was ready, and he opened his mouth and allowed the Elder to slide inside.

It felt incredibly different in this position with the Elder straddling him rather than him on top. He felt suffocated, but in a good way. The Elder entered him slowly, but kept going until Derek was on the brink of gagging. He seemed to know exactly when that was going to happen because he stopped and began pulling out right when Derek began to worry. Another long stroke that ended at the perfect time, and Derek began to relax. Clearly, the Elder knew exactly what he was doing.

It felt deliciously decadent getting taken like this and Derek enjoyed every moment, but he wondered if Chris would want to do this, and thoughts of Chris started dragging him down. Then the Elder approached him from a new angle and thoughts of Chris vanished, for a while at least. Every time the real world threatened to intrude, the Elder would force them away with a wave of pleasure. Derek wasn't sure how much more he could take, but he already knew without the Elder telling him that cumming without the Elder's permission was forbidden.

The Elder's thrusts came faster, filling Derek's throat in a glorious blaze of friction as he lay, helpless and hard, and he knew the Elder was about to cum. He wondered what it would taste like. Then the Elder grunted and his mouth was filled with a hot flow of masculine, tangy cum. Derek nearly came but managed to hang on as he swallowed quickly, then swallowed again. The Elder shivered and pulled away from him, aiming his body at Derek's still burgeoning cock.

"What a good boy," the Elder murmured.

The Elder reached out and wrapped his hand around Derek, and Derek cried out at the sudden pressure, again nearly cumming. The Elder began stroking him with firm, even pressure, from the base all the way to the tip, and Derek squirmed and lowered his arms. The Elder swatted his arms.

"Above your head," he commanded, and Derek bit his lip and returned his arms to their helpless position as he writhed in pleasure.

"You've been such a good boy," the Elder murmured. "I give you permission to cum."

The Elder pumped him faster and his permission was all Derek needed for his body to release its tension and explode outward. He went completely tense, then the tension released itself in a single point and for several long moments he felt his tension being released in waves that passed through his body again and again, crashing against him like a tsunami. Then the waves settled down and all was still, and languid. He took a deep breath and barely managed to open his eyes to see the Elder watching him.

"Let's go take a shower and clean up a little," the Elder suggested, and Derek realized his cum was all over both of them. He had managed quite an orgasm. He nodded and the Elder scooped him up again, carrying him to the bathroom.

They showered together but it wasn't an extension of their lovemaking, it was a genuine attempt to get clean. The Elder did spend quite a bit of time on Derek's lower regions, with a wink, but didn't seem upset when Derek was unable to respond. He was simply exhausted and spent.

They returned to the bedroom and rather than get dressed, the Elder drew him into bed and cuddled with him, spooning him with just a hint of possession in the position. The Elder cradled him sweetly, but Derek wondered if this was part of training him to be a submissive. He had no idea what it meant, really. He just wanted to be a master someday and order Scott into his bed. Chris, he assumed, would already be in his bed. If that wasn't his future, then why bother continuing?

"What are you thinking, little one?"

"About what I'll do when I'm master."

"And what is that?"

There was humor in the Elder's voice, but it was good-natured, not mocking.

"It's private."

"I won't tell anyone."

Derek paused. Who would the Elder tell? And what would the Elder gain? Nothing. There really was no harm in telling the Elder.

"I want Scott in my bed again."

There was a silence, but not a judgmental one. Derek looked back at the Elder and saw that he was thinking hard, as if trying to fit pieces together.

"Scott is the other Queen's mate, correct?"

"Yes."

"And he's been in your bed?"

"My first time was with him," Derek said, blushing just remembering his first time with Scott. "And more recently too."

He wouldn't mention the threesome, because that involved Chris and he knew better than to mention Chris in front of the Elder.

The Elder was silent for a few moments, stroking Derek's arm almost haphazardly.

"I would be willing to help you get Scott into your bed," he finally said. "He is an acceptable partner for you."

Derek was surprised, and felt a twinge of anger that Scott was acceptable but Chris wasn't. But he would take what he could get with the Elder. There was one question, though.

"Why?" he asked. "And tell me the truth. I told you the truth about Scott."

The Elder rolled away from him for a moment as if deep in thought, then rolled back and resumed his spooning position.

"Scott is the other Queen's mate, and I have a grudge against the other Queen."

"Jamie? I thought you liked him, just like everyone else."

"I respect him, but like is a strong word," the Elder said. "Jamie took something from me that can never be replaced, and for that he owes me greatly."

Derek could feel his forehead creasing. Jamie and the Elder barely knew each other, so how could Jamie take something from the Elder? Then he remembered what the Elder had said about Derek's father being like a son to him and he remembered that Jamie was the one to kill Ashton, and it all made sense.

"You know Jamie didn't want to be the one to kill Ashton," Derek said. "The council made him do it."

"As the Queen, it was his duty to do it. But I will still never forgive him," the Elder said. "And if I can disrupt his relationship by helping you seduce his mate, I will be happy to do so."

Derek smiled weakly. It wasn't the reason he wanted the Elder to be helping him, but it would get an end result that he wanted. He felt like he should tell Jamie to watch his back with the Elder, but if he told Jamie, then he would lose his chance with Scott. It was an impossible situation. Help Jamie, or finally get Scott. And what had Jamie done for Derek, exactly? Not much. Why should he feel loyalty to the man? But he did, and he couldn't ignore it. Well, nothing would happen for a while, so he would just put off his decision. He knew he couldn't put it off forever because he suspected the Elder was planning on something far more malevolent than simply helping to steal Jamie's mate, but he could put it off for now.

"You should get some rest, darling," the Elder said, kissing his cheek. "You've-"

A warning from the dragons sent them both upright. Someone had just bonded to a dragon in Portland, someone who was not a proper student, someone who was not part of the first year exam. It was too early, it was far out of season, something was wrong. Derek immediately contacted Marisol, but she was a blur of thoughts and sounds that meant she couldn't be communicated with – she was undergoing something and no one could contact her until she was back to normal. He tried Narné but the mate's dragon knew nothing more than he did, though Narné cautioned them to stay calm and not panic.

Jettie began to panic, however, as all the dragons in Spokane began contacting her and she didn't know what was going on. Derek soothed her and told her to repeat what Narné said about staying calm, that everything would be explained soon. Within five minutes, Marisol was back in communication. The dragons stopped worrying, though they didn't tell their human counterparts why. Suddenly it was a new game of missing communication as the dragons were no longer panicking but the humans still were.

Derek ran into the room where Jettie lay.

"Jettie, you have to tell me what happened. I'm the Queen! People will come to me for answers!"

I'm sorry, Jettie said. *Marisol said not until the council meets and decides what to do. Then you can know.*

"Jettie, that's totally unfair. You have to tell me. I won't tell anyone else if that's an issue."

Jettie snorted and looked around, focusing on the Elder who had followed Derek into the room. Both of them were still completely naked but Derek didn't feel any shame.

"If he has to leave, he will," Derek said without looking at the Elder. After all, being submissive only applied in the bedroom. Or at least he assumed it did. They would have to talk about that, because his role as a dominant Queen had to remain intact.

Jettie shook her head. *No one can know.* She sounded miserable and he knew she had been pleading his case with Marisol and had lost.

Derek and the Elder returned to their rooms and got dressed. Derek sent a note to the council members informing them that the Portland council was meeting and immediately after that, they would be meeting, though he didn't know what time that would be. He promised them answers, and only hoped he could deliver.

CHAPTER THIRTY-THREE

Fallout

Scott waited impatiently for the council to gather. Considering how anxious they were for answers, he would have thought they would gather a lot quicker than this. But they were taking their time getting dressed properly for the occasion. He supposed he didn't blame them – for the council, appearance was everything. Margot at least was prompt, but they needed a quorum before they could begin.

That foolish boy. That stupid, foolish boy. Scott's lip curled in disgust. Going to the mountain and infiltrating Marisol's nesting grounds. The nerve! And worst of all, he had found an egg that would have died if he hadn't been there! There had to be some sort of magic that had bound boy and egg together from the moment the egg was laid, because the coincidence was too strong. TK just happened to go into Marisol's nesting grounds right when she was deciding what to do with the egg? It had to be fate, but he didn't like to think that anything TK did was fated to happen. Because that meant TK was fated to be at the academy, and perhaps TK was fated to be with Jamie. Scott would never let that happen, no matter what rocks were in their relationship right now.

Jamie seemed deep in thought, and had been deep in thought since he had awoken from Marisol's mind. Scott had tried to talk to him, but he could barely get more than a few words out. Marisol had told Scott what had happened, with the warning not to tell anyone else. Not even the other queen, she had warned, and he knew Derek couldn't be pleased by that. He hoped Marisol had a good reason for keeping Derek in the dark because something like this could drive the boy into the Elder's arms, right where they were trying to keep him from falling.

And so he waited with a mostly silent Jamie beside him, not knowing what Jamie was going to say when the council started but knowing that whatever it was, he would support it. They couldn't afford to be divided about this. Even if Jamie announced that TK would be staying in Portland, Scott would suck it up and support Jamie's wishes. This was not the time for petty disagreements. That would come later, in private, when Jamie was back to himself and not so... quiet.

After what felt like hours, Margot finally approached them on the dais. She gestured to the many dark-robed people in the room.

"We have quorum," she announced, "From the male and female campuses."

"Thank you," Jamie said, sitting up straight.

With that simply gesture of sitting up, the entire room seemed to center around him. Scott felt himself slide away into the glory of Jamie's presence and the council went dead silent, all of them staring at Jamie in awe and a great deal of surprise. Jamie had complete control of the room in a way he had never had before. Scott wondered how he managed it, but his thoughts kept skittering back to Jamie and wondering what Jamie was going to say. He found he couldn't focus on anything else. Magic, he thought. Dragon magic. Jamie must have learned it from the dragons.

"Tonight, a visiting student found his way to the nesting grounds and successfully partnered with a dragon whose special ability is aging quickly. The dragons have confirmed that if this dragon, Devon, had been forced to wait until the usual exam, he would have died. This student saved his life."

There was a murmur of surprise at the words. No one had ever heard of a gift like that and there were significant consequences to be pondered. Would the dragon continue to age quickly? Would it die before its partner? Normally the partner died first, since dragons were so long-lived compared to humans, even humans partnered with dragons who had extended lifespans. How would a dragon with accelerated growth be trained properly and who would do it?

And of course there was the stance Jamie was taking. The student had saved the dragon. Not that he had nearly killed all the other eggs, which he had by being present in the nesting grounds, but that he had saved this one egg. It was a conciliatory and downright positive view of the event, and they would have to accept that view as well now. The student could not be punished in any way if they accepted Jamie's words here tonight.

"The student was trespassing on the nesting grounds," one voice called out, and there was a general murmur of agreement. Clearly the council was not going to accept Jamie's positive view without a fight.

"There will be some consequence to his actions," Jamie said calmly. "In the process of saving the dragon's life, he violated a sacred law and for that he will be sent to the Spokane campus to attend school. The teachers there are more than capable of training him and his unusual dragon."

There was another buzz in the room and Scott heard some jealousy and some relief in the voices. Jealousy that they wouldn't be taking care of such an exotic gift, and relief that they wouldn't have to deal with such a rebellious student.

"Have you already contacted the teachers there?" Margot asked.

"They will be informed shortly, if my decision meets the approval of the council," Jamie said, demurely lowering his lashes.

Immediately talk broke out in the room, all of it scrambled and in pieces so Scott couldn't piece together anything that was being said, but he did notice Margot's approving nod. The council talked and argued and debated, but it seemed like they did it more out of habit than anything else because the snippets that Scott did catch were all in agreement with Jamie. Finally, after ten minutes, Jamie looked up and the room seemed to zoom in around him again. He lifted his hand and silence fell.

"Have you reached a decision?" he asked.

Gerald and Margot stepped forward.

"We shall take a vote," Margot said. "Women first. All those in favor?"

There was a chorus of ayes.

"And opposed?"

Silence.

Gerald repeated the process for the men with the same result, and Jamie nodded.

"I shall inform the student that he and his dragon will be traveling to Spokane immediately for training, and that there will be no other punishment for saving the life of this special dragon. Thank you for your time."

He nodded and the room seemed to return to normal, without Jamie as the central focus. Whatever Jamie was doing, it was highly effective. It had to be dragon magic. He did have an incredibly close connection to the dragons and they considered him one of them, so perhaps he was learning how to use their abilities without even knowing it. Or perhaps he was all too aware of what he was doing, and simply hadn't told Scott about his new abilities, Scott thought bitterly. Either one could be the case.

Jamie tugged on his sleeve and led him back to their chambers.

"I need to talk to Derek now," he said. "Will you be at my side for this? I want to talk to him directly and it's very draining."

"Of course," Scott said, smoothing a strand of hair from

Jamie's forehead. "I'm always at your side."

Jamie smiled and laid down on the bed, closing his eyes. His brow crinkled in concentration and then his face went blank. Scott didn't touch him, not wanting to interrupt the connection between them. He waited for five minutes, wondering how long this would take. Jamie began to sweat and look pale. How much of this could Jamie take?

Ten minutes. Should he wake Jamie up? Pearls of sweat dotted Jamie's hairline and upper lip, and his eyelids flickered every once in a while. Was he trying to wake up but not able to? Did he want Scott to wake him up? Or was that part of speaking to Derek? He didn't know. Two more minutes, he decided. He would give it two more minutes and then wake Jamie up, and if Jamie wasn't done talking to Derek, then so be it.

He looked at the clock on the wall anxiously, waiting for two minutes to arrive. Thirty seconds. Jamie was so pale, so much paler than usual, that was. His tan from their summer together had worn off and he was far too pale. He hoped this summer would be spent outdoors again, but so far it didn't look like that would happen. They had responsibilities now, and training that went on even after school was out. Hardly any time for relaxing and sunbathing.

One minute. Was he really going to wait for some arbitrary time he had set for himself, or was he going to wake Jamie up early? He leaned forward and Jamie opened his eyes. They stared at each for a few seconds, then Jamie smiled at him.

"Thank you for not waking me up," he said hoarsely. "Derek needed a lot of explanation. I also needed a lot of information from him. Things aren't going well there, Scott. He's getting along with the Elder too well, it seems. He was quick to point out the Elder wasn't the monster we all thought he was. As much as I hate to do this, I might need you to go with TK and check things out."

"You're asking me to go visit Derek?"

Jamie's smile faded. "Derek's loyalty is important, Scott, more important than a lot of things. Now that I've met TK, I can see how the heart can have conflicting desires. I want you to do what it takes to get Derek on our side, do you understand?"

Scott flushed, his cheeks scalding hot. Jamie was essentially ordering him to have sex with Derek in order to get Derek back on their side. He had dreamed of having sex with Derek again, but being ordered to do so – by his boyfriend, of all people – felt wrong. They were trying to restore their relationship, not ruin it, and he knew this would ruin it if he went through with it.

"I'll go," he said. "But I won't do anything with Derek that a good friend wouldn't do. I'll talk to him, and that's it."

"It's okay, Scott, I understand," Jamie said, but he looked down as he said it and Scott knew he might understand but he wouldn't be able to accept. No, he would not cross that line again. Jamie was too precious to him.

"Jamie, I won't do anything to hurt you or our relationship, and I want you to know that," he said, tapping Jamie's chin so that Jamie looked up at him. "You mean too much to me."

"Even if our whole society is at stake?" Jamie whispered.

"I will find another way to convince him," Scott said.

A hint of a smile played around Jamie's lips. Scott leaned forward and kissed him, and as they kissed he felt the smile grow broader.

"I love you, Jamie," Scott said as they pulled away.

"I love you, Scott," Jamie said.

"I'll go to Spokane for you," Scott said, "But I will come back for you and I won't do anything to betray you while I'm gone. I know I haven't exactly been here for you lately but it's almost summer and I want you to know that I am here for you, that I will be here for you, whenever you need me. I want this summer to be a time when we're together."

"Just like last year?"

"Yeah," Scott said with a smile. "Except we won't be planning a war this time."

"We might be," Jamie said somberly. "If Derek continues the trend he's on."

"I'll talk sense into him," Scott said. "But for now, just relax. TK and I won't leave for a couple of hours and it's been a while since we've had a moment to ourselves."

He smiled seductively and Jamie hesitantly returned the smile. Scott held out his hand and Jamie took it, and together they laid down on the bed, looking forward to renewing their vows of love in harmony.

ABOUT THE AUTHOR

Elizabeth James

Elizabeth James hails from Portland, Oregon and spent many hours of her childhood tucked away in the Gold Room of Powell's Books, reading science fiction and fantasy masterpieces and hidden treasures. She writes romance with strong elements of science fiction and fantasy as a result, focusing on LGBT characters.

THRALL OF DARKNESS

Thrall of Darkness was founded because there is a shortage of good, quality literature featuring gay protagonists that does not reduce gay characters to stereotypes or dismiss them as secondary characters. Every story seeks to challenge the status quo by focusing on gay characters and combining drama, action, and sex into an addicting blend of fun-filled narrative.

You can find more information on Thrall of Darkness novels and short stories at thrallofdarkness.com.

BOOKS BY THIS AUTHOR

Demon Season

Taylor just wanted to bond with a regular demon during his first demon season, but instead he ends up with the prince of demons, an incubus! He fights through his fears of intimacy while battling past enemies as he and his demon come to a new understanding.

A Vampire's Desire

Kairos takes a job in an ancient vampire house knowing nothing about them and their society, and immediately falls in love with his boss, a powerful but cold vampire. As he tries to get closer, threats from a rival house threaten to tear them apart. Kairos pursues his boss's heart while struggling to protect himself and the ones he loves, and he wonders if he made the right choice entering vampire society.

Dragon Tamer

Luke has heard dragons all his life and when a dragon summons him to raise her dragonlings, he runs away to help her. But the world he enters is fraught with danger and he knows little of the outside world. As the dragons begin dying off and dragon tamers like him become scarce, a rival tribe kidnaps him and everything he knows is thrown into question.

Sagent

Gabriel is a sagent, a sex agent, at the start of his career, but he is already scarred by his previous agency. When he is sent on a dangerous mission to the underbelly of Destiny, everything starts to fall apart. Isolated from his agency and not knowing where to go, Gabriel must choose between returning to safety and Destiny, or staying and forging his own path.

First Prince

Wren is the beautiful yet rebellious first prince of Fontain, forced to move to the Imperial Palace as part of a treaty. Upon arriving, he receives a frigid welcome and realizes his stay will be fraught with danger. When he finds romance in an unexpected place, he realizes that his life may not be as dire as he imagined and pleasure can be found where it is least expected.

Prisoner Of Love

When Prince Tristan is captured in battle, he fully expects to be tortured and killed. But the torture turns to erotic pleasure as he learns that his enemy, Prince Ryan, is in love with him and has been planning his capture with meticulous care for years. Will Tristan hold firm to his principles, or will Ryan's forceful seduction overpower his senses?

Dark Offering

Nightmares are a nightly occurrence on the planet of Ylse, and they're strong enough to lure humans to be fed on by the creatures who haunt the night. Jarl is charged with risking the night to feed the colony. He comes across one of the creatures offering peace. Is the creature sincere or is this just a new way to lure the humans to their deaths on this inhospitable planet?

Bride Of Albis

Sam and his small crew of space-faring traders have their usual routine permanently shattered when they are kidnapped by pirates. Sam makes a deal with the head of the pirates: he will be sold as a slave in exchange for the freedom of his crew. But when he discovers that the pirate lied and sold his crew as well, he vows vengeance.

Seeking More

Seeking More is a collection of eight contemporary gay romance stories that range from the deeply emotional to action-packed, from hapless MFA students to couples on the brink of a new relationship. Each story is focused not only on steamy romance, of which there is plenty, but also on character development and an emotional connection between reader and character.

Eve Of Eternity

Sabine is a young woman searching for her identity while fleeing the powerful man trying to steal her heart and mind. She's almost under his control when she is kidnapped by a man with conflicting loyalties and a mysterious past who claims to kidnap her in order to rescue her. Will she break free from the men around her?

Treacherous A Dragon's Love

In the middle of the final battle against the great dragon Arostrath, a woman appears bound in golden chains. The King claims her as his reward but the youngest son has an unusual fondness for her that could cast the kingdom into ruin. Will his love for the beautiful and strange woman destroy the kingdom, or does her mystery hide the answer to all of their prayers?